DOMINION REQUIRED

Thanks for reading! Have fun.

DOMINION REQUIRED

A LOCHLAN ELLYLL NOVEL

BY

HS PAISLEY

J Sunley
PRESS

First edition

ISBN: 978-1-9995236-3-3 (ebook)
ISBN: 978-1-9995236-2-6 (paperback)

Hyacinth Agatha Paisley

CHAPTER ONE

Zemila

Blood covered the floor around her, but she was clean. A man reached for her. He collapsed. A second man cringed away. Her eyes fixed on him.

And look at that, she'd thought. He's made of stone.

Flesh tore. Rock crumbled. The stone man screamed.

"Ms. Alkevic?" said a voice through the dust and death.

His screams, Zemila thought. How do I stop hearing his screams?

"Ms. Alkevic, hello?"

Light quick footsteps. A hand on her arm.

"Zemila?"

"Huh?" Zemila snapped back to the present, back to her office, back from the memory of what she'd done. "Oh, sorry, Diana. Was I zoned out again?"

"That's quite all right," Diana, the department receptionist, said. "But Ms. Jace would like to see you up top."

"You didn't have to walk over." Zemila pushed her chair back from the Intelliglass desk and stood. "Why didn't you call?"

"I did." Diana tucked her straight black hair behind her ear.

Zemila looked down at her watch.

Four missed calls.

"Oh," Zemila said. "I'm sorry."

Diana's almond-shaped eyes looked sadly at her. Color rose to Zemila's cheeks.

"Don't apologize." Diana led the way out of Zemila's small office. "I know you've been . . . well . . ." She took a breath. "Ms. Jace is waiting."

Diana walked Zemila the short distance through the open-concept workspace to the elevators. Zemila was happy for the company, brief though it was.

"Ms. Jace," Diana said when the elevator door slid open. Zemila stepped in. Diana gave her a weak smile before turning back to her desk.

"Damnit," Zemila cursed as she watched Diana settle herself at her desk.

The elevator doors closed. Zemila squeezed her eyes shut and balled her hands into fists.

She knew why Ms. Jace wanted to talk to her.

It was the same reason Diana had needed to come to her desk. The same reason why she couldn't sleep. She was out of it. Really out of it.

"Damnit," she said again.

"Hi, Wendy," Zemila said to the pretty girl with dark skin sitting behind a large white desk. A fountain burbled in the corner of the reception area.

"Ms. Alkevic." Wendy popped to her feet. "I'll take you right in."

Zemila followed her down the white hall to a large double door. On a normal day, Zemila sympathized with poor Wendy, pulling open those huge doors over and over again. Today wasn't a normal day.

She hadn't had a normal day in months.

Wendy grunted a little as she pulled the door.

"Ms. Alkevic to see you," she said into the office.

Zemila walked in.

"Ms. Jace," she started. "I—"

Zemila stopped when her boss's critical dark eyes found their mark.

Sitting behind an Intelliglass desk three times the size of Zemila's, Ms. Adrienne Jace made an impressive figure. Framed by the enormous window, the bright blue sky behind her was clear of skyscrapers. Rumor had it she'd bought the airspace to keep the view. Adrienne's smooth terracotta skin, wide distinctive features, and jet-black hair showed her heritage. Even in the late 2040s, her indigenous lineage made her an outlier.

After a tap to a corner of the desk, scattered papers organized into folders.

"Sit," Adrienne commanded. "How are you?"

Zemila walked in and settled herself on one of the black leather chairs.

Adrienne Jace, the founder of JACE Co. was one of the wealthiest people in the city. Zemila searched her boss's face wondering how honest she could be. As far as Adrienne knew, Zemila was recovering from her roommate being murdered.

In reality, that was just the tip of the iceberg.

"Hmmm," Adrienne said when Zemila didn't answer. "That's what I thought."

"I'm doing all right," Zemila lied. "Really."

"Don't do that to me," Adrienne said. She stood and moved around her desk, sitting in the black chair beside Zemila.

"Do what?"

"Lie," she said. "This piece." Adrienne tapped her desk and an article appeared. Zemila recognized it as the one she'd submitted that morning. "It's not your best."

Zemila couldn't look at it. Her eyes flicked up and around the room, looking for something else to focus on. They settled on the large wall of books and an impressive collection of twentieth-century vinyl.

"Don't get me wrong," Adrienne said, pulling Zemila's attention back to her. "Even in this state you're good, but not your best. I think you need some time."

"No, I'm okay. I'll be better," she promised.

"That was not a request," Adrienne said coolly. "How is the new place?"

The new place, Zemila thought. It's lonely and foreign and doesn't feel like home.

"It's all right," she said aloud.

"Let's play a game," Adrienne looked at her sternly. "I'll ask questions, you'll answer honestly. When we are done, you'll have your job back in three weeks."

"Three weeks!" Zemila exclaimed. "I wanted to cover that Right Waters thing."

"Are you kidding me?" Adrienne scoffed. "Not a chance."

"I don't see a—"

"Three weeks," Adrienne cut in.

I want that story, Zemila thought, disappointed.

Right Waters party member comes home to find wife stabbed to death. She could see the headline. The byline.

The picture faded.

It was replaced by the bloody image of her roommate sprawled across a broken glass table.

Maybe it did hit too close to home.

"Three weeks, and be thankful it's not more," Adrienne continued. "Do you know how many people working for me have found their roommate just moments after she was murdered? How many of them are being stalked? One, Zemila. Just one."

"That's all behind me," she said, even though it wasn't.

Adrienne didn't know that she wasn't being stalked anymore. Zemila wasn't going to tell her. She wasn't going to tell her boss she'd killed the man who'd been following her.

"I shouldn't have let you come back so soon," Adrienne said. "You're valuable to this company. Valuable to me. I thought work might help you. Give you something else to think about. That was a mistake."

"It has," Zemila said, tears stinging her eyes. "I need to work."

"You need to process what's happened to you. What is happening to you. And unfortunately for you, my word is law here." Adrienne looked at her with concern. Zemila had to fight not to drop her eyes in shame. "So, let's play a game."

Zemila nodded again, breathing in deep.

"The new place feels empty, even though it's small," she said.

"I thought your brother was staying with you?" Adrienne asked. "And don't you have a dog?"

"He was. I couldn't stand him. And I do."

Nemo had come to visit after Zemila had found Tiffany's body. They'd only lived together for a couple of weeks before she kicked him out. He annoyed her. He was always around. He left crumpled, half-finished sketches all over the apartment.

But those weren't the real reasons she'd kicked him out.

11

"When he wasn't hovering over me, or asking if I was okay, he was off with Loch—" She cut off.

Not thinking about him, she mentally chided. I am not thinking about him.

Adrienne nodded.

"Siblings are hard sometimes. They know when you're lying. Are you talking to anyone about what happened?"

Zemila made a noncommittal sound.

Was she talking to anyone? Sure.

About what happened? Which part? Her roommate dying? Being stalked? Getting engaged? Finding out her new fiancé had been cheating on her for their entire relationship? Getting kidnapped? Almost dying? Being brought back from the dead? Learning her brother's best friend was in love with her?

Okay, she'd known that last one. She'd known it for years. That almost made it worse.

"Any word from Tyler?" Adrienne asked.

Zemila rolled her eyes.

"He wants the ring back."

"Are you going to give it to him?"

"I don't know. I was wearing it for two days before he—anyway. I don't know."

"Okay," Adrienne said.

Zemila was thankful she didn't push.

"Here's the deal," Adrienne said. "You are off for three weeks. I don't want to see you, but I do want you to see someone. Talk to someone, and maybe take a class where you can hit something really fuckin' hard."

"Ms. Jace!" Zemila laughed in surprise. She'd never heard her boss swear before.

"In fact," Adrienne said, drawing a rectangle on her Intelliglass desk and scribbling on it with a finger. "Here's the number of a friend of mine. She's good. Call her."

Adrienne tapped the rectangle twice and said, "Zemila Alkevic. Inbox."

There was a soft whooshing sound and the rectangle disappeared.

"Thank you," Zemila said, glancing down at her watch. The business card had appeared in her inbox.

"Last thing."

Zemila looked up.

Adrienne's dark eyes, usually so hard, softened. "Being around people who care about you is good. Don't isolate yourself. Don't shut down."

"Okay," Zemila said. "I'll ask Nemo to—"

"I'm not just talking about Nemo," Adrienne cut in, her gaze turning stony again. "That boy adores you," she said. Zemila knew she wasn't talking about her brother anymore. "The way he looks at you, Zemila, that's the real deal. That's the once in a lifetime stuff. The storybook stuff. Don't push him away."

The two stared at each other for a moment. Then Adrienne got up and walked back around the desk.

"Three weeks!" she said, sitting and opening a file on her desk.

Zemila stood. She'd been dismissed.

"Call Cam Hernandez," Zemila said the second she closed her office door. The call went to voicemail. "Call Tavius and Associates."

"Tavius and Associates, how may I direct your call?" a male voice answered.

Cam was in a meeting. Zemila left a message, then looked around her office.

Her desk took up most of the room. A small filing cabinet sat under a smaller window. There was a chair in the corner.

That was it. That was her workspace. Zemila could barely stand the thought of not being here for three weeks.

She sighed, and shut the door behind her.

Zemila tensed when a man stepped into the elevator with her. He smiled. She tried and failed to smile back. He returned his eyes to his watch.

He's not following you, she thought. He's not following you, he's not following you. He works here.

Elevators were bad. Hallways were bad. Hell, streets were bad if she was going in the same direction as a stranger for too long. A strange man. That was when her mind played tricks on her.

He's following you, her dark thoughts would say. You're going to be hurt again, taken again. He's going to kill you again.

Zemila rushed out of the elevator. Her body relaxed when she got outside. The crowded street was somehow easier to deal with.

Zemila could have taken the glass walkway connecting the two buildings to get to the underground parking in the adjacent building.

But hallways were bad. Besides, she could use the fresh air.

Not so fresh, she thought, as a bus passed.

She started to walk when a familiar figure caught her eye. If she had been anyone else, she might have missed him. If she had been anyone else, he wouldn't have let her see him.

She started towards the man, who ducked into a back alley half a block up the street. She took off her backpack and rummaged around in it as she walked. After a few seconds of digging, she found what she was looking for.

Zemila lit two cigarettes in her mouth and turned into the alley.

God, that's good, she thought, after taking a deep drag.

"I thought you quit."

Zemila handed the speaker her second cigarette.

"I did," she said, drawing on it again. "You look good, Billy."

"Been trying to stay clean," Billy said with a shrug. The hand not holding the cigarette pulled his navy-blue hood off and scratched his shaved head.

"Not trying anything new?" she asked, looking at him sideways.

"You mean that kid stuff all over the news?"

Zemila nodded.

"Hell no," he shook his head. "Candle coulda been my thing fifteen years ago, but now . . . nah, nah, I'm clean."

"It suits you," she said.

He gave her a shy smile.

For a second, Zemila saw the man Billy could have been.

Before the drugs and the misdemeanors. Before the ex-wife stopped letting him see his kids. Before he'd lost hope.

"I've been working," he told her. "Did like you said. Went to that Redford Outreach thing . . . it's not much. But it's work."

"That's great, Billy." She punched him lightly on the arm. "How long?"

"Five weeks for the job. About six months off the hard stuff."

"Billy," she said, excited. "That's great. Why didn't you tell me

15

sooner?"

He looked embarrassed, but pleased.

"Didn't want to jinx it," he said. "It's been a long time since I've been solid like this. You've been good to me, you know? I didn't want to jinx it. I didn't want to let you down. Not too many people have been good to me these last few years."

His blue eyes glanced up at her, then away.

"I'm really proud of you," Zemila said, meaning it.

"I got something for you." He flicked the butt of his cigarette away and ignored her praise. "Nothing big, but maybe something."

"You're timing isn't great," she answered, putting her own butt out under the heel of her black oxford. "I've been given a mandatory three-week holiday."

"That doesn't sound so bad," he said.

She shot him a look.

"All right, all right, I guess it's awful."

"I need to work," she told him truthfully. "I need to keep my mind off . . . things."

"Yeah," he said knowingly. "I heard."

"What did you hear?"

"Heard you got yourself kidnapped."

Her eyes narrowed.

"Where the hell did you hear that?"

They hadn't told anyone what happened. They hadn't even taken Lochlan to the hospital.

"Never mind where I heard it. This time off will do you some good." He turned away.

"Wait," she said. His sudden readiness to leave startled her. She was comfortable here in this back alley with this man she had grown to trust. "You said you had something for me."

"I'll tell you in three weeks."

"Will it still be relevant in three weeks?" she asked.

He paused. Considered.

"There've been fires," he said. "In Lowtown."

"There are always fires in Lowtown."

"In abandoned buildings, places where people are squatting, places where you wouldn't notice if people went missing."

"Are people going missing?" she asked.

"I guess you have a few weeks' vacation to ruin trying to figure that out," Billy said.

And he was gone.

Cam called Zemila back just as she got into Ida, her dark blue compact hatchback.

"Are you free tonight?" Zemila asked, putting Ida into reverse and backing out of her spot. Her heart was racing. She'd nearly sprinted from the underground parking stairs to her little car. When she heard Cam's voice, her stress eased.

"I can be," Cam said. Her light accent hinted that English wasn't her mother tongue. "What's going on?"

"Nothing really, I just . . ." she paused, driving out of the underground garage.

"Zemila? Did I lose you?"

"I just want to talk, or something," Zemila said in a rush. "I don't really want to be alone. I'd call Nemo but—"

"He has the sensitivity of a George R. R. Martin novel?" Cam said.

"You're such a nerd." A smile pulled at the corners of Zemila's mouth.

"Don't tell Jenner," Cam said. "I can come by now, if you'd like?"

"No, I'm going to hit at A&O's for a little while." Zemila moved slowly, joining the downtown traffic.

A&O's. Ace & Oakley's. It was a batting and pitching center that Zemila frequented.

"I need to work off a little frustration." Ms. Jace's words came back to her. She did want to hit something. "And you have clients."

"Sí, amiga, I do," Cam said. "How's 8:30? I'll pick up Chinese."

"You're a goddess," Zemila said.

"I know."

φ

With every swing, a bit of her mind cleared. With every hit, a piece of the world dropped away. It was just her, the bat in her hand, and the ball whizzing through the air.

Controlled. Steady. Consistent. She needed that.

The peace and clarity she'd felt as she swung at pitch after pitch stayed in the batting cage. Fifty minutes of tranquility. Then it was over. Reality slammed into her the second she left A&O's.

It had been sunny and warm when she'd parked her car two blocks away. She'd enjoyed the slow stroll then. She regretted the decision now. The low sun cast long shadows as it drew closer to the horizon. Hearing something behind her, Zemila quickened her pace. The sounds of harsh ragged breathing was getting closer.

It's your imagination, she told herself.

"Just keep walking, Mila," she said aloud. "Don't be ridiculous."

She would not turn around. She refused to give into her fear.

But she could hear the uneven gait of his walk, his heavy limp, his harsh breath.

Drag, thump. Drag, thump. Drag, thump.

The hair on the back of her neck stood up.

Drag, thump. Drag, thump. Drag, thump.

"Not real," she chanted. "Not real, not real, not real."

But it could be real, said a small voice in her head. You won't know unless you look. You killed a soldier. Just a soldier. More will come. More are coming.

He'd been created. Turned. She knew that. More are coming.

Drag, thump. Drag, thump.

Zemila walked faster.

Drag-thump. Drag-thump. Drag-thump.

She tapped her wrist to call Cam, but her watch wasn't there. It was in the bottom of her bag.

She cursed.

Drag-thump, drag-thump, drag-thump.

She was almost at her car. It was just around the corner.

She felt hot breath on her neck.

"Mine, mine, mine," the Famorian hissed in her ear.

"No!" she screamed, spinning around and raising her hands to fight him off again.

A hundred car windows shattered into a thousand pieces that encircled Zemila. Two loud cracks reverberated through the still evening air. Two chunks of concrete hovered in front of her.

A barrier between her and the Famorian.

But the street was empty. He wasn't there. She'd torn him into a million pieces and crushed him into powder. The Famorian had died screaming six weeks ago.

That Famorian, the small voice corrected. That one is dead. You killed a soldier. Just a soldier. More will come. More are coming.

"Damnit," Zemila said.

Carefully, she lowered her hands.

The concrete blocks fit neatly back into the craters they'd left behind. With another wave of her hand, the wall of glass fell.

She looked down at the deep grooves she'd made in the sidewalk. There was nothing she could do about that. There was nothing she could do for the many smashed car windows either.

She was losing control. She was gaining power. She didn't know what to do.

Zemila registered a stinging warmth on her forearms. She looked down. Tiny scratches from the glass window shards criss-crossed her arms. Blood welled in the jagged cuts. She tried to cover the scratches with her shirt. The sleeves of the baseball tee weren't long enough.

She let out a small whimper. Panic. Frustration. Fear.

Zemila jumped at the delayed car alarm systems. The street filled with noise. Her eyes filled with tears. She turned away from the destruction she'd caused, and sprinted the rest of the way to her car.

CHAPTER TWO
Zemila

Soap stung the small cuts on her arms. Souvenirs from the broken car windows. She scrubbed under the hot spray of the shower, trying to wash off the feeling of being followed. It didn't work.

She dried off with a fluffy white towel. Blood from her scratched arms speckled the towel. She pulled on sweat pants, a sports bra, and a thin long-sleeved shirt that Nemo had left. She was drying her hair when her home system announced a visitor.

"Camile Hernandez."

Oriole barked at the home system's announcement.

"Yes, yes," Zemila said, piling her long hair in a messy knot at the top of her head. Her hair was still wet and it dripped down her neck. "I'm coming," she called, though she knew Cam couldn't hear her.

"Oriole, upstairs," she said to the large black dog who'd followed to her front door.

After looking through the small peephole to make sure it was Cam, she unlocked the deadbolt and swung the door open.

"You're late," she said to the small curvy woman in a pencil skirt and heels. Cam Hernandez stood with a large paper bag at her door.

"But I have naan," she held up the bag. "I got Indian instead."

"From that place?" Zemila asked.

"Of course from that place," Cam replied in her sassiest voice.

"Forgiven!" Zemila pressed herself back against the wall. Cam squeezed past her and up the stairs. Zemila slid the four locks back into place before following her.

"You know where everything is," she told Cam as she walked into her bathroom to get a towel for her dripping hair.

When she came back out, Cam had placed several takeout containers and two empty plates on the white-topped island.

"It's cracked," Cam ran a finger along a narrow fissure in the marble. She followed the line to a large wooden cutting board. "Does it get worse underneath?"

"Kind of," Zemila said.

It got worse all right.

"What happened?"

"I dropped something."

Cam stared at her.

"You know I'm a lawyer, right?" Her tone was dry. "I get paid a lot of money to know when people are lying."

"Can we eat first?" Zemila asked, grabbing a bottle of Cab Sauv and two glasses.

"Sí, mi amiga," Cam said. "But there is a story there and I will hear it."

"Later," Zemila told her.

As they ate, they spoke of work. Zemila often reported on cases Cam worked on. They shared what they could with each other. Zemila did most of the talking. As a lawyer, Cam couldn't say much, but was good for a nudge in the right direction.

"Dios mio," Cam said when Zemila reached to take her plate. She grabbed Zemila's arm and pushed up the sleeve of her loose navy-blue shirt. "What the hell is this?"

Zemila pulled back her arm and repositioned the sleeve.

"It's nothing," she said, taking the dishes and bringing them to the sink.

"Nothing?" Cam repeated. "Your arm looks like a scratching post."

"It's not a big deal."

"For you or for the cats?"

"Ha," Zemila said, with little humor.

"Tell me how that happened." Cam started clearing the empty takeout containers and her eyes went to the marred countertop.

There was a minute of silence while the two tidied. Finally, with her wine glass in one hand and a second bottle in the other, Zemila went to the pair of white couches next to her floor-to-ceiling windows.

Cam followed.

Zemila sat down and stared into the depths of her glass.

"My gift has been acting up."

"What does that mean?" Cam asked.

Zemila's wine was halfway to her lips when she stopped.

She released the glass.

Cam gasped and lunged forwards to catch it. But it didn't fall. It just hung there, suspended in front of Zemila's open palm.

"I shouldn't be able to do this," Zemila said, swirling her wine without touching the glass. "Earth Drivers can't move anything manmade. This shouldn't be possible."

The glass moved back into her hand. She closed her fingers around it and took a sip.

"The countertop too?" Cam asked.

"That happened just after everything with Simmons . . ." she trailed off, fighting the images the memory brought.

"Have you told Nemo?"

Zemila looked at her friend.

"That's why you kicked him out," Cam guessed.

"He would go crazy with worry. Try to take me back to Erroin."

"That's the Luman School, right?"

Zemila nodded.

Erroin Peritia Academy. It was the first place that had felt like home after her mother died and her father left. She'd moved there ten years ago, when she'd been sixteen. She'd stayed for almost eight years.

"Maybe you should go. Would there be someone there who could help?"

"It's in India, Cam," Zemila said. "I have a job."

Not for the next three weeks, she reminded herself.

Erroin was where she'd met Lochlan. In a way, that was where this had all started. She'd met him and fallen for him without realizing it.

Not thinking about him, she told herself. Not doing it.

"Maybe Lochlan could help?" Cam suggested, kyboshing Zemila's efforts to keep her mind Lochlan-free.

And then he was all she saw.

Tall and lean, with his soft lilting Celtic accent, Lochlan was coiled strength wrapped in a human facade. His sharp features and piercing green eyes should have made him a standout. But he had the uncanny ability of blending into the background.

He would push his thick, black, square-rimmed glasses up his nose, hunch his shoulders, and step back into a corner.

She liked it when he didn't wear them. When he stopped hiding. Zemila thought that on those few occasions, she saw him the way he saw her.

"What are you smiling about?" Cam asked, derailing Zemila's train of thought.

"Nothing," she said.

"An Irish nothing?" Cam asked, her smile sly.

"I'm pretty sure he's older than Ireland."

"He probably is," Cam said. "Have you two spoken recently?"

"He came over after everything happened."

"That was over a month ago!"

Zemila shrugged. "He told me the truth about him being immortal and about his brothers. Told me he had to find the Tools of Lugh. It was after he left that I cracked the counter. He's called me a couple times since then, a few times this week. I haven't gotten back to him."

"Why not?" Cam took a sip of wine.

"I don't know what to say."

"Okay," Cam said.

Zemila appreciated that she didn't press.

"I've been helping him find his brother," Cam told her. "The one who's alive, I mean. Jenner's been helping him look for the Tools. He's planning to leave in a week."

"Really?" Zemila's heart sank. She didn't know why, but his leaving made her sad. It made it seem like there was a clock on when she could talk to him. But she wasn't ready, and she didn't think she would be in the next week.

We've got time, Lochlan and I, she told herself.

She didn't want to rush it with him. She wanted to work out her feelings, figure out her mind, then call him. She knew if she saw him, she would break. She would fall into his arms and use him as protection against the nightmare and against the world.

But she wouldn't do that. She wouldn't allow herself to do that. Not after Tyler. Not again.

We've got time, she thought.

"Could Lochlan help with your gift?" Cam asked.

"I don't know," she said, refocusing on the conversation at hand. "I don't know if he . . . if he caused this or maybe he made it worse."

Cam stared at her in shock.

"How?" Cam asked, tucking her ankles up on the couch. "How could he have done that?"

"Did he tell you about that spell he cast?" Zemila asked, her free hand drifting up to her neck. "The one that healed me?"

"Not really, just that when the guy had you, he did something, you needed help, and he cast some spell."

Zemila remembered the feel of the duct tape over her mouth, the cloth over her eyes, the strange hands on her skin.

Greg Simmons.

He'd kept her blindfolded and tied to a chair for the majority of her kidnapping. It had only been a few hours, but it had felt like years.

She remembered the fear when he'd taken her, the pain when he'd hit her, the panic when he'd sliced deep into her throat.

The glass in her hand shattered.

"Zemila!" Cam cried.

"Damnit."

"Are you okay?"

"Yes." Zemila looked down at her white couch, now sprinkled with red wine.

Lucky the glass was nearly empty, she thought.

"Zemila, your hand. Go to the washroom. I'll clean up here."

She looked down. There were bits of glass imbedded in her palm. She barely felt it.

"White couches," she muttered on the way to the washroom. "White carpets. Seemed like a good idea at the time."

She stood over the sink and picked at the glass. She hissed at the pain when she pulled out the largest chunk. Blood welled in her palm.

She stared at it, getting lost in it.

Her mind was sucked back to the warehouse.

Tied up, blindfolded, a blade at her throat. The hot pain. The warm blood. She clutched at her neck. Thick liquid spilled out from between her fingers.

She was dying.

Then something brought her back. She'd heard a voice. A rhythmic chanting. A heat hit her chest.

It was indescribable. It was electricity. It was ecstasy.

Then she was standing.

She removed her blindfold and took in her surroundings. There was a cracked symbol on the ground and a trail of gold. Lochlan was there. The golden light led to him.

Electricity. Ecstasy.

He'd tried to stand. Tried to reach her. Tried to protect her.

She'd turned her head to look at her abductor. The Famorian. Greg Simmons.

He'd writhed and screamed on the ground. He'd waved his arms like a toddler throwing a temper tantrum.

"Mine, mine, mine," he'd cried.

The memory seemed to echo off her bathroom walls.

"You're made of stone?" she'd said, catching sight of his grey hand smeared with blood. Her blood. "You're mine."

The feeling of ecstasy was gone. Anger was all that was left. Anger, fear, and a need to protect.

Lochlan had collapsed attempting to get to her.

He's not dead, she'd told herself. Not dead.

She hadn't known if it was true. In that moment, she'd needed to believe it was.

The memory drifted away. Zemila looked at herself in the bathroom mirror. Deep brown eyes looked back at her.

Maybe she should talk to Lochlan. Maybe Ms. Jace was right. Maybe what she felt was the real deal.

But that wasn't what weighed so heavily on her. What made her question herself, her gift, her sanity.

"You had to kill him," she told her reflection. "He would've killed you. He would've killed your friends. You had to kill him."

But you didn't have to kill him like that, said the small voice in the back of her mind. You didn't have to kill him like that.

CHAPTER THREE
Lochlan

As soon as my hands touched the edge of the community center pool, it all came rushing back. For thirty glorious minutes, I could forget that I hadn't seen or spoken to Zemila in six weeks. I could forget that my grandfather was still alive and trying to kill me . . . that he was getting stronger while I searched for the Tools of Lugh. No doubt he was searching for them too.

And why wouldn't he be? The Tools were the only way he could die. Or so the prophecy said. They were the only chance I had at killing him.

I paused on my way to the changeroom. Turning, I looked longingly over my shoulder at the water, now busy with the 6 a.m. crew.

There was a lengthy journey ahead. It was unlikely I would see or hear from Zemila before I left, and I wouldn't be in the water for a while. It would be nigh impossible to control my emotions without the calming effect of a hard swim.

I sighed heavily.

Mayhap it would be safer for the both of us if I just let Zemila go, I thought.

I hoped I'd be able to keep my emotions in check until I got back. I slung my towel over my shoulders and kept walking.

I'll figure something out, I thought. I always do.

I almost always do.

The blast of hot air from the sauna was more welcome than the cycle of theories about why Zemila hadn't returned any of my calls. I'd called a week after we'd talked. She hadn't picked up. I'd called the next week too. I was trying to give her space. One call a week wasn't too much, right? Week four was bad. I'd called her every other day. I knew I was being crazy. I knew she would pick up when she was ready. I just didn't want her to think she wasn't on my mind.

I'd stopped calling after that.

"New ink?"

The deep baritone voice made me jump.

"Sorry to startle you, Lochlan," said Tim.

Tim was a broad-shouldered Jamaican man who swam with a dedication I admired.

"Not at all, Tim," I said. It wasn't his fault I was jumpy. "I wasn't expecting anyone, least of all you. Short swim today?"

"Usman has signed us up for a sculpting class." Tim's disdain was obvious. "Twice a week at nine o'clock."

"Whoa." I caught my right foot in my hand for a quad stretch. "Contain your excitement."

"It's not my thing. He wanted to do something new so . . . for love, I go." Tim gestured to my arm. "But it appears art is your thing. I thought tattoos were out of style."

I glanced down, holding out my left arm. Though it had been two months, the dark pattern still surprised me. Faint at my inner left wrist, it grew darker as it worked its way up my arm, my shoulder, my pec, and finished over my heart.

"It was a little spur of the moment," I said with the same enthusiasm Tim had used to describe his art class.

"You regret it already?" Tim laughed, slapping his knee with the slowness of his front crawl.

"No," I said sharply, looking up from the twisting, knotted lines. "No, I don't regret it. It just hurt way more than I thought it would."

After I had stretched and wished Tim luck with his sculpting, I rinsed off, dressed, and ran home.

"How was the swim?" asked my elderly neighbour, Mrs. Abernathy, from her front porch. I opened my peeling front gate and closed it behind me before answering.

"Good!" I walked up the path to my door. Her dark chocolate skin wrinkled as a broad infectious smile greeted me. "Not too many people in the pool today," I told her. "How are you?"

"Oh, lovely. Just off to church," she said, hoisting her bright green handbag higher on her shoulder. "We are hosting a fundraiser. You could come, you know?"

"Thanks for the offer, Mrs. Abernathy." I adjusted a small chain around my neck. "I'd love to come, but I'm headed up—"

"Oh, yes," she interrupted. "Off to get your brother."

Mrs. Abernathy had been my neighbour for over three years now. Her strong southern drawl reminded me of an old friend. I liked that.

She liked my accent too. I think that's why she started inviting me over for tea.

"Shall I get your mail for you?" She flashed me a wicked grin.

"Ha ha," I said sarcastically. She knew very well that I didn't get mail. "Very funny."

I dropped my hand from the chain. I felt it like a weight around my neck. It carried a piece of the stone that had killed my grandfather the first time.

The time that hadn't worked.

"When can I expect you back?" she asked. "Hasn't it been a while since you've seen your brother? Not since Luis passed?"

Luis. The fake name I had given her for my eldest brother. Celtic God-King Lugh of the Long Arm wasn't exactly a name you threw out over sweet tea.

"Right," I said. "Not since he died. I'm heading up near Edmonton to get him, then we'll stay a couple nights in Toronto with an old friend."

"Heavens, boy," she said with shock. "Canada! Up near Edmonton! I thought you were taking the train?"

"I am."

"Edmonton is far."

"Since the MagLev got put in, it's not bad," I protested.

"How many stopovers have you got?"

"I go to New York, which only takes a couple hours. Then Toronto."

"Then across half of Canada," she said, incredulous. "Why don't you fly?"

"I like the train," I said.

It was true. I did like the train. But that wasn't the real reason.

I could count on one hand the number of times I'd taken a plane. Mostly it was fear that stopped me. I'd been told that water was the only thing that could end my life, but I was sure a plane crash would do the trick.

And if it didn't, well, I'd once healed from being crushed under a landslide. It had taken three years. I'd relearned how to swallow, how to walk, how to do everything. I had no interest in repeating the experience.

"So do I," Mrs. Abernathy told me. "Makes the trip quite long though."

"It does," I admitted. "I suspect I'll be gone for about ten days."

"That's not even long enough to ask for a postcard," she said, turning to make her way down the three steps from the porch to the walkway. Her thin hand gripped the railing with the strength born of a woman determined to live on her own.

"I'll send you a postcard," I promised. I pressed a hand to the scanner beside my door.

I heard the click of the lock at the same time as Mrs. Abernathy said, "Be safe now! I look forward to meeting your other brother . . . and to that postcard."

The smell of coffee greeted me when I opened my front door. One of the bonuses of having a roommate. Actually, I had two roommates.

I predicted it was Jenner in the kitchen and that Nemo was asleep on the pull-out couch.

I took off my shoes, crept forward, and peered around the corner into the living room.

Nemo Alkevic lay sprawled diagonally across the too-small bed. Standing a few inches taller than my six-foot-two, Nemo made an impressive figure, when he wasn't drooling on my pillow.

Nemo had been here for six weeks. He insisted he'd be out by the time I'd get back. I wasn't convinced.

"Coffee, amigo?" called my second roommate.

Nemo groaned and rolled over.

"Of course," I whispered, following my nose to the kitchen.

Jenner sat at the small table. In front of him, I saw an untidy stack of fifty-dollar bills. I rolled my eyes, guessing what it was.

"Oatmeal is on the stove," Jenner said, not lifting his gaze from the newspaper projection he was reading. Then he pointed at the cash. "That is from your second-favorite roommate."

"You made me oatmeal?" I asked.

"Favorite roommate equals me," he said, raising his coffee to his lips.

"Gracias." I reached into the cupboard beside the stove for a bowl.

"De nada."

I filled my bowl and sat down across from him.

"Hey!" he protested when I placed my oatmeal on top of the projection. "I was reading there."

"Use the wall." I took a bite of my breakfast, and pulled the cash towards me. There was a note.

Jenner gave me a scornful look, but flicked his fingers over his watch and redirected the newspaper projection.

LOCHLAN, the note read. HERE'S RENT FOR THE LAST MONTH. JENNER, HANDS OFF.

I frowned, counting the stack of fifties. Nemo paying rent for sleeping on my pull-out bothered me. His paying me in cash bothered me more.

"How's the world?" I asked, tucking the bills into my back pocket. Jenner always kept up to date with current politics.

"Still turning," he said. "There was a fire in a homeless shelter in Lowtown. They don't know how many died. And, read this," he said, zooming in on the relevant article.

I speed-read the top of it.

It was about the Right Waters Party, a small but aggressively right-wing group. They were bigoted, xenophobic homophobes with a specialty in playing on the fears of the public.

"So," I said. "What else is new?"

"I just don't understand how people are swallowing this," Jenner said. "I mean, come on. I would have to register as an immigrant if they got their way. My children would have to register! And both my parents were born here."

"You know I don't agree with them. Nor do most, which is why they resort to trash like this," I gestured at the paper and took a big gulp of my coffee. "But isn't that guy saying a 1stGen killed his wife?"

1stGen. First Generation American . . . as if America wasn't a country of immigrants.

Sighing, Jenner turned off the projection.

"Cam is going to be here in thirty minutes," he told me.

"I ordered a cab," I said, remembering Cam's offer to drive me to the station.

"And yet she will still be here in thirty minutes. Not everything is about you, you know? Many things are about me," Jenner said, a glint in his eye. "She's taking me to work today."

I squinted at him.

"Fine," he said. "She has those files you wanted. She said she would drop them by before she heads to the office."

"Does she know she's driving you to work?" I asked.

"It's possible."

"You haven't asked her yet."

"I haven't asked her yet," he echoed. "But it's not so out of her way, and I don't want to take the bus."

"Aye," I finished the last of my oatmeal and put my bowl in the sink. "Does Nemo know she's on her way?"

"Since he is still snoring," Jenner shrugged, "I'd assume no."

"You weren't going to wake him up, were you?"

"I think it's funny," Jenner said.

I shook my head at him.

"He's always so composed and Nemo-like," he went on. "I love it when my sister catches him off guard. He turns into an awkward teenager."

"Nemo was never an awkward teenager."

"He will be in about," Jenner looked at his watch, "twenty-seven minutes."

"I'm going to pack," I said, leaving the kitchen.

"You haven't packed? Dios mio."

Jenner's words followed me out of the kitchen.

I ignored them. I paused in the living room to throw a pillow at Nemo before continuing upstairs.

"Ah!" he said, jerking awake.

"Your girlfriend will be here in twenty minutes," I called over my shoulder.

"She's not his girlfriend," Jenner yelled from the kitchen at the same time as Nemo said, "Cam's not my girlfriend."

"Sure," I yelled back.

"Twenty minutes?" Nemo said, my words catching up to his sleep addled brain. "Crap!"

I pulled a duffle out from under my bed. My go bag. I added my favorite pair of jeans and a couple extra t-shirts. The white shirt I wanted to wear was looking a little grey and it had a stain. I threw it out. Then I took a real shower.

After changing into my second favorite jeans and a black V-neck long sleeve, I headed back downstairs. Nemo rushed passed me into the bathroom. Within seconds the shower was running again.

I smiled when I passed the living room. The pull-out was away. The clothing that had been scattered across the room was neatly packed. The coffee table was back in place between my mismatched couches.

I bent down to pick up a crumpled piece of paper Nemo had missed. Flattening it, I admired his skill with a pencil. Big eyes stared up at me out of a heart shaped face.

Cam.

He'd been drawing her a lot. I folded the paper and slid it into my back pocket.

"That was fast," Jenner said when I sat down across from him.

"I have a go bag," I told him.

"Oh," he said looking at me strangely. "That's so weird."

"Why?"

"I've only ever seen a 'go bag,' " he put air quotes around the word, "in the movies. Like, who actually needs that?"

"I'm the immortal grandson of Balor, Demon King, and secret brother to a Celtic god. I've been hiding from the Old World since before this country had its first immigrants."

"Hmmm," Jenner didn't look impressed. He took a sip of his coffee, then paused. Then he wiggled the mug in my direction. "Hey, superhero demigod magic man… be a pal?"

I smirked and placed a finger on the mug,

"Ignis," I said, and steam rose from the newly heated liquid.

"That will never not be cool," he said.

"I promise, it gets old."

"So, Dyson," Jenner nodded at me and raised his eyebrows. "She's the one you ran away with."

"It's not like that," I said.

"But you did run away with her."

"I did," I nodded.

"Isn't she a—" Jenner snapped his teeth together three times in rapid succession.

"Yes," I smiled. "She's a vampire."

"Sexy," he said. "How old is she?"

"Younger than I am."

"Dude, you can't even remember how old you are."

"I'm twenty-three."

"Oh, yeah?" Jenner asked. "How long ago were you twenty-two?"

"It's been a while," I admitted.

"*Camile Hernandez,*" my home system announced.

A hail of curses thundered down the stairs moments before Nemo sprinted into the kitchen, pulling on a deep red t-shirt.

"Unlock," I said through a laugh.

"Your shirt's on backwards," Jenner said.

"Crap." Nemo fixed it quickly, then tried to figure out what to do with his hands. He crossed his arms and leaned against the counter.

"Really?" Jenner asked.

"Leave him alone," I said. "Back here!" I called out to Cam when I heard the front door open.

Nemo huffed, pushed himself off the counter, and got a bowl of oatmeal.

"Hey, guys," Cam said upon entering the kitchen. "Do I smell oatmeal?"

"There's a little left," Jenner said. "Oh, it looks like Nemo took it."

Nemo froze, a spoon halfway to his mouth, horrified.

"Great job, Nemo," Jenner said.

"Do you want it?" Nemo extended his arms, offering her the bowl. "You can have it, if you want it, I don't want it, I mean, I'd eat it, but I don't want it, if you want it . . . I mean . . . hi."

"Awkward teenager," Jenner mouthed.

I couldn't help the grin.

"Hi," Cam smiled. "It's okay. I have to get to work. I'll pick something up on the way."

Jenner pretended to puke in the corner.

Cam dropped a heavy stack of papers onto the kitchen table in front of me and looked sternly at her brother.

"I guess that means you aren't going to ask me for a ride to work?" she shot at him.

Jenner's expression changed immediately to one of reverence.

"Camila," he crooned. "Mi hermosa e inteligente hermana."

"Oh, shut up," she said. He continued to praise her in Spanish. "Are you ready to go?"

"I'll go get my bag," he said, switching to English and leaving the kitchen.

Cam rolled her eyes before fixing them on me.

"The firm's P.I. said this is everything he could get. I didn't give him a ton to go on, so it wasn't easy. He got what he could about the names you gave me and those deaths in Canada."

"Prison records?" I asked.

"All in there," she answered. "When he went up for parole, when it was granted, the exact time and date of his release."

"Two days," I said. "That's why I'm going."

"Yeah," she answered.

My eyes quickly skimmed the files. "This is a huge help. Thank you."

"Don't thank me. He charges by the hour and the bill is in there."

"Not a problem." I opened the first folder. It was full of newspaper articles, most of which I'd already read.

"Cam?" Nemo asked, as she was about to leave the kitchen. "Are we still on for dinner tonight?"

I looked up in time to see Cam's lawyer persona melt away.

"Yes," she answered with a small smile. She took a few quick steps towards him, avoiding the still outstretched bowl of oatmeal, and kissed him on the cheek. "Text me later?"

Without waiting for a response, she turned and left the kitchen.

I heard Cam yelling up the stairs at Jenner. A moment later, he popped his head through the kitchen doorway. "Keep me in the loop, amigo. Call me if you need help."

"I will," I said.

"Safe travels, buena suerte."

"Gracias," I told him.

We clasped hands briefly and he left.

"Nemo?" I said after a moment of silence.

"Huh," he snapped out of whatever world he'd been in.

"Sit down," I said. "Eat your breakfast."

With a dreamy smile, he settled into Jenner's vacated seat.

"Where are you getting cash?" I asked, pulling the stack of bills out of my back pocket.

The dreamy smile vanished.

"I got a labour job with a guy who pays cash," he said.

I bet it sounded like a lie, even to him.

φ

I glanced at my ticket and walked down the busy stairs of Union Station. Finding my way to the map screen, I remembered the last time I was here.

Three months ago, I thought.

The prophetic dream of the train crash flooded my mind.

But I stopped it, I told myself. I saved those people.

And I'd played right into Balor's hands doing it.

"Edmonton," I said to the screen.

"*Train to Edmonton with stops in New York, Toronto, Winnipeg, departing in twenty-four minutes from Platform Nine,*" the automated voice replied.

I boarded the train ten minutes later and found my seat. There was something about the soft sway of a train that soothed me. MagLevs didn't move or sound like the trains of old, but there was still something nostalgic about them.

I loved traveling by rail.

"No, Olivia," I heard from the grouping of four seats across the aisle from me.

I turned to see a man and his young daughter. "You already have three trucks and your hover cube in your seat. You don't need the tablet."

Olivia wailed.

The man looked over at me apologetically.

"She'll quiet down once we start going," he told me. "She likes the way the train moves."

"Me too," I said, standing to put my messenger bag in the overhead compartment. I kept a few files in my seat.

Olivia did quiet down once the train started and fell asleep shortly after.

No rest for the wicked, I thought, as Olivia's little head settled on her father's lap.

I turned my attention to the papers in my hand. This one was from Jenner. It contained everything he could find about Megan Borde. My brother's new parole officer.

Princess Megan Borde grew up in Ontario. In university, she stopped using her given first name, Princess, and started going by her middle name only. After four years of post-secondary education, Megan Borde taught English in Mexico, then moved to Edmonton. That was fifteen years ago. She'd been a parole officer there for the last ten.

I looked through the file until I found a home address. That would be my first stop after renting a car. I wanted to learn who she was before walking into her office. I flipped back to the front of her file and started reading.

Olivia didn't wake up when we stopped in New York. She stayed peacefully asleep until the food trolley came by. Within minutes, she was eating a snack and driving one of her trucks around the small table in front of her.

"Vroom, vroom," she said with enthusiasm. She caught me watching her and smiled, apple sauce sliding down her chin.

I smiled back.

"You won't be the one," said a voice.

I jumped and my thick black frames slid out of place.

A middle-aged woman with almond-shaped eyes sat in front of me. When did she sit down? I thought.

Her long black hair was streaked white and grey. It was braided and came over one shoulder, falling to her waist.

"I'm sorry?" I said.

"Few young read off paper anymore." She gestured to the file in my hand.

"Oh," I sat up a little straighter, and pushed my glasses up my nose. "My parents were big readers," I lied.

I didn't know my parents and the Druids barely wrote anything down.

"Hmmmm," she said, staring at me as if she saw my falsehood.

"I'm sorry," I said again. "Do I know you?"

"Hmmmm." She looked out the window.

For the first time, I noticed how quiet everything was.

I followed her gaze. We were passing a small lake surrounded by tall trees. My eyes fell on a doe bounding away from the tracks.

But it wasn't bounding. It was frozen in midair. I looked to the sky and saw the slow-motion flap of a bird's wings. Turning in my seat I saw a toy truck was soaring off the table in slow motion. Olivia reached for it and her father reached for her.

My hand went to the piece of stone hanging from the fine chain around my neck.

"The Lady has your answer," the ivory-skinned woman said.

I narrowed my eyes.

"What are you?"

"The Lady has your answer and you will be found with the Collector," she continued, ignoring my question.

I gathered Magic to my core. I wanted to know what she was. I reached for the mental bonds that tethered me to my power. They weren't there. I had no connection to Magic. No power at all.

I started to panic.

"You will be found with the Collector," she repeated.

Her voice reminded me of water. It was smooth and strong and moved in strange places. Then something clicked, my panic faded, and she had my undivided attention.

"What Lady?" I asked, knowing she would not answer my first question. "What Collector?"

"The Virtuous Collector. Trust him with truth," she said.

"And the Lady?" I asked.

Time was short. The train was moving a little faster. The volume of the world grew. The doe's hooves lightly touched soft earth.

"The Lady of the Lake," she said, pointing out the window.

I followed her gaze and saw the lake disappear behind trees as we passed.

"Olivia, be careful!" her father warned.

Olivia started to cry.

I looked back at the seat in front of me. It was empty. The world had returned to its normal speed.

"The Lady of the Lake has your answer and you will be found with the Virtuous Collector. Trust him with truth," I whispered aloud. "What the hell does that mean?"

When I switched to a sleeper train in Toronto, I was still running over the riddle in my mind. The riddle she'd told me, and the riddle of who she was. Sleep took me in the wee hours of the morning. It came with strange dreams of fish and acorns. I dreamed of rivers with no end and of the woman from the train.

"You will be found," she told me. Figures appeared at her side. They echoed her words in voices that moved like water.

"You won't be the one," she said.

"You will be found," her companions told me. "You will be found."

Their voices, at first soft and melodious, turned cold.

"You will be found, you will be found, you will be found."

"You won't be the one," the woman from the train said. "You won't be the one."

Their voices grew louder. They stepped towards me. Behind them, I saw the flickering image of my brother Lugh with his sword. He was replaced by the Famorian, Simmons. Then the stone that had falsely delivered the true death to my grandfather. It lay broken in three pieces. I saw my brother Llowellyn with the spear.

Then I saw Zemila tied to a chair.

"Help me," she said. Before I could move, Simmons had a knife to her throat.

Not again, I thought. Please not again.

"You won't be the one," the women chanted. "You will be found."

"Help me," Zemila said.

"Not one more step!" Simmons yelled.

"No!" I cried. But too late.

"You won't be the one."

Zemila was dead. Again.

"You will be found."

Her limp body was in my arms.

"You won't be the one."

Her neck broken.

"What have I done?" I said. "Gods, I'm so sorry, Zemila. What have I done?"

The train jolted. I woke up.

CHAPTER FOUR
Zemila

Zemila looked at her watch. 2:10 p.m. Nemo was late.

The last of the lunch rush was leaving the small café. She envied the people going into work. But it wasn't like she hadn't been keeping busy. She'd spent the better part of the last week interviewing anyone in Lowtown who wasn't too afraid of the boogie man of Lowtown to talk to her. The Queen, or so she was called. Zemila had never found any proof of her existence.

Billy had been right on the money about the disappearances, though. Not for the first time, Zemila wondered where to go with what she'd learned. Nearly thirty people were unaccounted for after the fires. Their bodies could be buried under the rubble. But her gut told her that wasn't true.

One or two people per building? Maybe she could believe they hadn't been found yet. But six buildings in the last five months and thirty people missing?

That was too bizarre to let lie.

She checked her watch again. There was a notification. Her first thought was Nemo had cancelled, but it was just a reminder for her second therapy session with Dr. Danika Janson.

After taking Adrienne's advice and making an appointment, Zemila had spent an hour and a half filling in the therapist on her childhood trauma and the Human aspects of her life.

When she'd finished explaining her mess of a childhood, Dr. Janson had said, "That really sucks." Somehow, that had been exactly what Zemila needed to hear. She'd felt lighter walking out of the session than she had walking in.

But I need to talk about Simmons, she thought.

She needed to talk about how she'd developed a fear of unfamiliar men, and how she couldn't stop hearing Simmons' death screams. About her powers acting up. About how she needed help with her gift.

Are there Luman therapists? she wondered.

"Hey, Mila," said a voice from above her.

She looked up.

"Nemo." She stood to give her brother a hug.

"Sorry I'm late." He released her and they sat.

He looked tired, haggard. Dark sunglasses covered his eyes and there was an unusual slump in his shoulders.

"Don't worry about it," she said. "How are you?"

"I'm okay, looking for work." He settled into his chair.

After their mother died, and their father left, Nemo had worked as a dishwasher to put food on the table. He'd served for a while too, before he'd needed more money than he was making, and had found less legal means of putting food on the table. Zemila knew he didn't want to work in the restaurant business. She hoped he wasn't falling back into old habits.

"How bored are you without work?" Nemo smirked, changing the subject.

"Urgh!" She ran a hand over her tight ponytail. "You have no idea."

"I think I do," he laughed. "Remember the broken ankle when you were nine?"

"Oh God, that was worse."

She'd been trying to keep up with Nemo. He piggybacked her home. She cried silently into his shoulder the entire way.

"Thanks," Zemila said. "I needed some perspective."

"You were a monster," Nemo said. "Torturing all of us."

"It should've happened to you," Zemila said in jest. "You would have loved the time away from school."

"Are you kidding me?" Nemo said, his face going sour. The way it did whenever they spoke of their father. "He wouldn't have let me stay home."

"You're right," she agreed. "I miss you."

A beat of silence followed Zemila's words. She reached a hand out and placed it over Nemo's. He pulled his hand away.

"You're the one who kicked me out."

"Okay," she said, feeling defensive. "I'm trying to say something nice here. I miss you."

She waited.

He didn't speak.

"How's Lochlan's couch?" she asked. And why are you wearing sunglasses?

She didn't voice the second question. The day was overcast and his sunglasses were dark.

A gangly teenaged server came up to them and they ordered.

"You want to know how staying at Lochlan's is?" Nemo asked when the server left. "Or are you fishing for an update?"

"I'm not fishing," she said, picking at a spot on the wood table that matched the rustic décor of the café. "I'm asking."

"What are you asking?"

She flipped him off. "You're such a jerk."

"Can I just enjoy having the advantage for once?" Nemo's smile was genuine this time. "I never get this. You're always so put together. Even when we were kids. This," he gestured at her, "awkward version of you is so interesting. And satisfying."

"Are you done?" she asked.

"Okay, fine," he said, taking mercy on her. "Staying on the couch is okay. But since he left yesterday, I've been crashing in Loch's room."

"And at Cam's?" Zemila probed.

"Which story do you want here?"

"You're right," she said. "The Cam update can wait."

"I know you talk to her about me."

"I want to hear your side too," she said, meaning it.

"So nosy," Nemo said.

"I am a journalist. It's my job."

The server was back with their drinks and their conversation paused for a moment. Nemo took a gulp of water and continued.

"Lochlan headed to Edmonton yesterday," he said. "He's picking up his brother tomorrow from the prison, and taking him to his parole officer. Then they're finding their way back here."

"Is he allowed to leave the country?" Zemila asked.

"That's something Lochlan's going to have to figure out. I have no idea how it's happening. Jenner gave him some information on the parole officer, but you know Lochlan."

"He always finds a way."

Nemo nodded his agreement.

"Then he'll head to Toronto to see Dyson."

"Two pulled-pork sandwiches." The server slid plates in front of them. "Insider's tip," he said. "Start with the fries. The pork burned the roof of my mouth once when I dug in too quick."

"Thanks," Nemo said.

The server smiled and left.

"So, how are you?" Zemila asked, starting with a fry. "Cam told me you haven't been in touch with her much. That you bailed on a date."

"I didn't bail," Nemo said, defensive. "I rescheduled."

"And you bailed on me earlier this week."

"I did not bail. I rescheduled. I'm sitting right here!"

"Then things are good?"

"Yeah," Nemo said. "Things are fine."

"So why have you been paying Lochlan rent in cash?" she accused.

"How the hell do you know that?" he asked, getting heated. "You're not even talking to Lochlan."

That stung. She narrowed her eyes at him.

"Jenner mentioned it to Cam. Cam told me."

"Jesus!" Nemo looked out the window and shoved a few fries in his mouth.

"We're just worried about you."

"I'm not a kid, Zemi," he said, though the fries. He'd used to call her that when they were growing up. She hated it. He used it when he was pissed. "I can take care of myself."

"I know that," she said, trying to make eye contact with him. "I

51

know tha—Christ, Nemo. Can you take off the sunglasses?"

She reached forwards and he jerked his head away.

"Leave it, Zemi." His tone was harsh.

Her hand froze in the air.

"I just want to look at you." Zemila lowered her hand and clenched her jaw. Irritation at his stubbornness made her tone sharp. "I've barely seen you since you moved out—"

"Since you kicked me out."

"I needed some space to think."

"Well, I'm sorry I was such a burden."

"Oh, come on." She rolled her eyes. "It wasn't like that."

He looked out the window again.

"You were sleeping on my couch," she said.

"I'm sleeping on a couch now."

"Will you take off the damn sunglasses?"

"No."

"Come on!"

"No."

"Nemo," she pleaded and reached forwards again.

"NO!"

At the same time as he slammed his palm on the table, the sunglasses flew off his face and into Zemila's hand.

A stunned silence filled the restaurant. If she hadn't been so distracted by the black eye marring Nemo's good looks, she would have been worried about using her gift in public. She would've wondered how she'd moved the plastic frames.

"How the hell did you do that?" he demanded.

"Who the hell gave you a black eye?" she shot back.

"Are you kidding me?" he hissed as the low chatter of the restaurant picked up again. "I knew there was something weird going on with you. I knew you were keeping something from me." He glared at her. "No secrets, remember? That's the deal we made when Mom died. Or did you forget?"

"No, I didn't forget," she said, guilt welling up inside her. "I just needed—"

"That's why you kicked me out." It was a statement. Not a question. "You knew your gift was acting up and you didn't want me to notice."

She looked down at her hands. She felt nine years old again. All she wanted to do was cry into her brothers' shoulder.

"How long?" Nemo demanded. "Since Simmons? Lochlan?"

"Before," she said in a small voice.

"And when were you going to tell me?"

"Are you going to tell me about your black eye?" she asked.

He scoffed. "You're kidding right?"

She stared at him. He shook his head, stood, and reached into his pocket for his wallet.

"Now I need some space to think." He threw a few bills onto the table and turned away.

"Nemo, wait!" she called.

He didn't turn back.

CHAPTER FIVE
Lochlan

Dark liquid spilled onto the tiny white saucer. I moved the postcard out of the way. "Coffee. Grilled cheese."

The waitress left without another word. The service at this greasy spoon left something to be desired. I signed my name in the small space left at the bottom of the card for Mrs. Abernathy.

"You're late."

I looked up.

A red-haired teenager sat down across from the person in the next booth over.

"Yeah, but I'm always late, Meg," she said. "I think it's safe to assume that I come at four and you come at 3:45."

"Just gives me time to read the paper." Megan closed the pages, but the girl reached for it.

"Crazy business about this guy, right?" She gestured to the politician and child on the front page. It read 'Widowed US Senator Still Grieving.' "The poor kid."

"I know," Megan said. "Still no idea who killed her, but he's gunning for a 2ndGen. Anyways, how are you? I missed you last week."

Though my eyes were on my sandwich, my ears stayed on the conversation. I hoped to learn something, anything I could use to my advantage.

Megan and Sabrina Borde met at this diner once a week. Sabrina, Megan's wayward niece, had gotten into a spot of trouble with the law and Megan had been able to pull some strings. The weekly meetings with Megan had been court-ordered for six months.

That was three years ago.

"How's school?" Megan asked.

Sabrina shrugged.

"Specifics."

"It's good," Sabrina said. "Nothing really new."

"Well, that's a lie," Megan said.

I looked up to see Sabrina flash a small smile.

"There is this boy," Sabrina said.

I sipped my coffee and listened.

Thirty minutes later, the server brought my bill. Though I had a better idea of who Megan Borde was, I had learned nothing of real value.

"I couldn't go," I heard Sabrina say.

"Oh?" Megan answered.

I don't know what I was expecting to learn here anyways, I chastised myself. Something that could help me, or something I could use as leverage?

"I couldn't!" Sabrina insisted.

"Okay," Megan answered in the same knowing voice.

"Why do you always do that?" Sabrina said.

"Do what?"

A small black box was shoved under my nose. The server wordlessly asked for payment. I placed my thumb on the pay pad.

"Answer like that."

"Like what?" Megan's tone was innocent.

"Like you know I'm lying," Sabrina said.

"Are you lying?"

I slowly moved my thumb towards the five-dollar tip button. The server squinted at me.

If looks could kill, I thought.

I hit the ten.

"You knew I was lying," Sabrina said. "You always know when I'm lying."

I drained my coffee before standing. I glanced at the pair on my way past, just in time to see Megan give Sabrina a devious smile.

"Then don't lie," Megan said. "I always know."

My hand froze on the door.

"Impossible," I whispered and turned to stare at Megan.

Four percent of eight billion, I thought. That was the estimated Luman populations. Small odds of running into one here.

She must have felt my eyes on her. Megan looked up. I dropped my gaze and hurried out the door.

I stood just outside, pretending to be on my watch, but I called for Magic. I reached for the bonds. In my excitement, when I pulled, more Magic came than I'd asked for. It sparked between my fingers. I looked up nervously. Luckily, there was no one around to see. I centered myself and fixed my intention on discovery.

"Mór-amarc," I whispered. There was a small whooshing sound as

I sent the revealing spell in Megan's direction.

It came back with welcome news.

Megan was Luman.

φ

I left the Yellow Head Motel at 6 a.m. the next day. The June morning air was cool and I could see a storm rolling in.

I waited for a line of driverless transport trucks to pass before I pulled onto the highway. A highway lined with motels and empty parking lots. Business was slow.

The sky ahead of me was clear and bright. Behind me, cloud cover slowly darkened my rear-view mirror. I would beat the storm.

It followed me the whole way there.

So did images of the dream I'd had. It wasn't like the other dreams, the ones I thought were prophecy. This one didn't reek of redemption, or salvation, or the lust for power I had so long ago . . . no. This one seemed like a warning.

The idea of Zemila lying dead in my arms turned my blood to ice. I had no idea what this warning could mean, or who it could be from. But the more I thought of it, the more I realized she would be better off without me. She would be safer if I wasn't around.

Just before nine, I pulled up in front of Grande Sky Institution.

It had been hard not to build up this moment, the reconnection with my brother. I'd imagined and re-imagined what it would be like. The knot of anxiety in my chest squeezed tight. My emotions were mixed.

He was hiding in this place. Hiding from the world. From Balor. From me.

Then again, I thought, I'd been doing the exact same thing.

I parked in the visitor lot and walked to the gate. I pushed the intercom buzzer.

"Please wait," a female voice said.

"Oh. Okay," I answered awkwardly.

The sky was dark now. I hoped it would hold. I didn't want to drive back in the rain.

"Visiting hours don't start until nine," said the voice.

"I'm here to pick up my father."

That's what Jenner had told me to say. We'd gotten a current image of Llowellyn. He'd cast some kind of aging spell.

"My name is Lochlan Ellyll. My father is Leo MacEthan."

"Please wait."

A soft rumble crossed the skies.

"Scan your palm and look into the camera," the female voice directed.

I did. After a few more questions, I was buzzed through the fence.

I went through a second identification process inside. I sent a prayer of thanks to Jenner when I was directed to sit in the small waiting area.

My mind raced over how he might react, how I might react. Would we give ourselves away somehow?

A door opened. My head snapped up. There he was.

An old man with long grey-streaked hair braided down his back. He dipped his head as he walked through the door. Tall and broad, he dwarfed the guard bringing him out. A beard covered most of his face. A face I barely recognized.

But his bright green eyes told me he was kin.

I dropped my head into my hands and started to cry.

φ

Mist clouded the horizon as a dark shadow fell over high stone walls. A boy followed his feet down a corridor. He moved quietly; he always moved quietly.

Light and sound came through the crack between door and frame. Something called to him. He pushed open the door and the call grew louder. A fire crackled in the hearth.

The boy tilted his head. The fire was black.

How odd, he thought.

"Little Lochlan," said a voice behind him.

The boy whipped around.

"Little One." The hulking figure of his brother watched from the end of the hallway.

"Don't call me that!" Lochlan snapped.

"What are you looking at?" said a second, equally large figure. Though all three of them were twelve years old, Lochlan was much smaller than his brothers.

Lochlan turned back to the hearth. It was empty.

"Nothing," he said.

φ

Long and lean, he moved quickly, twisting out of the way. The spear point missed him by inches.

"Close, Little One," said the spear's wielder.

"Don't call me that," he said, rolling away from the advancing attacker.

"Lugh, don't," said the broad-shouldered teenager, watching from under a nearby oak tree. "I can feel his anger from here."

"You cannot protect him forever, Llow," Lugh said.

"Lochlan does not need my protection." Llowellyn smiled lazily. "I am warning you."

"Warning me?"

In his arrogance, the future King straightened out of his fighting stance.

Lochlan saw his moment

φ

"Where is he?" Hands on Lochlan's shoulders held him back.

"No. Stop."

"Llowellyn, release me! Tell me where he is."

Tears slid down his face.

"Lochlan, please."

"Llow, by the Gods, I swear—" Lochlan tried to push passed his brother.

"Little One," Llowellyn said. At those words, Lochlan became a boy again.

"Don't," he said weakly.

He saw the truth in his brothers' eyes. Their King was dead. He didn't want to believe it. It couldn't be true.

He slid to the floor, knees unable to support the weight of his anguish. A large hand rested on his head as he wept.

"Little One," Llowellyn said, sadly.

"Don't call me that."

60

φ

A large hand rested on my head. I looked up into the bright green eyes of my King.

I blinked. Llowellyn. Not Lugh.

"Llowellyn," I said to the greying man.

"Little One," Llowellyn said. My heart swelled at the old nickname. I stood and embraced my brother. "It's been an age," he said, hugging me back.

Llowellyn didn't speak as we left. Nor did he speak as we started to drive. He just looked out at the world. Or he looked at me.

I understood.

If I wasn't driving, I would have been drinking in the sight of him too. He'd said it had been an age. It had been longer than that.

"You look good," he said, finally breaking the silence.

"You look old."

"Yes." He sniffed and adjusted a thin gold chain around his neck. "It was a hard spell."

"Not a binding?"

A binding was easy enough—I'd used it many times. It was a way to grow old with someone. A common practice for immortals who used our type of Magic.

"Not a binding," he said.

"Then how did—" I sucked in a breath, not wanting to finish the question. Fearing the answer. "All this time?"

"All this time," he said with a slow nod.

"Because of the children," I assumed.

"That was part of it," he whispered. "That was part of it . . ."

Llowellyn, a man of endless patience, had loved working with children. He had always taught the young soldiers when we were with the Tuatha Dé, when we were at war with Balor the first time.

In 2009, under the name Leo MacEthan, Llowellyn had graduated from teacher's college. Teaching work had been hard to come by back then. Llowellyn had been happy to take a job in a small northern community in need of educators.

He'd packed his bags and moved to Cold Lake, Alberta. He'd been there for seven years as a beloved Arts teacher before tragedy struck.

Six students were found brutally murdered in one of the school portables. Slowly, evidence that the gentle giant Mr. MacEthan was the leader of a small, but aggressive, cult, came to light. The papers said he'd been recruiting students, and their deaths were a cult ritual gone wrong.

In the end, the crown prosecutor was only able to charge him with one murder. Samantha Ouako. She hadn't been found with the others. She'd been found later, buried in a shallow grave not far from where Leo MacEthan had fished on the weekends.

Llowellyn had pled guilty. The case had never gone to trial.

I knew my brother had the ability to kill. We'd all been trained fighters. But Llowellyn killed to protect. He killed because he had to. He'd never taken to war. Not like I had.

Where the Druid Priestess gave our King the gift of strength and leadership, where she gave me wit and defiance, she'd given Llowellyn compassion and reason.

For him, violence was always a last resort.

"Was it hard?" I asked. "Giving up Magic?"

That was the only way he could have aged without a binding spell.

He'd blocked his connection to Magic.

"No," he said. "The spell was hard, but giving it up? After everything that happened." He took a deep breath. "Giving it up was easy."

I didn't ask what "everything" meant. He would tell me when he was ready. I tried to reach out with my mind to sense how he felt.

In the Old World, we were linked. It had started when the three of us had hit puberty. To say it was awkward would have been an understatement. We had only felt strong emotions at first. As we got older, as we'd trained, the ability had developed into whole conversations. And when we fought—

Oh, when we fought, I remembered. We were one mind. We were unstoppable. When Lugh died, my heart had hurt so much I didn't notice the empty space in my mind for a century. I longed to feel that closeness again.

But without a connection to Magic, Llowellyn was a blank wall. The emptiness of that was a loneliness I hadn't expected.

Llowellyn's hand drifted up and touched what I knew was a stone pendant hiding under his shirt.

"Here," I said, pulling mine over my head and handing it to him. The power of the Magic would help him recover his connection faster.

"Lochlan, no," Llowellyn said, pushing it back to me. "You keep that piece of him."

"Much has happened, brother," I said, not sure how to start. "I'm sorry to say, but you need your Magic back."

"They mean nothing together until you tether all three pieces of the stone," he said. "I will take it then."

He looked out the window, ending the discussion.

"All right," I said, returning my eyes to the road. "First your parole officer, then everything else."

"Megan Borde," Llowellyn said. He gazed out the window like he'd never seen the prairies before.

"She's Luman," I said.

His head snapped up. "You're joking."

"A low-level Gifter," I told him. "I don't think she knows."

"What is she?"

"A Truth Seer."

He made a small huffing sound before turning back to the window.

"How do you know this?" he asked.

"I followed her."

"Of course you did."

I could hear the smile in his voice.

"Did you expect anything less, brother?"

"No, Little One," he said, a smirk firmly in place. "Your predictability is a warm comfort. Tell me what you learned."

Once I started talking, I couldn't stop. I told him about Megan, then my life. Of traveling to the New World, and how strange everything had seemed. I told him how lost I'd been, and the people who helped me.

I told him about Erroin Peritia, the Luman school in India where I'd met Zemila. About the nightmares that had started there. Horrible nightmares where I was as out of control as I was when Lugh had died. When I had killed the men who killed him. I explained that the dreams had left when I left school, and I explained why they'd come back.

I spoke of Simmons, and the spell that had saved Zemila's life. He knew what it meant that I had resorted to Blood Magic. That I'd risked Blood Magic.

I told him about the prophecy and why we needed him. That he too, like I did, had to kill our grandfather Balor for him to truly die. And we needed the Tools to do it.

"Lugh's Tools," he said, fingering the chain at his neck. We pulled into a parking spot. "We have two of three pieces here."

"We do." I laid a hand on my chest.

"And the third is with a Vampire?" he asked.

"In Toronto, yes. When this is done," I nodded to the front door of the rundown building, "we'll go there."

"Good she is a Truth Seer. Better if she knows about the Luman world."

"Yes," I agreed. "Let's hope she trusts her gift."

"Let's hope," he echoed, getting out of the car. "I don't suppose we have any other options, do we?"

We walked towards the door.

"I could spell her, go into her mind, and plant a false—"

"No." The word was sharp and stern. It stopped me in my tracks.

"Llow, I—"

"No," he took two long strides towards me and laid a hand on my chest. "You cast a powerful blood spell not two months ago."

"It wasn't like that—"

"You do not know what it was like. Nor does anyone else," he said. "You know how wrong it could have gone. Imagine if that spell had taken you instead of saved the girl."

"She's not just a girl," I told him.

"You said she won't even speak to you. You said you think she would be safer without you!"

"She's overwhelmed," I protested. "She needs time, and when has our presence made anyone's lives better?"

My brother's eyes were shards of emerald ice. I realized too late what saying that would mean to him.

"You've seen with your own eyes what horrors that spell can bring," he said calmly.

"Llow, I didn't mean—"

"You have seen," he interrupted me. "Yet you cast it anyway."

"She would have died!"

"Little One—"

"Don't call me that," I said instinctually.

"Little One." He cupped my cheek like he'd done when we'd been boys. "Do not start down that path again."

Shock and hurt ran through me.

"You think I would enjoy playing with Megan's mind?" I shook off his hand. "You think I've learned nothing in all this time?"

"I think," my brother said, looking down at me. "Especially if Balor is truly back . . . I think it's beyond your control.

CHAPTER SIX
Lochlan

I was frustrated and angry. After lifetimes apart, my brother thought I was still the same boy. He thought I had no control over my power. No will of my own.

Dark Magic no longer held sway over me. He should have known that.

"Hello," said a young man in the parole officers' waiting room. He wore a dark blue floral shirt and a warm smile. "You must be Mr. MacEthan?"

"That's me," Llowellyn answered. "Leo MacEthan."

"Have a seat," he said. "I'll let Ms. Borde know you're here." He eyed me as he rose from the plain wooden desk. He walked to the farthest left of the three doors behind him.

"MacEthan is here," he said into the room. I couldn't make out the muttered response. After a moment, he turned and said, "You can go right in."

"Thank you." Llowellyn passed with a nod.

I followed.

With a much sterner expression than she'd worn yesterday, Megan Borde sat behind a wooden desk, writing furiously on a notepad.

"Have a seat," she said without looking up. "Just a moment."

We sat.

"Terribly sorry," she said. When she looked up, she reached out a hand. "My name is Megan."

"Pleased to meet you Ms. Borde. I'm—"

"Leo MacEthan," she cut in. "Yes. And you must be his son."

"Lochlan," I supplied and shook her hand. Her grip was strong.

"As I'm sure you're aware, I'm going to be your parole officer while you're here in Edmonton. I took a look at your case; there is nothing too pressing. Tell me a little bit about the current goals you are working on?" she asked.

Getting your Magic back and hunting down an ancient deity, I sent to my brother.

My thoughts met the blank wall of his Magic-less mind.

Of course, I mentally chided.

"Do you want to tell her," I asked. "Or should I?"

Llowellyn looked blankly from her, to me, and back.

"Mr. MacEthan, I think its best if you tell me yourself what—"

"I've been locked up for three decades," Llowellyn spoke over her. "Maybe you should do the honors."

"Mr. MacEthan, I really think—"

"Suppose I'll start with what she is?"

"Yes," Llowellyn agreed.

Megan sat back in her chair, arms crossed, glaring. Men crumbled under that stare, I was sure. I nearly did.

"Ms. Borde," Llowellyn said, unsteadily. The stare worked on him too. "Why did you become a parole officer?"

"We are not here to talk about me, Mr. MacEthan."

"Please," he said. "Humor me."

"I don't—"

"It's important," I interrupted.

She froze.

"Ahh," I pointed a finger at her. "There it is."

Llowellyn nodded. "Yes, I see it too."

"See what?" Megan asked.

"Truth," I told her. "You heard Truth."

"I believe," she seemed to choose her words carefully. "That you believe, whatever is going on between the two of you is important."

"No," I slowly shook my head. "You heard Truth. That's why you paused."

She stared blankly at me. Clearly not having any of it.

"You became a parole officer," Llowellyn said. "Because you are, at your core, good. You want to help people. But there are lots of jobs where you can help people. You chose this one, because you connect with this part of the population in a way other people don't. Because you always know when someone is speaking Truth."

There was a beat of silence.

"Lots of people can tell when they're being lied to," she said.

"He didn't say that." I told her. "He said you can hear Truth. Not my truth, not your truth. You can hear, capital T, Truth."

"There is no such thing as absolute truth," she said.

But her arms weren't crossed anymore, and she was leaning forward.

"Isn't there?" Llowellyn asked.

"No." She said the word without a hint of a question.

"Magic is real," I said. "True or false?"

Her eyes went wide.

"And there it is again," Llowellyn said. "Shall I have my brother show you?"

"Your brother?" she said.

"Aye, my twin brother."

He didn't even stumble on the word, I thought. Twin.

I guess I was a twin now. Being one of three was a distant memory. Another life. I had been a twin for a very long time.

"Impossible," she whispered. She didn't sound certain.

"Do you believe me?" he asked.

"I don't . . ." she said. "I . . ."

Her eyes moved back and forth between us. Searching for answers. Searching for reason. There was only Truth.

"We need your help," I said.

"If you're twins," she pointed first at Llowellyn, then me. "Why the hell are you so much older than him?"

"Ahh, well, that is interesting," I said, leaning back in my seat and gestured for Llowellyn to speak.

His eyes narrowed, but he consented.

"I cut myself off," he said, elbows going to his knees. "While I was in prison, I cut myself off from Magic. I haven't cast in over thirty years. I haven't had Magic in my body, so I've aged."

A small tilt of the head was all the confusion Megan showed. I was impressed at her composure, whether or not she trusted her gift.

"Magic heals our cells, keeps us young. Kept me young," he corrected. "Until I stopped using it."

"Right," she said, skeptically. "Sure."

"She doesn't trust her Gift," he said over his shoulder to me.

"I can see that," I responded.

"Maybe you could restore part of my connection."

"I thought only the caster could break this type of spell," I said. "Or one of the Old Gods."

"Magic ties to the body in three ways," he explained.

Megan watched, eyes wider than usual.

"Body, mind, and soul," he said. "The spell I cast blocked all three. The connection of Magic to my body can be restored with an infusion of power and intention. It should work. For all three, we may need an Ancient. But you," he nodded at me. "You can restore my body."

"Ummm . . ." Megan said. We both looked at her. "What?"

"What if we were the same age?" Llowellyn said. "Would you trust us? Would you trust yourself?"

"If you de-aged thirty plus years before my eyes," she scoffed, "I guess I wouldn't have much choice."

Llowellyn nodded, then stood with the speed of an old man. He held a hand out to me.

"Power and intention," he repeated.

"Isn't that how it always is?" I asked, standing as well.

"Yes, Little Lochlan." He closed his eyes. "Yes, it is."

I took in a deep breath.

"And the word?" I said, asking for the spell.

"Ros-éaraid," he answered.

I pulled on the bonds tying me to Magic, requesting power.

Feeling the steady build in my core, I fixed my intention on my brother. On my desire for him to connect to Magic. And to me.

I felt a spark between my fingers.

I heard a gasp from the other side of the desk.

With one last request, one last pull on the bond to my power, I clasped my brother's hand and pushed the Magic into him.

"Ag mo caitheamh, ros-éaraid cagair," I said. "Ros-éaraid cagair."

All the energy, all the Magic, all the power and intention I'd pulled to my body, I then pushed into his. A great whooshing sensation racing through my body and into Llowellyn.

Our bond was restored.

My eyes snapped open. A flood of emotions hit me. Anger, frustration, hopelessness, pain, and grief. It washed over my body and forced me back into my chair.

On the heels of that grief was love. Such deep love—and even deeper loss. I squeezed his hand, then released it as the connection broke.

"Oh. My. God." Amazement colored Megan's words.

I turned to look at my brother.

The slightly bowed figure straightened. His chest filled out at the same time as his lined face smoothed and his grey hair darkened. He took in a deep breath and grew. Not in size, but in energy. The energy of a young man. The power of potential.

He stretched. A few things cracked and popped.

This was the man of my memory, I thought. Taller and broader than I. His features were wider, softer than mine. I had rarely worn my hair so long.

He looked like Lugh.

We'd noticed we weren't aging when we were around twenty-five or twenty-six. Llowellyn always thought it had stopped at twenty-three. That was the man I saw before me now. The gentle giant, the empath, the first brother of the King. The second son of Cian and Ethinn.

He looked around, searching for something.

"I don't suppose there's a mirror in here?" he asked. "It has been a while."

Megan shook her head slowly, mouth hanging open.

"That's all right," he said, sitting down.

"Ms. Borde?" I asked.

"Huh?"

"How are you feeling?"

She gazed at Llowellyn, eyes wide.

"Start from the beginning."

"So, let me see if I get this," Megan said after nearly three-quarters of an hour. "You two are gods—"

"Demigods," Llowellyn corrected.

"And I'm a Gifter."

"Low level," I said.

"Your grandfather came back from the dead—"

"He was never really dead," I repeated.

"To take over the world."

We nodded.

"You need me to disappear you," she pointed at Llowellyn. "So you can help him," she pointed at me. "Your twin-slash-triplet brother, track down a spear, then a sword, to kill your grandfather again—"

"Never actually dead."

"So that he doesn't . . . What? Enslave humanity? Kill us all?"

"We aren't clear on his intentions beyond gaining power," Llowellyn said. "But yes."

"This is a lot." She let her head fall into her hand.

Then she laughed. Hard.

The shift in tone was unnerving. Llowellyn and I shared a nervous glance.

"Did we break her?" he asked me.

"Christ," Megan said. "My mother would go nuts if she knew I could tell when she's lying." She shook her head. "She's so good at it!"

A light bulb went off in my mind.

"She's why you were resistant," Llowellyn said, apparently having the same thought. "She's had you questioning yourself your entire life."

Megan shrugged.

"Parents have a way of messing us up," I said. "Or grandparents, in our case."

"Okay." Megan took a deep breath and held up a finger. "Question."

"Just one?" Llowellyn asked.

She smirked.

"Can you be old again?" she said. "Because you're going to have to die."

Llowellyn looked from Megan to me.

"It's possible," I said.

"What do you mean die?" he asked.

"Right now, with your parole," she explained, "you're being tracked. You were implanted with a tracking device that only turns off when you die and the officer responsible for you, that's me, verifies your death and disables the device."

"So, I have to be dead to not be tracked," Llowellyn stated.

"Yes," she confirmed. "And you should do it in here . . .right now. Die."

"Not demanding at all, this one," I said, hooking a thumb in Megan's direction. The words were casual, but my stomach dropped. I saw fear behind my brother's eyes.

"Says the guy I met an hour ago, asking me to break the law," she countered.

"Touché," I said.

"And it should be a heart attack," she added. "A real one. Is that possible? Paramedrones will scan the body and produce a report. That will come to me and I'll be able to deactivate the tracker."

"I can do that," I said.

"That's Blood Magic," Llowellyn told me.

"I am aware." My tone was dry.

"There has to be another way," he said. "How long would I have to be dead?"

"If you, old man you," Megan said, "die of natural causes here in this office, if you had a heart attack or something, the Paramedrones would come in, pronounce you dead, do an autopsy scan, and leave. Human paramedics wouldn't even show up."

"There wouldn't be an autopsy or anything?" I asked.

"If the drones say it's natural causes, and the next of kin says they don't want one, no. The next of kin could call a funeral home and make arrangements for the body."

Llowellyn looked from her to me. I knew what he was thinking.

"This sounds like a good plan," I said, trying to allay his fears. "I can do this."

"And the funeral home?" he asked Megan.

"Easily bribed. Some move bodies full of drugs, others do low-level smuggling. Falsify records of cremation . . . The right one won't be hard to buy off."

"You're sure?" he asked her. "Ms. Borde, you're sure this is the only way? The best way?"

"No," she answered. Her light brown eyebrows drew together. "But it's the only way without hurting anyone or burying me in paperwork."

"Someone is getting hurt," Llowellyn said.

"I don't count," I told him.

"I was talking about me."

My eyebrows popped up in surprise.

He made a joke, I thought.

If he was joking, he agreed. That was always how he'd dealt with pressure in the old days.

Llowellyn ran a big hand through his hair. The action revealed the tones of dark brown streaked through the black. "I'm not sure about this. It's dangerous."

"I'll be fine," I told him.

"I don't mean to rush you two," Ms. Borde said, "but we have been here a while. If this is going to happen—"

"Right," I said, clapping my hands together and standing. "I'll need a knife, or something sharp enough to cut skin."

"Don't look at me." Llowellyn raised his hands in a gesture of surrender. "I just got out."

We both turned to look at Megan.

She pushed back from her desk and rolled her chair to a safe in the corner. With her back to us, she keyed in a ten-digit code, scanned her palm, and her eye.

A moment later she handed me an eight-inch, black-handled hunting knife, still in its protective sheath.

"Ahhh, thanks?" I reached for the blade with obvious hesitation.

"What did you expect, a little switchblade? This is Alberta, not West Side Story."

"Right," I said, pulling the knife from the cover.

The blade was hot pink.

"Problem?" She narrowed her grey eyes at me.

"Your real first name is fitting a little better now," I said, tossing the cover on her desk.

"Only my mother calls me by that name," Megan said,

"I need this too." I picked up a small bowl of paper clips, dumped the clips beside the blade cover, and took the bowl. "I will have to cast the entire time to keep him dead. I'll cloak myself. No one will be able to see me. It will seem like you and my brother are in here alone."

"Okay." She nodded, looking pale.

"I'll tell you when to call for help."

"Okay," she said again.

"Ready?" I asked, looking sideways at Llowellyn.

My brother stood.

"This will be worse for you than it will be for me," he said. "Are you ready?"

I called enough Magic to power an aging spell for Llowellyn, a cloak for myself, and the Blood Magic of a death cast.

"Aye," I told him. "I can handle it."

"All right," he said.

"Aois nascair," I cast.

Within seconds, the old man was once again at my side.

"All right," he repeated, offering his big hand for the blade.

I pricked the end of his finger. A few drops fell into the bowl.

The spell didn't need much. Not like last time. Not like when I had really taken a life with it. The thought that Llowellyn was right and this was a bad idea flashed through my mind.

I ignored it.

I watched the drops of my brother's blood fall into the small glass bowl. I thought of what I had to do: move my brother's soul right to the brink, and hold it there.

Not like all those years ago when I'd moved a soul—and eaten it.

Bile rose in the back of my throat at the memory of consuming not one, but three souls. I had been in a blood rage that Llowellyn had barely been able to pull me out of. But that had been a long time ago. I had more control now.

I hoped I had more control now.

Pulling a lighter out of my pocket, I looked for something small to burn.

I'd never used a sticky note in a spell before, but there's a first time for everything. I peeled one off the stack. It was an indication of the Department of Corrections' budget that they had to use sticky notes at all. The rest of the world was digital.

"Ag mo fol, mair mé t'anam," I began to chant. "Ag mo fol, mair mé a brach."

I said the words again and cut my finger. I let a few drops fall on the sticky note. Megan sucked in her breath as the air in the room changed.

"Ag mo fol." I lit the sticky notes on fire and placed it into the glass bowl. "Mair mé t'anam, ag mo fol, mair mé a brach."

I paused.

The curling black edges of the paper were consumed by flame.

"Ahh." I doubled over in pain, clutching my chest.

Llowellyn fell forward at the same time, catching himself on Megan's desk.

"Ag mo fol, mair mé t'anam, ag mo fol, mair mé a brach."

"Now?" Megan asked.

I shook my head, straightened, and walked backwards. I leaned on the wall.

"Ag mo fol."

A memory surfaced in my mind.

"Mair mé t'anam."

I pull my dagger from my belt and drive it into his stomach, twisting it when I feel it hit bone. I hear the splinter of his spine.

"Ag mo fol," I whisper. He crumples forwards on to me as his Spark is pulled into my blade.

"Mair mé a brach," I said, trying now to keep myself in the present. Llowellyn slipped onto the floor, clutching his chest. I tried to stay there instead of with the memory of the men, long dead, who had killed my kin.

"Now?" Megan asked again.

Again, I shook my head.

I drive my blade through the soft flesh under his jaw. I kick his legs out from under him and pull back before driving my dagger into his heart. He falls. "Ag mo fol," escapes my lips. His life force joins his brother's.

Llowellyn's eyes gazed blankly at the ceiling.

A tingling sensation flows up the arm holding my dagger. It is still buried to the hilt in the man's chest. The color of stone tints my skin. The soft call of remorse grows faint.

Llowellyn's hand slid off his chest.

I am dancing with Dark Magic. I do not care. I am stronger this way. It is easier this way.

I throw myself on top of the third man responsible for the death of my King. No need for my dagger. I eat his Spark.

"Now?!" Megan asked urgently for a third time.

I wrenched myself back to the present—I locked eyes with Megan.

"Dortha mo Gotham."

Megan's eyes went wide as the cloaking spell fell over me. I wasn't invisible, but I was close.

"Now," I said.

"Help!" she screamed. "Brady, get in here!"

I continued to cast under my breath as the man who had greeted us upon arrival rushed into the room.

"What the—" he said, skidding to a stop. He looked down at the old man dead on the floor.

Megan was on her hands and knees over Llowellyn's limp form.

"Call 911! Get me the defib!" she yelled at him. "This man is in cardiac arrest!"

"Oh my god, oh my god, oh my god," Brady chanted. He hurried back to his desk. "Why the hell doesn't the government have more money?" I heard him call from the other room.

"Hello, 911, what's your emergency?"

It must be on speaker, I thought, still muttering the incantation.

Not sixty seconds after Brady left the room, he was back with the defibrillator. Megan had already cut Llowellyn's shirt open in preparation.

"Here," Brady said, shoving the small box into her hands.

She twisted the top before placing it in the center of my brother's chest. Thin wires with small pads on the ends snaked out of the device. They fixed themselves on Llowellyn's skin.

"What can I do?" Brady asked as the little machine started its analysis.

"Go downstairs. Make sure the drone comes to the right office," she ordered.

"Where is his son?" Brady asked.

"What?" she spat, whipping her head up to look at him.

"Didn't this guy have his son with him? What happened to his son?" Brady said, confused. "They looked so alike."

"What are you talking about?" Megan snapped. "That wasn't his son. Just someone dropping him off. He left right after."

"*Shock in 3-2-1,*" the little machine said. A loud beep filled the room.

"Brady, downstairs, drone, now!"

"Oh crap! On it!" he said, and he rushed out of the room.

CHAPTER SEVEN
Lochlan

I woke up with a hangover.

The Blood Magic I'd used to hold my brother on the cusp of death hadn't been as strong as the cast with Zemila, but I still had a pounding headache. Getting in at 2 a.m. and waking up at 6 a.m., didn't help. We had taken the train to Winnipeg as soon as we'd finished with Megan. The ride had felt long.

After throwing up what felt like my stomach lining, I brushed my teeth and left the motel bathroom.

"The coffee was better in prison," Llowellyn said. He sat by the window and slowly brought a paper cup up to his lips.

"I don't think I could handle coffee right now," I said, turning on the kettle, then looking at the limited supply of tea the pay-by-the-hour motel offered.

"You shouldn't have done that yesterday," Llowellyn said.

"Gods below, brother." I didn't even try to hide my exasperation. We'd spent the better part of last night arguing.

We'd argued about the spell, the Blood Magic, the past. Llowellyn feared I was vulnerable, and easy to corrupt. He feared that the more I used Dark Magic, the easier that corruption would be. A part of me feared he was right.

"You shouldn't have done that," Llowellyn repeated, still looking out the window. "But I am grateful."

I froze, the teabag halfway to the paper cup.

"I'd forgotten about the outside world," he said. We were on the ground floor. Asphalt and a diner. That was the view. "I made myself forget."

I put the mint tea bag in the cup.

"Forget the world. Forget the Magic." He sipped the bad coffee. "Forget you were out there on your own. It was easier that way. He came to me first, Little One," he said.

A warmth spread through my chest. I had hated that nickname. Hated that I was the smallest, the weakest of us three. Hated that I was the little one. Now it brought me warmth.

"I suppose," he continued, "you did a better job of hiding from him. I got sloppy. He found me. Attempted to take my mind. To force me to . . ." He trailed off.

The kettle popped.

I filled my cup with the hot liquid. Taking my tea, I sat on the edge of the bed.

"I was a teacher," he said, still staring out the window. "It was a small town. I was making a difference. I thought I was making a difference," he corrected, and a shadow crossed his face. "All I did was bring them pain."

"No," I said. "No, that is not fair."

"Is it not?" He looked at me with tears in his eyes. "Had I not gone to that school, those children would be alive. They would have had children of their own by now."

"We cannot blame ourselves for his actions," I said, as much to myself as to Llowellyn. "We cannot take on that burden along with everything else."

"You sound like Lugh," Llowellyn said.

"He told me that once."

"Me as well." Llowellyn's gaze went back out the window. "After Balor left that family. Do you remember that?"

"Aye." A chill went down my spine. "How could I forget?"

Lugh had steadily risen through the Tuatha Dé ranks, with Llowellyn and me following right behind him. We had been sent on a mission. Something trivial. We'd taken a night's shelter with a young family on the outskirts of a nearby village. On our way back, we'd passed them again to relay our gratitude and seek another night's shelter.

They had been ravaged, slaughtered. Nine people. Five of them children. It was a warning.

Help an Ethinsonn, face the consequences.

We'd spent many a night under the stars after that, not wanting to risk any more lives.

"I should have tried to find you then," Llowellyn said. "When he first came for me. But I knew you were the one he truly desired. He craves you. I didn't want to lead him to you. Then I was arrested. I was sentenced. I thought, mayhap he'll forget me. Mayhap I could be safe in prison. I could keep people safe that way.

"But the truth is," he said, turning his green eyes to mine, "I was scared. Scared of him, scared of you, scared of myself."

"Scared of me?" I said.

"Scared of what he could force on you." He lifted a big hand to my cheek. "Force out of you. After seeing what he almost made me do, I was scared of what he could turn you into."

I wish I could have been hurt by these words. I wish I could have shaken off my brother's touch, yelled and screamed. Ranted about how I was different, how I was better. How Balor could never corrupt me.

But I couldn't, because he was right.

"I don't know how long it will take to fully recover my Magic," Llowellyn said, dropping his hand. "When I was a teacher, it was overwhelming to feel what my students felt." He smiled and shook his head. "Teenagers. It was an experience, but I got used to it, with time. It helped me understand them . . . as much as anyone can understand the little monsters."

The shadow was back over his face. "But prison. Nothing could have prepared me for that. It was too much. The anger, the fear. Gods, the hopelessness. It was paralyzing."

"Hey," I said, shaking his big shoulder. "You did what you had to. You survived. There's no shame in that."

Llowellyn nodded and wiped at his eyes.

"I've missed you, brother," he said.

"And I you. Stronger together?" I said.

His response was steady and reassuring.

"Not alone."

Llowellyn drained his cup and went into the washroom. A few moments later, steam from the shower, along with his deep melodic voice, drifted through the crack between door and frame. I didn't recognize the song he sang, but his voice comforted me. Many of those nights under the stars had been filled with songs around a crackling fire.

Pulling my mind from the past, I tapped my watch, taking advantage of the time alone.

"Tjart Tech and Security. My name is—"

"So you don't even look at the screen when you're working anymore?" I said, interrupting Jenner's practiced opening line. "Why do you stay?"

"Amigo!" Jenner smiled. There was a quick glitch in the image and Jenner's face disappeared. "I just started! Give me a break."

At Tjart Tech and Security, all calls were recorded and stored forever. The glitch was Jenner cutting this particular call out of the recording. His image returned in a moment.

"Does this mean you're headed back?"

"We're going to stop in Toronto first, see Dyson," I said. "She wants to meet Llowellyn. I'd like him to have contacts outside of D.C. in case . . ." I trailed off.

"Okay," Jenner said, knowing me well enough to leave it alone. "How is he? How was the big reunion? Did you bring him flowers?"

"What?"

"Everybody likes flowers, Lochlan," he said. "You never get me flowers."

"Why in Danu's name would I ever get you flowers?" I laughed.

"How is he?" Jenner asked again, ignoring my question.

The smile slid from my face.

"He's . . . different." I looked at the bathroom door.

"He's been in prison a long time," Jenner said. "You haven't seen him in a long time."

I nodded.

"And you'll stay in Toronto fooor?" dragging out the o.

"Just a couple of days," I said. "If that."

"You're not worried that so many new faces will overwhelm him?" Jenner asked.

"Maybe," I said, running my hand over my rough chin. I needed a shave.

"Didn't you say he's an Empath?" Jenner leaned forward. "Won't so many connections wear him out?"

"He doesn't have his Magic right now," I told Jenner.

"What?" His eyes went wide. He knew how much we needed Llowellyn.

"I'll explain later." I'd heard the shower turn off. "I have to go. Have you heard from Zemila at all?"

"No. Have you talked to Nemo since you've been gone?" he asked.

"No," I squinted at him. "Why?"

"Oh, that beautiful idiot. It's nothing, just further proof that I am the superior roommate." He pointed both of his thumbs at himself. "I am the greatest."

"Goodbye, Jenner," I said, rolling my eyes.

"See you in a few days, amigo. Don't miss me too much."

The hands of a clock replaced Jenner's face. I put my watch back on my wrist. At the same time, Llowellyn exited the bathroom with a towel wrapped around his waist. He looked thin, but strong. Scars tracked themselves across his body. Some looked decades old, others just a few years. But they all looked painful.

"Gods," I breathed as my eyes roved over the thick raised marks on his chest, and arms. My eyes flicked to the mirror on the wall behind him, and I saw the scars tracked over his back too. "What happened?"

He looked down at himself.

"Life," he said.

"They didn't heal?" I asked.

"They are healing," he told me. "They used to be bigger. There used to be more."

"Here," I said, standing quickly and emptying the bag of clothing I'd bought the day before. "I brought a couple different things."

The scars crossed his chest and forearms. I wondered what they were from, but I dared not push. He'd tell me when he was ready.

Our bodies were as close to human as an immortal's could be. We felt pain like a human, we bled like a human, and we healed like a human. But we didn't scar. Our healing process, though not instantaneous, did exceed that of a human body.

"Side effect of locking away my connection to Magic," Llowellyn said, no doubt feeling my eyes on him. He chose a pair of forest green pants, a white undershirt, and a cream long-sleeve shirt. "Aging that way was strange. Not like the other times . . ."

I wondered what the other times were. I wondered who he had aged with.

"We'll need my Magic back, Little One," he said, shaking himself out of his memories. He fiddled with the button at his collar. "I'll need it for the battles to come."

"It will come back," I said. "The Gods be willing, it will come back."

CHAPTER EIGHT
Zemila

A wet hairy face plopped itself onto Zemila's leg.

"Ori." The black Akita mix looked up at her. "I'm working."

Papers on Celtic folklore and profiles on wealthy collectors were strewn across her desk. She'd been reading for the last three hours, totally absorbed. Where most people read off their watch, a projection, or an Intellidesk, Zemila was an old soul. She liked paper.

Zemila had printed profiles on people who collected antique weapons. She'd also printed every iteration of the legends of Lugh she could find. Idly scratching her dog behind the ear, her eyes drifted from the papers in her hand to the plastic sunglasses on her desk. She put the profile of Kennedy Virtue down and looked at the glasses. It had been two days since her lunch with Nemo. She hadn't heard from him since.

He's pissed, she reminded herself. Then she took in a slow deep breath and raised her hand.

With every ounce of focus she could muster, she tried to call the plastic sunglasses to her. Her arm shook. She willed the frames to move. They remained still.

She let her hand drop to the table.

Her eyes found the small ring box tucked under some papers. She glared at it and cursed herself for not returning it sooner. She'd ignored Tyler for the first week of three calls a day. The messages he'd left had begged her forgiveness. When she'd finally spoken to him, she'd told him it was really over. He'd asked for the ring back.

She had every intention of returning it. She just needed her hands to stop shaking before she saw him.

For the three weeks following her capture, she could barely stop shaking. Smoking had helped. Throwing herself into new projects had helped more. Tyler would know something was off. She didn't want him to feel protective of her. She didn't want to cry in his arms because she was afraid of the world.

So, she waited.

The longer she waited, the angrier Tyler got. At some point, she'd started threatening to sell the ring instead of giving it back to him.

But she would give it back. Eventually.

Zemila had more important things to worry about right now. Her brother, for one. She picked up her phone to call Nemo, but it started to ring as soon as her hand touched it.

It was her office.

"Diana?" Zemila said, surprised. The face of her office secretary filled the screen.

"How much do you love me?" Diana asked.

"You know I love you, baby," Zemila said, a smile breaking across her face.

"Well, it's good and bad," she said.

"Hit me," Zemila said.

"Ms. Jace wants you in for an interview. Vacation's over. That's the good news."

"When?" Zemila asked, excited.

"That's the bad news. It's with Redford Justal and it's in four hours," Diana said. "Can you make it?"

"Four hours? I haven't prepared anything!"

Adrenaline flooded her body. It pushed away the constant nagging fear. Her mind started to race over what she knew and what she needed to know. She looked at her watch. It was almost eleven.

"The interview is set for 3:30 p.m. Can I tell Ms. Jace you'll take it?"

"Of course! Does she want me to come in to see her first?"

"You know her so well," Diana said in a sing-song voice. "She wants you in her office at 2:30."

"Okay," Zemila shuffled papers on her desk. "I'll take it! Of course, I'll take it."

"It's so cute that you still use paper. I'll see you soon."

"Diana, wait!" Zemila said, pausing. "Do you know why?"

"Why?"

Zemila hit her with a look. Diana laughed.

"Of course, I know why," she said.

"Are you going to tell me?"

"For a price."

"Name it," Zemila said.

"Your undying devotion."

"You already have it. Share."

"All right," Diana sang. "Spoilsport. Turns out Justal didn't know it wasn't you doing the interview until about thirty minutes ago. Caused quite a stir."

"Really?" Zemila's eyebrows popped up.

"Really," Diana repeated. "He refused to do it with anyone else."

"Thank you, My Love," Zemila said. "My Queen."

"Oh, stop." Diana waved off Zemila's adoration.

"I'll see you soon."

"Yes, Ms. Alkevic," Diana said in her most professional voice.

Zemila smirked and hung up.

"Real quick walk before I go?" she said, looking down at her dog. Oriole wagged her tail in response.

φ

"I'm so happy you could come in on such short notice," the city councillor said. They stood on the front steps of the JACE Co. building. Zemila's camera woman was packing up. Redford Justal's people were a few feet away.

"To be honest, Mr. Justal," Zemila responded, raising her voice over the sounds of a passing bus, "I'm surprised Ms. Jace gave in."

"Me and Adri go way back," he winked.

Adri? Zemila thought.

"She's like family. I didn't have to pout for too long before getting my way."

In all Zemila's research she'd never learned that Justal and Jace had a personal connection.

"Oh no," he said with a smile. "She didn't tell you."

"She most certainly did not!"

"I guess she didn't want it to affect your reporting," he speculated. "Maybe I should have told you our grandmothers grew up on the same reservation before the interview."

"And what difference would that have made?"

"Maybe you would have gone a little easier on me."

"Oh no," Zemila smiled. "If I'm going to be calling you Mr. Mayor, I have to ask the tough questions."

"The election isn't for another two years," he laughed.

One of his aides broke away from their huddle and tapped Mr. Justal on the shoulder. He turned away from Zemila and spoke briefly with the young man.

"Thank you for your time," Zemila said, sticking out her hand when he turned back.

He shook it.

"I'm sure the residents of Lowtown appreciate your concern, Mr. Justal. One last question, off the record. Would soon-to-be 'Senator Justal' be closer to the mark than 'Mr. Mayor?' "

Redford Justal laughed, put a finger to his nose, and pointed at her.

"See you around, Ms. Alkevic," he said, and turned away.

Zemila stood for a moment, smiling after him. She looked around, not surprised that she was alone. Natalie must have left as soon as the camera was packed. Natalie had worked with Zemila too many times to get stuck waiting around for the end of the post-interview interview.

An anxious knot started to form in Zemila's chest. She tried to ignore it. The street was busy. The city noise comforted her.

I'm okay, she told herself. I'm okay.

"Come along," said a man who brushed by Zemila, jarring her from her thoughts.

Zemila blinked and turned. He was walking away from her.

Billy, she thought, following after him.

He didn't stop in their usual alcove. Instead, Zemila ended up following him for nearly five minutes.

Must be big, she thought, if he's acting this way. She gritted her teeth against the anxious feeling that they were being followed.

"Hey, Billy," she said, after he turned into an alley and finally stopped. She pulled out a pack of cigarettes and tucked a hundred-dollar bill in the lining, then pulled two out.

Lighting them, Zemila passed the pack, and one of the smokes, to Billy.

"Okay," he said, reluctantly taking the cigarette and the money. "Okay, thanks."

"What's going on?" she asked, after taking a long drag.

He moved nervously from one foot to the other, pulling on the cigarette.

"What's going on, Billy?" she asked again. "And what's with the hike?"

"Ohhhh, ZeeZee," he said. "I really, ummmm." He took another long pull. "You know I come to you when I know stuff, right? I don't sit on important things . . . My intel is good, right?"

"Yeah, Billy, it's good. You're always good."

He looked nervously up and down the empty alleyway. A stray cat hopped from a fire escape onto a dumpster. The sound, though light, made Billy jump.

"Always good, always good," he repeated.

He was starting to make her really nervous. And her nerves were already shot.

"I don't want to be right," he said. "I don't want to be right on what I got right now."

"What do you 'got?' " She stepped forward and laid a hand on his arm. "It's okay, Billy. You're okay."

"It's . . . I mean, it's a rumor, ya know?"

"The rumors you hear tend to be on the money."

He sighed deeply.

"Just tell me," she said.

There was a long pause. The cat yowled.

"You got a brother, right?" Billy said.

Zemila took a step back and let her hand fall off his arm. She hadn't been expecting that.

"Yes," she answered. "Why?"

"Have you heard from him recently?" Billy took another long drag before crushing the butt under the heel of his boot.

"Yes," she said.

Billy's shoulders seemed to sag in relief at her words.

"I had lunch with him a couple of days ago," she finished.

He froze midway through pulling another cigarette out of the box with his lips. His hands dropped to his sides, real worry in his eyes.

"Billy," Zemila said in a wary tone. "What's going on?"

"I heard—" He paused. "I heard there was a Gifter caught in Heaven."

Zemila's blood turned to ice.

"Yeah, I know about you." Billy scratched his head with the hand that wasn't holding the cigarettes. "I hear things. There are no real secrets in this town. Not if you know where to look."

She inclined her head in a stiff motion. Billy continued.

"A Gifter going by Kevic."

Her heart sank.

"Tell me everything," she whispered.

"That's all I know," Billy said. "A Gifter going by the name Kevic is being . . . held." He said the word like it hurt him. "In the basement of Heaven. You being Alkevic, being a Gifter too, I thought maybe you knew him. I thought you should know where he was."

Tears stung Zemila's eyes. She blinked them away. If Nemo was going by Kevic, he wasn't up to anything legal.

"Also," Billy hesitated again. "They say she's dealing with him herself."

"What?" Her panic leaked into her words. "How is that possible?"

"I don't know," Billy said. "She doesn't usually get her hands dirty. I'm just repeating what I heard. I heard that name. I came straight to you."

"Billy, thank you," Zemila said, pulling another hundred out of her wallet and handing it to him.

He tried to shake it off, tried to not take it. She shoved it in the pocket of his plaid shirt.

"Thank you," she said again.

Her mind was already racing. Thinking of people she could call, contacts she had. Her mind kept going to one name. One person she knew could help her.

"I hope you get him back," Billy said. "Be careful."

"I hope so too," she said as she turned away. Then to herself she said, "if I'm not too late . . . if he's still alive."

She left the alleyway and headed to Lochlan's house.

CHAPTER NINE
Lochlan

The trip from Winnipeg to Toronto was just over fourteen hours. We boarded the 8:20 a.m. train and were to arrive in Toronto at 10:35 p.m. Dyson insisted we take an early train and sleep the whole way.

"Just remember you have to stay up all night with me!" she'd squealed excitedly into the phone when I'd called to confirm.

I smiled at the thought, then looked across the small train table at my brother.

Even in my earliest memories of him, Llowellyn's hair had been long. Though breaking the binding spell had changed its color from grey to the many hues of dark and darker brown, it did nothing to change the length.

He'd pulled half of it into a knot to keep it out of his eyes while he read a newspaper abandoned by a previous passenger. The rest of it cascaded over his shoulders.

"This planet," he said, looking up from the paper and out the windows at the city we whizzed through, "we are killing it."

I glanced out the window too.

"I fear you're right," I looked at the article he was reading. *The Big*

Five Lobby Against Further Tax Increases, the headline read. "I fear humanity will kill itself before long."

"No." Llowellyn shook his head. "I have faith."

I raised an eyebrow at him. He caught the look and gave me a brief smile.

"I have faith that humanity is mostly good," he said. "And there are more things in this universe than even you or I know."

"More things in heaven and earth, Horatio?" I asked, remembering a conversation I'd had with Jenner not so long ago.

"Indeed," he said. "I have faith."

"You've been gone too long," I told him.

"And you, Little One, have always been a cynic."

"My cynicism saved our lives a time or two, as I recall," I said.

"Wit and cynicism are not the same thing." He looked out the window as the city raced out of view.

I nodded in agreement.

"There was a politician a few decades back who said 'cynicism is the refuge of cowards.' "

"Are you calling me a coward?" I asked.

"Only when you're being cynical."

I tried to smile, but it got lost somewhere between thought and expression. I ran my hand through my hair.

"Are you all right?" he asked me.

"I miss Lugh," I said.

"As do I, brother mine. As do I."

We sat in silence for a moment, no doubt both thinking of our King, our protector, our brother. Then I stood.

"That one is from yesterday." I gestured at the paper. "I'll print today's."

He nodded and kept reading.

I left the grouping of four seats and headed for the back of the train. There was a printer in one of the last cars. Briefly checking a map, I found what I needed and walked through a pair of sliding doors.

The newsstand screen was brightly lit with images of every major news outlet. I pressed my thumb to the JACE Co. logo before saying, "Print Issue, June 28, 2047."

A sharp whirring sound came out of the machine. The narrow horizontal slit spit out the newspaper. I took it and walked back through the cars to my seat.

An image of a man and his son covered the front page. *Maggie Cartwrytte Killer Still at Large*. There was a subheading that read, *Grieving husband hard at work to advance Right Waters protection bill*.

Sliding back into my seat, I took a better look at the image. The man's face looked haunted, like he hadn't slept in weeks.

His poor child, I thought. He would never be the same again.

The boy looked like he'd had to grow up too fast. Like his childhood had been stolen. I shook my head at the senseless violence, then looked up at Llowellyn.

"Llow," I said. "What's wrong?"

His green eyes were wide with shock. His mouth hung slightly open. He stared at the empty seat in front of him.

"Llow," I said again, looking between the empty seat and my brother. My eyes narrowed. "You saw her too."

At my words, his eyes snapped to mine. He nodded.

"What did she say?" I asked.

"The Lady has your answer," he said. "And you will be found with the Virtuous Collector. Trust him with truth."

"Is that all?" I asked, leaning forwards.

"She said my Magic will be back. Soon."

CHAPTER TEN
Zemila

"Call Cam Hernandez," Zemila said, moments after throwing herself into the driver's seat of her car. She scanned her thumb, turned the key, and Ida roared to life.

"*No device connected*," the automated voice replied.

"Connect device," Zemila instructed. She pulled out of her parking spot and maneuvered her way out of the lot.

"*No device connected.*"

"Connect!"

"*No device—Device connected.*"

"Call Cam Hernandez."

"*Disconnected.*"

"Damnit, Ida, why?" Zemila banged on the dashboard.

She stopped just before exiting to put on her earpiece. Within a minute, Zemila was zipping out of the parking lot and an outgoing call was ringing.

"This is the last car I buy," she muttered to no one. "You suck, Ida."

"Hey," Cam said, when the call picked up. "What am I looking at here?"

"Hi, Cam, you're still on my watch, so it's the car door."

"You're driving without connecting your phone? Are you trying to get a ticket?"

"She wouldn't connect," Zemila whined.

"You need to quit that car."

"Have you spoken to Nemo recently?"

Cam huffed.

"What?" Zemila asked.

"We were supposed to go out last night and he didn't show."

Zemila's heart sank. The sliver of hope that Billy had bad information was shrinking rapidly.

"Did he call?" Zemila asked.

"I love you, Mila, and you know how I feel about your brother, but sometimes, sometimes . . ." She said the next part in a rush. "Sometimes he can be a real dick, you know that? No, he didn't call, write, send a messenger pigeon, nothing. I haven't heard from him . . . Wait. Why? Is everything okay?"

"I'm sure it is," Zemila said, though she wasn't sure at all. "You're probably right and he's just being a dick. I'm headed over to Lochlan's to talk to him."

"Message me when you track him down?"

"Of course," Zemila replied.

"Talk soon."

"Hang on!" Since Zemila was still driving, she couldn't see if Cam had disconnected the call.

"Yeah?" Cam said.

"It's your birthday in a few days, right?"

"Who told you?"

"Do you want to do anything special?" Zemila asked.

"I'll get back to you," Cam said, and hung up.

φ

Zemila parked a block away from Lochlan's semi-detached house. She walked along the empty street, feeling thankful that the summer days were long. It made walking alone a little better.

But she still walked quickly.

"Well, aren't you a picture," said a small voice as Zemila opened the gate leading to Lochlan's porch.

Her heart jumped into her throat. She hadn't been expecting anyone. Looking up, Zemila saw an elderly woman with chocolate skin and grey-streaked curls. Sitting in a chair on her porch, she had a jug of what looked like iced tea on a table beside her. The woman's hand moved a large yellow fan lazily back and forth in front of her face.

"Hello," Zemila said.

"Hello, dear," the woman answered. "I don't suppose you know who I am."

Her southern drawl made Zemila smile. The woman reminded her of a friend from her school days.

"No, ma'am. My name is Zemila. Zemila Alkevic."

"Nice to finally put a name to the face," she said. "I'm Louise Abernathy. I saw a beautiful picture of you once. You and Lochlan." She nodded and made a small sound of affirmation. "Picture didn't do you no justice, though. It didn't capture your aura." She waved the fan in Zemila's direction.

"My aura?" Zemila asked, walking up the steps and leaning on the little wall separating Lochlan's porch from Louise Abernathy's.

"Oh, yes, I can feel it from here." She nodded again. "You look like you're in a bit of a tizzy though, so I won't keep you."

Zemila smiled.

"Is it that obvious?"

"Oh, yeah, but I have a gift for these things. You run along now," she said. "If you have a moment you should come sit with me. Have some of my sweet tea. I'd insist if I didn't think your tizzy was important."

"I'll take you up on that," Zemila said. "Thank you, Mrs. Abernathy."

"You're welcome dear. Now run along."

Zemila pushed off the wall and pressed her palm to the scanner pad before knocking. She heard her name being announced by the home system.

She waited to hear her brother get off the pull-out couch with a groan. She waited for him to answer the door. She waited to hear the sarcastic tones of Jenner complaining that Nemo wasn't moving fast enough.

She knocked again. More frantically this time.

Nothing.

The last strings of hope she was holding onto seemed to slip from her fingertips. She looked at her watch. 6:10.

Jenner finished at five, she thought. Where is he?

"Call Jenner," she said.

"*Calling Jenner Hernandez,*" her phone answered.

It rang. Seconds felt like years.

"Chica, chica, chica," Jenner answered. His tone was so contrary to her mood, she was stunned into silence. "Yes," Jenner nodded sagely. "My beauty has that effect on people all the time."

"What?" Zemila snapped.

"Madre de Dios, woman, you called me! I should be what-ing you. Don't you know I have a very important job?"

"You finished an hour ago," she said, finding her voice and glaring down at her watch. "You're playing frogger."

The high-pitched beeping sounds in the background stopped.

"You have no way of corroborating that," Jenner said, turning to face the camera.

"Am I wrong?"

"Why are you calling me?" Jenner demanded.

"Have you seen Nemo in the past two days?" she asked.

"I saw him after his lunch with you," he said. "What did you say to him? He was pissed and wearing some really dumb cheap sunglasses. Then he went over to Cam's, I think."

"And since then?"

"With Cam?" he shrugged. "I try very, very hard to not think of my sister in that way."

"When was the last time you spoke to Cam?" she asked.

"It's been about a week. I'm supposed to cook for her for her birthday. But maybe I will order in and put it in a casserole dish."

"But you can cook," Zemila said. "I've had leftovers at Cam's. She said you made them. They were amazing."

"As am I, I know, I know," he said with a mock bow of his head. "I just don't always have the urge, the feeling! Plus, I've been sewing so much lately, and I can't find the right hat." He scrunched up his face like he was thinking hard. "Maybe I'll make one . . ."

"What time will you be home?" she asked, trying to stay on task.

"I finished ten minutes ago. I was just on a roll, so I kept playing. If

I leave now, maybe forty-five minutes. Why?" he said. He seemed to register Zemila's worry for the first time. "What's this all about?"

"I have a contact, a guy who gives me information."

"Okay," Jenner said, waiting for the punch line. "And he said . . ."

She took a deep breath.

"He said Nemo is being held in the basement of Heaven. He said Queen Anne is taking care of him herself."

Jenner turned his chair to look at her fully. His face now totally filled the small square watch. "Queen Anne is a myth."

"Are you willing to bet Nemo's life on that?"

"I'll be home in twenty minutes," he said. Jenner disconnected and the image of a clock filled the screen.

Zemila shuffled awkwardly on the porch and looked around for a place to sit and wait.

"Might as well come and have a glass of tea, dear," Mrs. Abernathy said from her rocking chair.

Zemila didn't know how Mrs. Abernathy did it, but once the two of them started talking, Zemila's thoughts eased. Everything except the old woman, her sweet tea, and her stories, seemed to melt away.

It didn't last long.

As soon as the cab pulled up in front and the lanky caramel-skinned man stepped out, tension filled her body.

"Thank you," Zemila said to the elderly woman.

"Any time, dear. Any time," Mrs. Abernathy answered. "The old, like me, need to keep up with the young, like you. That's what my Harvey used to say. Have friends of all ages."

"He sounds like a wise man," Zemila said.

"Hello, Mrs. Abernathy!" Jenner jogged up the stairs.

"That he was, dear, that he was. And hello, Jenny-love."

Jenner beamed at the nickname.

"I hope this one," he hooked a thumb at Zemila, "isn't bothering you?"

"Oh, no, I had to absolutely beg her to come sit with me."

Jenner froze. Mock outraged covered his face.

"You made my one true love beg you?" he demanded.

"I–I was—" Zemila stuttered.

"No excuses," he interrupted. Then he turned his attention to Mrs. Abernathy. "Forgive her. She knows not what she does."

"Nothing to forgive, lovey. Now get out of here." Mrs. Abernathy shooed them away like a swarm of flies. "That girl is in a tizzy. I've distracted her as much as I can."

"Thanks again for the tea, Mrs. Abernathy," Zemila said. Placing two hands on the little wall separating the porches, Zemila hopped over it and followed Jenner through the front door.

"And an athlete too," she heard Mrs. Abernathy say to herself, fan moving slowly back and forth. "No wonder he's mad about her."

"Dios mio, Mila, I hope you're wrong about all this," Jenner said, leading her into the living room. "Queen Anne. I thought she was a myth."

"Me too." Zemila followed him in. "But my source is good."

She paced the small space as Jenner started to connect his system. A projection appeared on the large blank wall across from him. It looked like a map of the city. A second later, it was replaced with a length of code.

"I've been looking into the fires in Lowtown," Zemila said. "Her name has come up a few times. But I didn't really think it was her. Just a scary story, ya know?"

"Yeah," he said. "A boogie man for the bosses to tell their minions about."

"Word is she's been relocating survivors. Those that weren't . . . anyway, it's all very quiet."

"The greatest trick the devil ever pulled was convincing the world he didn't exist," Jenner said.

"What's that from?" Zemila asked.

"Me, right now," Jenner replied. "I just said it."

Zemila crossed her arms.

"A movie from the nineties—¡No mames!"

"What?" Zemila asked, turning to the projection.

"No, no, no." Images, maps, and code flashed across the wall. Jenner spoke in rapid Spanish as his fingers moved faster than Zemila could track. "Call Cam Hernandez."

"*Calling Camile Hernandez*," the home system responded.

"Jenner," Zemila said, trying to remain calm. A ringing sound filled the room. "Please explain to me what's going on."

Cam's face appeared in a small square on the wall when the call picked up.

"Jen, hey, I'm in the—"

Jenner cut her off with a stream of Spanish.

Zemila couldn't understand the exchange, but the urgent tones did nothing to assuage her concerns.

"She is going to send us everything she can on Queen Anne and Heaven," Jenner explained when Cam disconnected the call.

"What?" Zemila said. "How does she have information on Queen

Anne?"

"A rival of my father's from law school was a professor when Cam went to Stanford. She was two years younger than everyone else when she went. Some of the other profs had been giving her trouble. The skinny little engreída trying to make it at Stanford. The prof called my dad and looked out for Cam a bit after that."

"Okay," Zemila said, waiting for the punch line.

"Dad never told Cam that Chadwick Martínez—"

"Jesus," Zemila said.

"—was an old classmate. He and my dad are cool now. But Cam speaks to him regularly."

"She regularly speaks to the Associate Attorney General?"

"She doesn't like to tell people."

"I understand why," Zemila said.

"She'll reach out to him and will send me what she can," Jenner said.

The Tjart Tech logo flashed on the projection, then the logo of a phone provider.

"What can I do?" she asked.

"Unless you have some discreet way to get any intel . . ." Jenner trailed off, fingers flying.

"I could reach out to a few contacts, but word would get back to her," she said.

"Dios," Jenner said, shaking his head. "Queen Anne. She's really real."

"Yeah," Zemila said, solemnly. "She's really real."

"Why don't you go upstairs and lie down in Lochlan's room," Jenner suggested. "Nemo has been staying up there while Loch is away. It's not that I don't want you here, I just—"

"That's okay," she interrupted.

He was hacking into the city surveillance, Tjart Tech, Heaven, and Nemo's cell phone provider, all at the same time. If she stayed, his attention would be split.

She turned to leave the room.

"We'll find him," Jenner said, fingers stilling.

She turned back and looked at him. "I know."

At the top of the stairs, the bathroom door was open. She went in and washed her face. When she straightened, she surveyed herself in the mirror. Plain brown eyes looked back at her.

Unbidden, the image of Simmons, with one arm missing and one leg turning to dust, flashed through her mind. She closed her eyes against the memory and left the room.

Zemila looked around the little hallway for a distraction. She'd never been inside Lochlan's house before.

Jenner's room, she thought, when she peeked into the first bedroom.

The walls were covered in early 2000s memorabilia. Posters of old TV shows and shelves of action figures, books, and DVDs. She remembered watching DVDs as a kid. Jenner had a stack of them next to an old plasma screen in the corner.

She stepped back into the hallway.

The walls of the hallway were bare, like Lochlan had just moved in.

You're always ready to leave, she thought.

It had been the same at Erroin. She remembered sitting on her brother's bed, looking across the small room at Lochlan. It felt like a hundred years ago.

Nemo's side of the dorm had been plastered with posters and

scattered with personal effects. Lochlan's side had looked like a hotel.

Zemila had been sixteen. Lochlan had been eighteen.

Well, she thought. He hadn't been eighteen. I'd only thought he was.

He'd helped her with her English. She'd helped him with his Serbian. He'd started to learn when Nemo had moved in. He'd been horrible at it.

Maybe that's why he never told Nemo, she thought absently.

She pushed open the door to Lochlan's room.

It was as sparsely decorated as the hallway. The walls were empty but for a cartoon poster of a girl in a short red dress with fairy wings. She flew against a forest backdrop. There were other flying creatures in the background too.

Zemila noticed a handwritten addition to the poster. It read, "Fern Gully and the Last Rain Forest starring Lochlan Ellyll." Looking more closely, she saw someone, probably Jenner, had glued a picture of Lochlan's face over one of the winged animals being ridden by a fairy.

She smiled, despite her mood, then turned to take in the rest of the room. Her eyes went from the hastily made bed—Nemo never did like to do that—to the corner where his unfolded clothes were piled high on an open suitcase.

There was a chair beside the window. A sweater sat crumpled on the rust-colored armchair. She picked up the black thin knit top.

It was Lochlan's.

Sinking on the bed, she brought the sweater to her nose and inhaled. It still smelled like him. Like wild forests and quiet nights.

Him.

She inhaled again, and lay down.

Pulling her knees to her chest, she hugged the sweater under her chin. The pillow smelled like Nemo's shampoo. He'd been right there not long ago.

I need him to be safe, she thought. I need them both to be safe.

Surrounded by the feeling of the two men on earth she would do anything for, and who would do anything for her, she drifted off to sleep.

Pain and confusion. And then she was fine.

Her eyes drifted away from Lochlan, nearly dead on the ground. She looked at the thing responsible.

"You're made of stone?" she asked, her voice as cold as ice. Her thoughts were on vengeance.

If he dies . . . she thought. Out of the corner of her eye, she saw Lochlan collapse.

"You're mine," she said to the cringing excuse for a human on the ground beside Lochlan.

She squinted her eyes at him, her intentions clear.

Pain, she thought.

Simmons screamed. Her thoughts became his reality. She stared at him and slowly made a fist with her hand. It may as well have been the hand of God reaching down and tearing at Simmons' stone arm.

He screamed. She pulled. Stone ripped from flesh, and flesh ripped from more flesh. All the while she watched. All the while he cried.

When the arm was fully detached, she did the same with his leg. A slow pull. A slow rip. An agonizing scream.

The detached stone arm and leg circled around the pleading man. They smashed together violently, breaking into smaller pieces, then smashing together again. He flinched with every loud crash. Tears fell down his face. Chunks of stone hit the weeping man, again and again.

He cried for mercy. She didn't care.

Eventually, the arm and leg were gone. Only powder remained.

The powder froze in midair, and for a moment, the man looked relieved. Perhaps he thought he'd been spared. His weeping quieted. His pleading ceased.

Then the powder started to press in around him.

With the flexing of her hand, Zemila forced the dusted remains of the limbs into his nose and down his throat.

The screaming, gagging sounds he made were inhuman. But he was inhuman, so she didn't care. This man had hurt her. Hurt Lochlan. She didn't care.

She watched him struggle to breathe. She watched him twitch on the ground. She watched life leave him.

"Zemila," someone said in her ear.

Look what you did, said a small voice in her head.

"Hey, Zemila."

You are a monster, the small voice said.

"Zemila!" Jenner shook her awake. She opened her eyes and looked up at him. "We've got something," he said.

CHAPTER ELEVEN
Lochlan

We waited for Dyson outside the subway station. Llowellyn was absorbed in his book. I was pacing back and forth, thinking in circles.

Who was the woman on the train? I thought. No, not a woman. She only appeared that way.

"The Lady has your answer," I muttered to myself. "The Lady of the Lake has your answer and you will be found with the Collector. Trust him with truth."

The sorceress of Arthurian Myth, I thought. The one who brought Lancelot back from the dead. She was the Lady of the Lake. She gave Arthur Excalibur. I'd brought Zemila back, I was in search of a sword. That fit.

I made a mental note to look into Arthurian mythology, then looked over at my brother.

"How can you possibly be reading?" I asked him.

"What should I be doing?" He didn't look up. "Staring at the ground and pacing? Shall I mutter to myself about the intervention of Old World Mystics, hmm? Have you come to any conclusions you wish to share?"

He waited for a response.

"Do you feel better?" he asked.

I mumbled a response.

"I'm sorry?" he said, looking up.

"No," I said louder.

"What was that an answer to? I asked several questions."

"All of them . . . Nothing . . . Shut up."

"Then, alas," he returned his gaze to his book, "I will read."

"Danu," I cursed, and kicked at a pebble near my feet.

"Brothers, if ever I saw them," said a familiar voice.

I turned. Hazel eyes met mine and a smile broke over my face. My old friend momentarily drove the riddle out of my mind. She took long graceful strides towards me, her curly brown hair bouncing behind her.

"Dyson," I said. "It has been too long."

"You haven't aged a day," she hugged me.

I laughed. Of course, neither had she. Releasing my hold, I took a step back and looked at her properly. She looked exactly the same as she had the day I'd met her almost ten years ago.

Pale with a distinct caramel undertone that gave away her mixed heritage and an infectious smile.

"Let me introduce my brother, Llowellyn," I said.

He stood and offered his hand. She shook it.

"Nice to meet you, Llowellyn, I've heard almost nothing about you." She gave me a sideways look. "I look forward to getting to know you."

"I knew a vampire once," Llowellyn said. "I already like you better."

Dyson's smile widened. It showed white, Human teeth.

"We're headed this way," she gestured back the way she'd come. "Let's walk."

"How fare thee, old friend?" I asked, as we walked.

"Things are good here." Her sad smile gave more truth than her words, but I wasn't going to push. "And you?"

"Did you bring it with you?"

"Right to business, eh?" she said.

"Eh?" I mocked. The ground slanted up under our feet. A streetcar trundled out of its alcove to our left. I spared a moment to wonder why we weren't taking it. But the night air was cool and I didn't mind the walk.

"Old habits die hard," she said, pulling a silver chain from around her neck. A stone wrapped in gold wiring hung from it.

"How did you get that?" Llowellyn asked, as she handed it to me.

"My maker," she said. "He gave it to me a long time ago."

Dyson hadn't spoken to her maker in over five years. Not since we'd left school.

"And where did he get it?" Llowellyn said.

"I think Niloc gave it to him, but I don't know where he got it."

"Dyson and I met at a Luman university in India," I said, answering my brother's unasked question. "Erroin Peritia Academy. Niloc Erroin is the founder and protector of that school."

Llowellyn nodded.

I put both chains around my neck and tucked the small stones under my shirt. There was a slight vibration against my chest. Those two pieces were closer than they had been in millennia.

We had the first of the three Tools of Lugh.

"Dyson," I said, "a weird thing happened on the train."

I launched into my encounter with the woman and Llowellyn filled in his parts. When I was done, Dyson nodded and smiled like she knew something I didn't.

"What?" I asked.

"Supernatural aid," she said.

I looked at her, confused.

"Did I ever tell you that I minored in English Literature when I was Human?"

"I remember you reciting Shakespeare at Erroin," I said. "Ad nauseam."

"Which is your favorite?" asked Llowellyn, interested.

"*Midsummer Night's Dream*! 'If we shadows have offended,' " she threw out her arms as if performing for an audience, " 'think but this and'—and I won't bore you with that."

"Maybe later," Llowellyn smiled.

"Why are you bringing up your English minor?" I inquired.

"I'll tell you inside," she said. "We're here."

The fifties-style diner looked right out of a movie. A neon sign over the entrance read Thav's.

"Whatever you do," she said, resting her hand on the door, "don't mention the jukebox."

She pushed the door open and we walked in.

CHAPTER TWELVE
Zemila

Zemila rubbed her eyes and followed Jenner downstairs.

"Cam got back to me with—well, we know more now." Jenner flopped down into his usual seat across from his projection.

"Jesus." Zemila's eyes went wide. Blueprints covered the wall. "We have the layout of Heaven?"

"Queen Anne is under heavy surveillance by the FBI."

"You got all this from Cam?" Zemila asked.

"Not exactly," Jenner said. "The FBI is kicked out of the Heaven system every so often. They'll get back in, but they don't have this."

He tapped a few times on the glowing blue keyboard and the blueprints disappeared, replaced by security camera footage.

"Oh God, Nemo." Zemila sank onto a couch, eyes roving over the wall. "Is this live?"

"There is a three- to five-second lag," Jenner said.

"He looks bad."

A square at the top right showed her brother. He was tied to a chair, slumped over, beaten, and bloody.

For a moment, she was tied to the chair, duct tape over her mouth and fabric tied over her eyes. Then Simmons was dying again. She was killing Simmons again.

Zemila squeezed her eyes shut. She shook off the memory.

He's alive, she told herself. Nemo is still alive. And I'm going to get him back.

"How do I get in?"

φ

Heaven. The word was illuminated in elegant wing-tipped letters above the entrance. Two bright spotlights lit up the sky, directing wayward travelers to the only cash casino in DC.

Zemila had spent a lot of time in Lowtown over the past two weeks, but she'd never been to Heaven. With the few shortcuts she'd learned, the drive was thirty minutes. It took her longer than that to convince Jenner not to call Lochlan.

He would help her. She was sure of that. But it would take him too long to get back. Time was something Nemo didn't have.

Like the flame calling the moth, Heaven's bright lights beckoned all those who dared test their luck. Many a fortune had been changed inside those walls. Some for better, more for worse.

"Time to test my luck," she said, exiting her car.

She pressed a button on the side of her watch and two small disks popped out. Placing one under her jaw and the other behind her ear she said, "Call Jenner."

"*Calling Jenner*," answered the androgynous voice.

"You're there," he said after a half-ring.

"Walking up to the doors," she answered.

"You got this," he said. "Nemo is still alone in that room. There are a few guards in the hallway. They look like a regular patrol."

"I guess they're not expecting a rescue mission," Zemila said.

Jenner grumbled something that sounded suspiciously like "suicide mission."

Zemila ignored him.

The luxurious hotel attached to the three-story casino jutted up into the sky. From rock stars to athletes, foreign diplomats to foreign royalty, Heaven had played host to them all. Once last year, Zemila heard the entire hotel was booked by one person. She never found out who.

Stone lions guarded the entrance. Each had an eight-pointed star hanging around its neck and wore battle-ready expressions.

Cool air hit her when the doors slid open. Zemila paused a few paces into the grand foyer. There was a lobby bar to her right, a restaurant-lounge to her left, and a golden fountain right in the middle. Water cascaded around a beautiful man in battle armor riding a lion. He had an eight-pointed star carved into his breast plate.

Taking a step closer to the fountain, she saw that the lion had a giant forepaw on the head of a slain man.

"Have you been here before?" Zemila asked Jenner. She stared at the face of the man beneath the lion's paw. His headdress and long beard triggered something in her memory.

Something old, she thought.

A class she'd taken at Erroin on ancient dynasties was tugging at her attention.

"No," Jenner said. "But I hear the gentlemen of the night are top shelf."

Zemila's eyes flicked back to the men and women leaning seductively against the lobby bar.

"Pick one," she tried to joke. "I'll bring him back for you."

"I pick Nemo," Jenner said. "We'll worry about my sex life later."

"Yeah," she said. "Good plan."

Zemila walked towards the sounds of slot machines and soft music. Pure white linen hangings covered an archway. Zemila stepped onto a moving sidewalk.

"Welcome," said a seductive female voice. Zemila closed her eyes as the soft linen hangings brushed over her. "Welcome to Heaven."

The moving sidewalk turned into an escalator, bringing her down a level. She gripped the handrail, not for balance, but to steady her mind. The high-ceilinged room was dimly lit and it smelled like home. It calmed her. She inhaled deeply.

"There's something in the air here," she said.

"What do you mean?" Jenner asked.

"I smell home. I feel . . . safe," she explained. "I shouldn't feel safe right now."

Doubt crept into her mind. Should she have waited for help? Waited for Lochlan?

"No, you should not feel safe," he said. "Maybe if you were with a demigod, you would—"

"Enough," she said.

He stopped.

Her eyes were drawn to the balconies that extended out of the wall far to her right. They were attached to hotel rooms. Each had a small glass elevator to the casino floor.

Her eyes widened. She turned away from a couple using the elevator for . . . other things.

"Where do I go?" Zemila stepped off the escalator.

The casino was a maze. Jenner directed her through arcade games and slot machines, through winners and losers, drinkers and lovers. She made two wrong turns, but eventually found where she was going.

"Now sit down at that bar and order a drink," he said. "I need you to wait there for a couple minutes."

"Rye and ginger," Zemila said. "Light on the rye."

"Not a drinker, huh?" said the bartender, an exceptionally beautiful woman with the darkest skin Zemila had ever seen.

"Not today," she replied.

"All right, hun," the bartender said in a smooth voice.

Zemila looked for a scanning pad when her drink arrived.

"Cash only, baby," the bartender said. "Is this your first time?"

"Right," said Zemila, reaching into her pocket.

"Hey," the woman said. "Aren't you—?"

"No," Zemila said, sliding over the cost of the drink plus two hundred dollars. "No, I'm not. And I was never here."

"I must be mistaken," the woman said, slipping the extra bills into her pocket. "You look like a woman whose show I really liked."

She winked and left.

"Aren't we popular," Jenner said in her ear.

"Shut up," Zemila muttered, taking a sip of her drink.

"You see that man who's playing roulette?" Jenner asked.

"There are three tables of eight men playing roulette," Zemila said. "Which one am I looking at?"

"Middle table, across from the dealer. Sandy hair and the most forgettable face I've ever seen."

"Yes," she said.

"He's a security guard. Behind that table is a door. That's where you're going."

"How do I get through it?" she asked.

"That guy is going to be replaced. When he is, he'll head through that door."

"Okay."

"Do you carry a bag of rocks or anything?"

"What?" she asked.

"Find something you can move with your teenaged Luman ninja powers. Prop the door open when he goes through," Jenner explained. "I copied some code to loop on the door's sensor so it will look like it's closed. The loop will only last about sixty seconds before someone notices."

"Why didn't you tell me this earlier?" Zemila asked, looking around for something she could use.

She finished her drink. The bartender brought her another.

"On the house," she said, before sauntering off.

Zemila downed the second drink, regretting her "light on the rye" comment.

"Two minutes," Jenner said in her ear.

Zemila's eyes scanned the bar top, the tables, the floor. She even checked the bottoms of her shoes to see if there were any pebbles stuck there.

Nothing.

"One minute," Jenner said.

Zemila looked at the glass in her hand. An idea born of an angry night at Once More With Feeling flashed into her mind. She placed the glass on the floor at her feet.

She didn't know what made her new abilities work, when they worked. But whatever was in the air, along with the small amount of alcohol she'd consumed, made her feel more relaxed than the situation warranted. For this, it would help.

You can do this, she thought. You can do this.

Taking in a deep breath and pushing the fear of her ever-changing gift aside, she envisioned the glass breaking clean at the base.

Zemila heard a soft chink and knew it had worked. The base of the glass slid free.

"Thirty seconds," Jenner said in her ear. "Are you ready? What are you using to prop the door open?"

She stood and walked a few steps away from the bar. With her hand down at her side, she used her gift to drag the nearly transparent circle behind her.

"Zemila?" Jenner asked.

"I'm ready," she said.

She walked to the roulette table and watched the little ball bounce.

"His replacement is on your left," Jenner said.

The action was smooth. The sandy-haired security guard got up. A man of similar description sat down.

Zemila leaned against a pillar, half in shadow. She kept the door in her sight line as she pretended to check her watch. Out of the corner of her eye, Zemila saw the guard at the door. He scanned his palm, then his eye. It opened. He slipped through.

Zemila centered her mind and flicked the glass discus in the direction of the door. It zoomed through the air, an inch off the ground and wedged itself between door and frame.

"Is that . . . glass?" Jenner asked.

"There was nothing else to use around here."

"But . . . it's glass," he said. "I thought—"

"Not the time, Jen."

"Okay," he said without hiding his uncertainty. "Remember, there is a lag in the video. Be careful."

"Yeah, just tell me when to move," she said, only half-hearing his warning.

"Twenty seconds," he said.

She tried to shake off her anxiety and reign in her control.

"Ten . . ."

She walked in the direction of the door, checking her watch.

"Go through in three . . ."

With forced calm, she leaned against the wall beside the door.

"Two . . ."

With her index finger, she moved the glass circle just enough so she could slip her fingers through the door.

"One . . ."

She took in a breath.

"Now!" Jenner said in her ear.

She pushed with her mind, moving the glass disk at the same time as she snuck her fingers around the door. Slipping through, she closed the door, pulling the small piece of glass through with her.

"That was the easy part," said Jenner. "There aren't many places to hide, so I'll have to take you to him the long way."

"Why?" she asked.

"To avoid any guards," he answered.

She looked down the white-walled corridor.

"Get to the end of that hall, make a left, then another left. I'm going to open the first door you see. Go now, someone's about to come in behind you."

She sprinted down the hall and was just about to turn the corner when Jenner frantically said, "Zemila! The glass!"

It was lying on the ground next to the opening door.

Damnit, she thought as she spun on her heel. With her right hand, palm up, she frantically whispered, "get over here." The glass disk flew through the air, and straight into her palm.

She closed her hand around it, and started to run.

"First door on the right," Jenner said.

Zemila heard a beep and moved through the now unlocked door. Once inside, she felt a stinging sensation in her hand.

"Damn," she said.

"What?" Jenner asked.

"The glass," she told him, examining her palm. Blood slowly bloomed in a jagged circle. "It cut my hand when I caught it."

"Better find something to wrap it with," he advised. "The last thing we need is you leaving a trail of blood wherever you go."

"Right." She looked around the room. A desk and a single chair sat on one side, a pair of uncomfortable-looking straight back chairs on the other. She went over to the Intelliglass desk.

No drawers. Nothing to stop the bleeding. She pressed her hand to her dark jean pants and her eyes roamed the bare walls.

"Jackpot," she said to the necktie hanging on the back of the door.

It was too long to just wrap around her palm and there were no scissors to shorten its length. Giving a silent nod of thanks to an old classmate who'd shown her the basics of boxing, she used the tie like a wrist wrap.

Tucking the bit of glass under the wrap on her forearm, sharp side up, she looked around the room, trying to see where the security camera was. The glass cut into the fabric of the navy tie, but not enough that she feared she'd lose it.

"Ready?" Jenner asked. "Back right corner."

Zemila nodded at the pinhole camera in the wall.

"Ready," she echoed.

"Then let's go."

Jenner directed her through the labyrinth that was the basement of Heaven. She had to double back twice and was nearly seen once, but Jenner got her there.

"On the other side of that door, there is an apartment . . . kind of," he said.

"Kind of?" She waited for a response.

"It's not just white walls, anymore. There's a kitchen and stuff . . . I don't know. Nemo is being held on the other side of the apartment."

"Okay," she said, hurrying down a flight of stairs.

"It's the hard part now," he said.

"I know," Zemila agreed. She'd have to do this all again in reverse—and with the dead weight of her brother. "How's he doing?"

"Still in there alone," Jenner said. "You'll be able to see him once you're through the next room."

"Okay," she said, excitement and apprehension coursing through her. She pulled open the door in front of her.

Jenner's sharp intake of breath was all the warning she had. By the time she'd registered his cries of "wait," a fist had connected with her jaw, and pain exploded across her face.

"What the hell do we have here?" said a gruff voice above her.

Zemila shook the stars from her eyes.

"I don't think I've ever hit a girl that hard, Jago," said a man leaning against a marble counter. "You're kind of a bastard."

Zemila looked up at the big man who'd knocked her off her feet.

"Am I?" the man called Jago said. He considered her, sprawled on the ground. "I guess you've never had the shit kicked out of you by a girl. I respect the strength of a woman." He wound up for another hit. Zemila scrambled to get her feet under her. "I don't go easy on them."

"Good," Zemila said, finding her feet and delivering a vicious upper cut.

He stumbled backwards.

"See what I mean?" Jago rubbed his jaw. "I should have kicked her while she was down."

"What are you doing here, girly?" the second man asked. "Get lost on the way to the ladies?"

Zemila narrowed her eyes at him.

"You know what, Karl, I think you should take this one. She looks like she could teach you a thing or two about power. I'll be here to clean up your mess."

Despite the pain in her jaw, Zemila smiled at Karl. He pushed himself off the counter and approached her.

"What are you smiling at?" he said. "You're about to get locked in the basement. And there is already someone in there."

"My brother," Zemila told him.

Jago's face went pale. He took a step back.

Karl quirked a smile and stepped forward.

"Oh, so you think you're on a rescue mission," he said.

"Easy, Karl," Jago warned. "She ain't what she looks like."

"And what do I look like?" Zemila asked, gathering her strength.

"Human," Jago said.

Karl looked at him sideways.

"You're right," Zemila answered. A loud crack filled the room. "I'm something else."

Zemila threw her hands forward, then back into fists at her sides. Two hunks of marble were ripped out of the countertop and soared through the air. One hit Karl in the shoulder when it flew past him to hover at Zemila's side. Jago ducked and the second piece just missed him.

"Christ," Jago said.

Karl used cruder language.

The pieces of marble circled Zemila as she walked slowly towards the men. They drew their weapons. Both had a finger on the trigger.

Her eyes flicked from one man to the other.

Silence. Tension. No one moved.

"Boo," she said.

Karl screamed and fired.

As quick as he did, the two pieces of rock slammed together, creating a protective shield as both men emptied their clips to zero effect.

Pushing her hands out in front of her, she drove the slabs of marble forward, knocking the men off their feet.

Six security guards came at her from the hall to her left.

Right it is, she thought.

"Jenner, where do I go?" she asked.

Silence.

"Jenner?"

Gunshots rang out behind her. She threw herself sideways. A hot sting on her shoulder told her she was hit. The bullet had grazed her.

Lucky, she thought, as she dove over a sofa. She crashed into the wooden coffee table on the other side.

"Why?" she whined at the sharp pain in her side. "Why did I wear this shirt? I like this shirt." She pulled a splinter of wood out of her hip. It hurt like hell and her shirt was ruined.

Scrambling to her feet, she ignored the pulsing pain of her jaw, shoulder, and side. She felt behind her ear and under her chin.

Nothing.

"Damnit," she said, looking down at her watch. Not only had she lost her CommuniDisks, but the call was disconnected.

She looked around the room at the walls for a pinhole camera. A beep sounded behind her, and she turned. A door on the opposite wall popped open.

"Thanks, Jen," she whispered—and sprinted for the door.

Running from the voices echoing behind her, she made it through another door whose lock flashed green at her approach. She heard a click and a beep when she closed it behind her.

Feeling someone slam against the other side, Zemila backed away and looked around. She was in another hallway. It was brightly lit with cream-colored walls and gold accents. She walked slowly, wondering where she was, wondering where Nemo was. Both questions were interrupted by the pair of men who stepped out in front of her.

"Here," the first called. "She's here!"

She tried to escape in the opposite direction. It was blocked too.

I'll have to fight my way through, she thought.

Adrenaline coursed through her. She scanned the hallway for something she could control with her gift. She found nothing.

The first of her attackers ran at her. Ducking his first punch, she quickly caught him with a right upper cut, left hook, then moved on. She made short work of the next man and sent another silent prayer of thanks to her university MMA coach.

It wasn't until she backhanded the fourth guard, that she remembered the glass disc tucked away in her makeshift wrist wrap.

After leaning into a jab she knew she couldn't avoid, she shuffled back and loosened the circle of glass. Catching with her gift, she threw it forward to smack the next attacker squarely in the forehead. Before he could recover, Zemila picked up a decorative vase and smashed it over his head. He crumpled.

She repeated a similar process with the next guard and was about to do it again when someone grabbed her neck and lifted her off the ground.

The glass disc fell to the floor. She tried to call it back to her, but as her panic rose, her control seeped away.

One hand around Zemila's throat became two. She was slammed against the wall. He squeezed.

She choked for air, feebly smacking at his thick hands around her neck. She tried to turn. She was barely successful. Out of the corner of her eye, she saw bulging, wild eyes. He was going to kill her.

Unsure of what possessed her to do it, Zemila slowly raised a hand to the level of the man's face. Then, she pulled. At what, she didn't know. All she knew was that, if she died, Nemo died too.

Small dark dots began to speckle the man's face. His grip faltered. She slid down the wall. Her feet found the floor. A red mist broke through the pores of the man's skin as if called by her hand.

He was taller than her by several inches, but as she pulled, he shrank. Dropping to a knee, he moaned. Standing tall above the man, Zemila pulled. The man's moaned turned to a yell, and then a vicious scream of pain.

"Enough!"

Zemila was flung off her feet, as was everyone else in the room who wasn't standing behind the speaker.

"Bring her to my office," said a woman's voice.

CHAPTER THIRTEEN
Lochlan

Thav's Diner had checkered floors, pale pink walls, and the nostalgic feeling of the 1950s. A few fans turned lazily overhead as the big jukebox behind the door played "Cry to Me" by Solomon Burke.

"Whoa," Llowellyn said from behind me. "Time warp."

He wasn't wrong. I'd gone east after the war. But on the few occasions I'd visited this part of the world, it had looked just like this.

Dyson led us to several black and chrome barstools. I shoved my bags under the bar and sat.

"Isn't it great?" Dyson said, spinning her stool to lean back on the bar.

"It really is," I said, copying the motion. I took in the records and posters on the walls and did a double take at the man who walked past us. He was carrying several takeout bags.

"Gods below," I said, staring at the blond server. He chatted animatedly with a few customers.

"Yeah," Dyson's smile was no longer sad. "He looks great, doesn't he?"

"Who's that?" Llowellyn asked, following my gaze.

The server said goodbye to the couple he'd delivered the takeout bags to. The old-fashioned door chime rang as they left.

The server turned and I met his eyes.

"Umm, Dyson," I said. The man made a beeline for me. "He doesn't know me, does he?"

"Ahhh," Dyson said.

"Hi!" I stood, extending my hand.

He knocked it away and gripped me in such a tight hug I could barely breathe.

"Lochlan," he said and squeezed tighter.

"Hi . . . David . . ." I managed to get out.

"What's happening here?" Llowellyn asked.

"It's a long story," Dyson said.

"David." A lanky man with dusky skin came out from the kitchen. "David, let the man breathe."

The newcomer poured a cup of coffee and slid it to Dyson.

"Oh, sorry." David released me. He turned to my brother. "It's not that long of a story." He stuck out his hand. Llowellyn shook it. "I'm David."

"Llowellyn."

"Nice to meet you," David said. "Nutshell version: seven years ago, I took a bad job that landed me in India with debt up to my eyeballs and a needle in my arm. Dyson found me. Lochlan helped get me out. He paid off my debts, paid for my rehab. He brought me home."

"And," Dyson said.

"You helped," he said to her, snaking an arm around her waist. He pulled her to his side, looking at her like she was the only person in the room. Like she was the only person in the world.

Then he planted a kiss on her cheek. She looked embarrassed but pleased.

"Well," said the man behind the bar. "Since no one seems to want to introduce me, I'm Thav. This is my place. Welcome. Can I get you some coffee?"

"Sorry, Thav!" David tore his eyes from Dyson.

"Tea, if possible," Llowellyn said, extending a hand. "I'm Llowellyn."

"Not to be rude, secondborn Cianson, Ethinnson, Balorson," Thav said, eyeing the outstretched hand. Llowellyn let his hand fall. "But I think it would be better to shake hands when the place is empty," Thav winked, and slid Llowellyn a cup of tea.

"Okay," he said, looking at Thav with narrowed eyes.

I noticed David staring at me, eyes wide. Dyson saw it too.

"Honey, you're being weird," she said. "Stop it."

David blinked and looked away.

"David," Thav said. "Table two."

"Right," he said. "Still on the clock."

He grabbed a pot of coffee from behind the bar and headed over to a table of security guards.

"They're here every night," Dyson told me. David laughed at something one of them said as he filled a mug with coffee. "They get breakfast before their shift. They tried to get David a job, but with his record . . ."

I nodded. I too was haunted by my past.

"Nice to see you again, old friend," Thav said to me. "Ember misses you. She won't be back until two or three in the morning. She's out of town, letting off some steam."

A month after Dyson had officially met Thav and Ember, she'd called me to ask a favour. Ember, a Fire Gifter, had been having trouble controlling her gift. Though Thav was more than capable of helping, he felt she'd be better served by someone who didn't raise her.

She didn't need help anymore.

"Hungry?" Thav walked back into the kitchen.

"Starved," I said. "How is Ember doing?"

"Good!" he answered through the large cut-out between kitchen and bar. He put two bowls of chili on a ledge. Dyson hopped over the bar with inhuman grace. I looked around the diner.

"Don't worry," she slid me and Llowellyn a bowl of chili each. "There's barely anyone here."

"Her control is exceptional," Thav told me, then gave Dyson an exasperated look.

"Any idea what time she gets in?" I asked, pulling the chili toward me. Llowellyn attacked his like he hadn't eaten in years.

"Tonight," Dyson said. "No idea when."

She walked slowly around the bar instead of hopping over it again. She looked mockingly at me the entire time.

"Better safe than sorry," I told her. "How many angry mobs have you run from?"

"None," she said.

"Well, neither have I. But it doesn't sound fun."

"I have," Llowellyn said. "And it's not fun at all."

Dyson fiddled with the coffee mug in front of her. It was a prop, like my glasses. It helped her blend in.

"Ember will be happy to see you," Dyson said, ending the discussion of mobs and exposure. "She wanted to wait for you, but didn't know when you would be here."

"I don't think Llowellyn will be up for it, anyway."

"Can I have more chili?" Llowellyn asked. "It's amazing."

"It's my favorite too," David said, coming back around the bar.

Llowellyn was looking at me, as if I could make it appear. I could, but that was beside the point.

"I don't work here," I said.

"Oh, right." He turned to David, like Oliver Twist, bowl in his outstretched hands, but David had already gone back to the table of security guards.

"Is Katye back tonight too?" I asked after Ember's sister.

"Katye won't be back for a few weeks. She's on the East Coast with her mother's family."

I nodded.

Moments after the security guards left, David joined us at the counter. "Can I have some chili too?"

"You're still working," Thav said from the kitchen.

David made a show of looking around the empty diner.

"Well, lock up then," Thav ordered.

David turned off the OPEN sign and locked the door.

Thav and Dyson returned with bowls of chili balanced on a tray and we moved from the bar to a large table. Llowellyn beamed when an even larger bowl than the first was placed in front of him.

"Dyson tells me you are on a quest." Thav poured himself a cup of coffee, then joined us.

I tilted my head from side to side, not able to speak through chili. I swallowed. "I don't know that I would call it a quest."

"A journey then?" Dyson asked.

"Aye, but we're all on a journey," I told her.

"Sooo deep." Her words dripped with sarcasm.

"Your grandfather," Thav said, "is alive?"

"He is," Llowellyn said. "I got that happy news upon release. And do I get to shake your hand now?"

"No need for dramatics, Thav." Dyson rolled her eyes.

"His Magic isn't fully connected," I told him. "He won't be able to sense your power level."

"Ohh." Thav looked like a child being denied a treat. "I suppose I was being a bit dramatic." He stuck out his hand to Llowellyn. "I'm Thavaindor of the First Line."

"Holy shit," Llowellyn shook his hand. "Are you really? I haven't met an Ankhian in years."

Thav smiled.

"'Thavaindor of the First Line,'" David mocked. "Show off."

"Hey." Thav released Llowellyn's hand. "There are few alive now who know what that name means. Who know that my people once—"

"Walked with dinosaurs, ruled the earth, yeah, yeah, Gramps. But we have visitors," David said. "I want to hear their quest story."

"Hmmmm." Thavaindor of the First Line surveyed David of equal parts disapproval and affection.

Llowellyn was still looking at him with awe. The first time I'd learned who he was, I'd done the same.

David's glib attitude was understandable for a human who saw Thav as a father figure and friend. But as Ancients, we knew better. We knew that, as old as we were, if Thav called us child, he wouldn't be wrong.

I was surprised at how well Thav fit in. It was rare that an Ancient of his power didn't go mad after a few hundred millennia. He was so well-adjusted.

"Quest?" David looked from Llowellyn to me.

"Dyson didn't tell you?" I asked.

"Dyson doesn't know," she said.

"Yes, you do," I accused.

"Only bits and pieces," she answered. "You're pretty tight-lipped."

"I've been told that before," I said.

"I could have it from the beginning too," Llowellyn said.

"You lived the beginning," I shot at him.

"It was a long time ago . . ." he said through a full mouth of chili.

"The short version," David said, scrapping the bottom of his bowl.

"The short version," I said, organizing my thoughts. "A long time ago, there lived a man called Balor, King of Demons. He led an army of Famorians, man-beast hybrids who had one arm, one leg, and one eye made of stone. His wife gave a prophecy that he would die at the hand of his grandson. Balor had but one daughter. He locked her away to avert the prophecy.

"It didn't work. She bore triplets. Balor commanded his grandsons be drowned at sea. He gave them to a Druid Priestess who, unknown to Balor, was allied with the triplets' father. Though Balor thought them dead, she spared and blessed the three babes. The firstborn was named Lugh and he grew up to be a great leader and king. One day in battle, he killed his grandfather, fulfilling the prophecy."

"Wait a minute," David said. "I thought Balor was alive."

"Aye," I nodded.

"Then how could the prophecy be fulfilled?" he asked.

"We were wrong." I looked at Llowellyn. "The true prophecy states that Balor must die three times. Once at the hands of each grandson. Only then will he be truly dead."

"What did you call those part-stone, part-man things?" Dyson asked.

"Famorians," Thav and I answered in unison.

I looked up into his dark eyes, for a moment getting a glimpse of his true power, before he blinked and it was gone.

"Arm of stone and a leg of stone," Dyson repeated slowly. "I've seen one of those."

A stunned silence met her words.

Not possible, I thought.

"Not possible," Llowellyn said. Thav slid a fresh bowl of chili to him. Llowellyn thanked him before turning back to Dyson. "How old are you?"

"Old enough!" her tone was defensive. "You Ancients are so touchy about age. We can't all be older than the wheel." She gave Thav a pointed look.

David snorted a laugh into his chili.

"Hmmmm," Thavain squinted at her.

"I did see one," she continued. "I fought one."

"When?" I asked. There was no way Dyson was old enough to have fought a Famorian. She'd been born in the late 1980s.

"Here, in this city, not long after you left," she told me.

"Not possible." But the words didn't come out as certain this time.

"Balor is not the only God left from your world," Thav said.

"That is a frightening thought," Llowellyn muttered.

Silently, I agreed.

Balor alone, having to work to hold each mind he overtook, was one thing. Balor with another Old God, was quite another. But, no, Balor never did like to share. Most of the Old Gods had hated him then, and they would hate him now.

Why else would he be working so hard to get me, I thought. He wanted to corrupt me, turn me. He thought it my destiny to help him gain power.

In a deep dark corner of my mind, I feared he was right.

"No," I heard from beside me. Llowellyn stared at me. "Don't go there. Don't think that."

He always knew when I was spiralling. He always pulled me back.

"I don't think any of the Old Ones would help him," I said, breaking eye contact with my brother and turning to Thav. "You must have been fighting some kind of Gifter," I told to Dyson. "Also, why were you fighting Gifters?"

"After you left, I needed to make money," she explained.

"If you needed money, you should've come to me," I said.

She looked at me like I'd just told her two and two make five.

"I like being able to make my own money, Lochlan. And you'd already helped so much. I needed a job that was only nights, with people who wouldn't expect much. I started fighting."

"You started fighting?" I echoed.

"Yes. It was a Human cage at first, then I got approached by a Seraph who ran a Gifter ring."

"A Seraph," Llowellyn slowly shook his head. "I hate Seraphs."

Seraphs claimed to be the descendants of angels. Though their glowing white hair and skin made them look ethereal, their views of right and wrong made them anything but angelic.

"Okay," I was still confused.

"That's where I fought one of those stone-man thingys."

"When was this?" I asked.

"A little while after you left," she said again.

"This was all around the time that Dyson first introduced herself to us," Thav explained.

"Introduced?" Dyson scoffed.

"I had never put it together with you," Thav went on, ignoring the interruption. "There was something off here around that time."

"Off?" I asked.

"A new power in the city. It didn't stay long. I never thought anything of it, but now it appears—"

"That Balor found you here first," Llowellyn finished.

"He found me in India first," I said. "I didn't know it was him then. I only realized he was active about two months ago."

"Two months ago," Dyson smirked. "That's when you got something of a call to action?"

"I guess you could say that," I said, looking at her sideways. Thav rolled his eyes. My eyes darted between the two of them. "What am I missing?"

"Dyson thinks she's funny," Thav said.

"I am funny," Dyson told him.

"Meh," David added.

She shoved him lightly.

"Would you say you had some hesitation when this first started?" Dyson asked, ignoring my question.

"Of course," I responded without thinking. "My first instinct was to run."

"A refusal of the call," she nodded, sagely.

Llowellyn let out a bark of laughter. I still didn't get the joke.

"Dyson," Thav warned.

"What?" she said. "He left his known world and, on the train ride here, he got supernatural aid! He and Llowellyn both."

"Did you now?" Thav looked at me with interest.

"I don't know if I would call it supernatural aid," I said, before recounting the story of the woman on the train.

"A hero's journey indeed," Thav chuckled, when I'd finished.

"Right!" Dyson said enthusiastically.

"Do you know what's going on?" I asked David.

"Nope." David shook his head.

"I get it," said Llowellyn.

"Don't rub it in." I elbowed him in the side.

"There are some similarities throughout all hero myth narratives," Dyson explained. "The stages of the story, I guess."

"In the Western world," Thav corrected.

Dyson nodded in agreement.

"I'm still missing something," I said.

"You're still mything something?" Dyson laughed.

"You're not funny," Thav told her.

"Not funny," David echoed, but he was smiling.

"I think it's a little funny," Llowellyn said.

"Don't encourage her," David told him.

"The hero's journey, stage one, a call to action," Dyson recited, unphased. "Stage two, refusal of the call. Stage three, supernatural aid—"

"Oh, come on," I interrupted.

"Stage four," she spoke over me. "The hero leaves his or her known world."

"I'm no hero," I said.

"You said it, not me," Llowellyn mumbled.

"You're my hero," David said with a nod.

"Easy." Dyson winked at him. "Sitting right here."

"Sorry, babe," he said. "But he kind of is."

Rain pounded on the windows as we talked around the table. When the full-table discussion had devolved into side conversations, David and Llowellyn moved over to the bar. Each with a mug in hand, one tea and one coffee, both wrapped deep in discussion.

"They seem to be getting along well," Dyson said. "How has it been, having him back?"

"It's only been a couple days, but it's nice. Feels like home."

"That's what it's like having you around," she bumped her shoulder against mine.

"Haven't talked to Sahrias recently then?" I asked.

Her expression went blank.

"No," she said. "No, I don't think that will be happening any time soon. Thav knows him, you know?"

"Really?"

"He's filled me in a bit on why Sahrias reacted the way he did, but . . ."

"But it doesn't change what happened," I finished for her.

"It doesn't change what happened," she repeated.

"Pa," I heard from behind me, as the old school bell over the door chimed. "Pa, can't you do anything about this rain!"

A smile broke over my face. I knew that voice.

"It's a tsunami out there," she said.

Ember.

I turned in my seat to see a short, round-faced woman with hair the color of fire. Her dark roots bled smoothly into a deep red, that seemed to melt into tones of orange and yellow through her curls.

"You know I can't," Thav said, standing to greet his granddaughter.

"I know you won't." She shook off her umbrella, and did the same to her raincoat.

"How was it?" Thav asked.

"Good," she responded, hugging him. "Challenging in the rain. It was raining at first, but it was fun. Is David here? I want pie."

"He is," Thav said, releasing her. "And a few others."

"Others?" Ember asked, looking around. "Lochlan!" she ran the few steps between us. Launching herself into the air, I got to my feet just in time to catch her.

"Ember, I've missed you," I said, feeling her heat in my arms. A thin stream of steam rose from her clothes as they dried. "How do you fare?"

"Better now."

"Careful you don't burn off your clothes." I put her down.

Ember was still steaming.

Suddenly, a wave of heat and lust washed over me. I watched her walk away from me. She bent down to pick up her jacket, and I almost groaned aloud.

Hang on, I thought. Sense breaking through the cloud of need.

I tilted my head.

Lust, so strong a moment ago, turned to embarrassment. Embarrassment and guilt. It was fading from my mind.

Because those aren't my thoughts, I realized.

I turned to look at Llowellyn, who was staring fixedly at the ceiling. I closed my eyes and tried to press into his mind.

145

"Ahh," he said, turning to look at me.

"That was . . ." I laughed. "Intense?"

"You felt that?" he asked, embarrassment growing.

"I wasn't expecting it. I haven't had to keep my guard up in a while, but we can talk about it later," I said, trying to conceal my laughter.

"Talk about what later?" Ember asked.

"Ember, this is my brother Llowellyn. Llow, this is one of Thav's granddaughters, Ember," I said, ignoring her question.

Ember's eyes shifted from me to Llowellyn, she extended her hand. She looked him up and down appraisingly.

"Well, hello, gorgeous," she said.

"Ember," I scolded.

Then my knees gave out, and I collapsed.

I was barely able to stop the ground coming up to meet me as a chorus of cries rang out. Pain ricocheted through my body.

"Jesus, man," David helped me up. "Are you okay?"

I looked up at my brother.

"It wasn't me," Llowellyn said. "But I feel," he closed his eyes. "I feel something."

"Something's wrong," I told him. "Something's happened to Zemila."

I tapped my watch.

"Call Zemila Alkevic," I said.

"*Calling Zemila Alkevic.*"

Her phone rang and rang and rang. No answer. I tried again. Still nothing.

"What is happening here?" Ember said, concern in her eyes.

"I don't know," I said. "I don't know what happened. I just know

Zemila is in trouble."

"Who's Zemila?" David asked.

"A friend from school," Dyson answered.

"Well, that's the short version," Ember rolled her eyes.

I shot her a look.

"We don't really need to get into all that now," I told Ember, then to my watch I said, "Call Jenner."

"*Calling Jenner*," it responded.

CHAPTER FOURTEEN
Zemila

The adrenaline had worn off. Zemila's whole body ached. Not even the gun pointed at her head could keep the pain at bay.

Zemila followed the guards through the winding halls and into a small office. Once inside, she saw the person who'd spoken for the first time. The woman was short with honey brown skin and cold dark eyes.

Queen Anne.

"So," the Queen said, taking her time to settle behind an ordinary wood desk. "You are the one who tore me away from my thriller."

"Ahhh . . ." Zemila said, trying to figure out what she was talking about.

There was a squashy armchair in the corner. Beside it sat a small table with an open book. Floor-to-ceiling bookshelves lined the walls. The room looked more like a library than an office.

Zemila looked back to the Queen. She didn't think "yes" was the right answer. She wished she still had Jenner in her ear.

"You have my brother," Zemila said, finding her voice, and her courage. "I want him back."

"I see," the Queen said, she tapped her gold-painted nails on the gleaming wood. "Do you know who I am, little girl?"

"You're Queen Anne."

"That's right." Her voice was silky and dangerous. "Do you know what I do here?"

"Read, I imagine." Zemila eyed the walls.

Queen Anne's thick eyebrows popped up in surprise.

"Here at Heaven," she clarified, seemingly taken aback by Zemila's sarcasm.

"Run a casino," Zemila answered obediently.

"That's right. This casino is my dominion, my home. These people who I employ are my family." She gestured at the guards lining the walls. "Your brother came into my home, cheated at my tables, and stole from me. You came in to my home and tried to kill my family. What am I to do about this?"

Zemila was silent.

She didn't know what to say. If Nemo had stolen from Queen Anne, things were much worse than she'd feared. She'd heard what happened to thieves in the basement of Heaven.

"He cheated?" Zemila asked, not really expecting an answer. How could Nemo have been so stupid? So desperate? Why hadn't he come to her, to Lochlan . . . to anyone?

"He used his telekinesis at my craps tables. Went on a quiet winning streak," the Queen said. "He almost got away with it. That makes it worse. Heaven has a strict policy about thieves."

Her deep grey eyes scanned Zemila.

"We make examples of them. We let others know that we don't take such transgressions lightly," the Queen continued. "I've never had anyone brazen enough to try and kill my family for a thief."

"I wasn't trying to kill anyone," Zemila stated.

I was trying to stay alive, she thought. I have the bruises to prove it.

"Then what, exactly, were you trying to do to poor Otto?"

"Otto?" Zemila asked.

"The man whose blood you were pulling through his face."

"I . . . I . . ." The image of the man's cringing face as red mist rose from his skin flashed before Zemila's eyes.

"I didn't mean to . . . I don't know what I did," Zemila answered truthfully.

"Well, well, well," Queen Anne's tone lifted. "Aren't you interesting?"

She pushed back from the desk and walked around it. She faced Zemila. They were roughly the same height, although the Queen wore four-inch heels and Zemila wore flats. Standing eye to eye, Queen Anne stared at her.

"What are your gifts, little Luman girl?" Queen Anne asked.

Zemila wasn't particularly fond of this nickname, but she answered the question.

"I'm an Earth Driver."

"Earth Driver," repeated the Queen. "But don't all things come from the earth?"

That thought scared Zemila. But she couldn't say the thought had never crossed her mind. No Earth Driver in recorded history was ever able to control anything man-manipulated.

"Does that frighten you?" Queen Anne asked, correctly interpreting her silence. "It does, doesn't it."

"You don't know my thoughts," Zemila tried to keep her feelings hidden.

"Don't I? It's all right here," the Queen said, lifting a hand. "It's written on your face." Her fingertips moved towards Zemila's cheek, and brushed it softly.

A painful shock ran through Zemila's body.

She stumbled backwards, almost losing her footing. The Queen was thrown backwards as well and collided with the desk behind her.

There was a beat of shocked silence.

Zemila broke it.

"What the hell was that?" Zemila cupped her cheek. It stung like she'd received an electric shock, drowning out the dull pain of her other injuries.

The Queen righted herself. She straightened her suit jacket.

"Aren't you just full of surprises." Her tone was no longer light. "How long ago did you die, little Luman girl?"

Zemila's hand fell from her cheek, to her neck. She felt for the gash that wasn't there, the scar that didn't exist.

"How do you know th—"

"Answer the question," the Queen interrupted.

"Two months ago," Zemila whispered, her fingertips still on her neck. She realized what she was doing, and let her hand fall.

"Who was the Caster?"

"What?" Zemila's journalistic mind woke with the question.

"Who cast the spell that brought you back?"

Leverage, Zemila thought, hope flaring in her chest.

"Why?" she asked.

"Whoever it was will be worried about you," the Queen said.

Zemila's phone started to ring.

"I bet that's them now. Check her watch. Who's the caller?"

A large man with a thick neck stepped forward. Zemila released the glass disk she'd hidden back under her wrist wrap and held it in the air with her mind.

"One more step," Zemila said, "and this goes through your skull."

The man paused and looked at Queen Anne.

"That's quite all right, George," the Queen said. "I can see that this little one is smarter than she looks. She knows she has a bargaining chip now."

The confirmation was welcome news.

"Erase call log," Zemila said.

"Call log erased."

"What happened when you touched me?" Zemila asked.

"You know that erasing your call log won't stop me from getting hold of your records," Queen Anne said.

"You think I came here alone?" Zemila asked. "You think I don't have outside help? Someone who can make sure you never get that information, someone who has been watching us the whole time?"

The lights in the office flickered on and off.

"Say hello, Your Highness." Zemila's voice was cool. Much cooler than the internal happy dance she did at the proof that Jenner was still with her. "That's my angel playing with your lights and recording everything we say."

The plan was, get in, get Nemo, get out. And, when that fell apart, try to bargain. Their only hope was that the Queen valued her anonymity above making an example of Nemo.

But now Zemila had something else the Queen wanted.

Lochlan.

Queen Anne narrowed her eyes. She looked quickly at one of her guards, who left the room. No doubt to try and get Jenner out of the Heaven system. Zemila knew he'd fail. Jenner was too good.

"If you don't want the whole city to know your face, you will give me my brother, and let us leave, unharmed," Zemila said.

"Blackmail," the Queen observed. "The boogie man Queen Anne was bound to become fact eventually. Though, this would be a little sooner than I'd like. Are you prepared to deal?"

"Depends on the deal," Zemila said.

Queen Anne laughed.

"I like you," she said, her voice lifting again.

The tonal shift made her hard to read.

"What happened when you touched my face?" Zemila asked for the second time. "How did you know that I had—" Her hand moved involuntarily to her throat. "How did you know?"

"I'll tell you how I knew and I'll give you the opportunity to work off your brother's debt," Queen Anne said.

"And in return?"

"You will not release any image of my likeness. You will bring me whoever cast that spell, and that person will do me a favor. When the favor is complete, I will release your brother."

"I will bring you the person who cast the spell. I will turn over any recordings we have. I will take my brother with me now, and we are both free to leave."

"Not a chance," she said. "If he doesn't stay here, I have no way of ensuring your return."

"I'm not leaving him tied to a chair in your basement," Zemila said.

"I don't think you have much of a choice."

"How badly do you want to meet this Caster?"

Queen Anne smirked.

She's enjoying this, Zemila thought.

"I will let you see your brother. He will be treated by our in-house doctor and moved to the hotel. When you wish to leave, you may do so. I'm not stupid enough to think that you would actually turn over every recording you have of me, but I will take your word that my likeness will not be released."

Zemila nodded.

"You will bring the Caster here in the next forty-eight hours. He or she will complete a favor and I will release your brother."

"What kind of favor?" Zemila asked.

"My kind of favor," the Queen answered. "Do we have a deal?"

"You will tell me what just happened? How you know?"

The Queen nodded.

"Then we have a deal," Zemila extended her hand. She was gambling on Lochlan's willingness to help her.

Queen Anne and Zemila shook hands.

The bargain was made.

"It didn't hurt that time," Zemila observed.

"Yes," Queen Anne said, then she turned to one of the men lining the walls. "Take our guest to Dr. Nassar. When he's done being looked over, move him into the silver suite." To Zemila she said, "I'm assuming you'll wish to stay the night with him."

"I'll be able to leave in the morning?" Zemila confirmed.

"I am a woman of my word," Queen Anne said.

"Is that a yes?"

"That's a yes."

Zemila nodded.

"Then the doctor should see you too," the Queen said, surprising Zemila. "Get you some ice, stitch up your wounds."

Zemila looked down at her shirt. It was covered with blood where the wood had pierced her. The Queen ordered a change of clothes for both Zemila and Nemo to be brought to the suite, as well as a meal prepared.

"Sit down," the Queen gestured at the chair in front of her desk. "Your wounds are of no immediate concern. Tea?"

"Okay." Zemila was thrown off by the tonal whiplash. One moment her brother was being made an example of and the next she was getting tea and a change of clothes?

"Two chamomile teas, some disinfectant, and gauze. Thank you, George," the Queen said. "After that, you can go home. The rest of you, to your posts."

There was a muttering of, "Yes, Queen," and, "Thank you, Highness," as the room emptied.

After a few minutes of awkward silence, George came back with two mugs of steaming tea, some wipes, and a pack of gauze.

Zemila's bloody shirt had dried into her wound. She winced as she peeled it up. Gingerly, she dabbed at it with the disinfectant. Moving her shirt and cleaning the wound had opened it again. She pressed the gauze, stemming the flow of fresh blood.

"Mmmm," the Queen said. She handed the mug she'd sipped to Zemila and took the second. It unnerved Zemila that the Queen knew she wouldn't put anything in her body that hadn't been tried first.

"Now to business," Queen Anne said, sipping her own mug. "First, I'll tell you whoever cast that spell loves you and loves you deeply. You both could have been sucked into some hell realm or worse. I've seen many a soul corrupted by that spell."

"He does," Zemila said, knowing it to be true.

"He," the Queen echoed. "Now we're getting somewhere. And you love him." It wasn't a question.

"I do," Zemila said. She'd never admitted that to anyone before. It was surprisingly easy.

"Well, isn't that sweet," the Queen's words were laced with sarcasm. "As to what happened, all spells leave a mark. Sometimes the mark is visible, sometimes it is not. It can be etched into the Caster's skin, or—" She hit Zemila with a look. "It leaves a residue in the essence of the being touched by it. That's what my Magic reacted to. The residue of the spell."

"Why?" Zemila asked. "Why would your Magic react to that spell?"

"Well," Queen Anne gave Zemila a wry smile, "because that spell is mine, little Luman girl."

CHAPTER FIFTEEN
Lochlan

Jenner's face filled the screen of my watch.

"What the hell is going on?" I demanded.

"Oh, hey, pal," Jenner said awkwardly. "Not a—nothing, not at all, nothing is going on here . . . How are you?"

"Jenner," I said, my tone a warning.

"Yes?" he said meekly.

"Is Zemila with you?"

"Why would Zemila be with me, mi amigo? She is her own woman, she does her own thing, she is strong and independent and very frightening and threatening, when she wants to be. Very threatening and I am afraid of her."

"What?"

"I just mean . . . she has a dominant personality, you know. She tells you to do something, and you do it. She tells you to keep a secret, and you keep it because you're afraid."

"Jenner," I repeated.

"Yes?" he squeaked.

"Tell me. Now."

"Okay," he said. "But you have to protect me from her."

"Sure." As if I could, but he didn't need to know that.

"Right, well, Zemila went to lunch with Nemo a few days ago. He had a black eye and was super cagey about it. That was the last time she saw him. This afternoon, one of her contacts told her he had been taken by Queen Anne's people, and was being held in the basement of Heaven."

"What?"

Jenner kept going as if I'd said nothing.

"Cam went to her contact at the DOJ and got some intel on Heaven, and Zemila went there about three hours ago to try and break Nemo out. I hacked into the system, but I lost verbal connection with her. Then someone kicked me out. I just got back into the system, but I can't see her on any of the cameras."

"What!"

"I know, I don't know how I got kicked out. Whoever it was must be—"

"Jenner," I said.

"Yes?"

"WHAT?" I yelled.

"Oh, you mean Zemila. Well, she made me swear not to tell you, and she's so scary with that hair and those cheekbones and the whole being able to move mountains—"

"WHAT?"

"I am looking for her now, amigo. But I don't think it would be a bad idea for you to get here as soon as inhumanly possible. Can your Magic teleport you? Oh my God," he said distracted. He looked straight at me for the first time. "Can you teleport? But if you could, then why would you take the train? Why were you late for work so many times when those fake-real vision things star—"

"Jenner, focus!"

"Right, okay," he said. "I can see you're upset. I think you should come home now. Bye-bye."

He hung up. I looked up blankly from my watch to the stunned faces surrounding me.

"Wha . . . I . . ."

Llowellyn spoke first. "What's the fastest way to get us back?"

"To fly. But that will still be a few hours," Dyson said.

"Is it really going to make a difference if you get back now or then?" asked David. "I'm not trying to be a jerk here, but it sounds like the damage is already done."

"If Jenner gets a lead on where Zemila is," Dyson said. "Maybe Lochlan can get to her."

"Queen Anne is ruthless," Thav said. "But she's fair. If Zemila goes to her with something to offer—"

"How the hell," Dyson turned to look at Thav, "do you know who Queen Anne is?"

"She won't kill your Zemila outright," he said, ignoring Dyson's question. "Even if she has nothing to bargain with, she would sooner make your friend an example than give her an easy death."

"Somehow that doesn't make me feel any better," I said.

"Pa," Ember said. "You can send them back now, can't you? I mean Katye isn't here, so she can't help. But Dyson could fill her spot. We can do it, right?"

"Do what?" Dyson and I asked at the same time.

"With her lineage, yes. Yes, my girl that could work." Thav looked quickly between Dyson and David. "But she would need to feed afterward and animal blood won't do. Ember will be too exhausted, so it can't be her. David, I'm sorry."

"That's okay," he said. "Who should I call?"

"David, no." Dyson turned to him. "No, we can find another way."

"I am so confused," I said as Dyson and David started a quiet argument.

"Likewise," Llowellyn added.

"My race can bend time and space to our will in a more lasting fashion than most Lumans can. But in these new times, I am weak."

"Of course," Llowellyn said. "Ember is your bloodkin. She lends power to the Magic. But Dyson?"

"There is an Ankhian at the top of her line." A shadow passed over Thavaindor's face at the words.

Llowellyn's eyes went wide.

"I've heard this myth," he said.

"Not a myth," Thav told him. "Just a story for another time. We should be able to send you home, if Dyson is willing."

"Yes," David broke away from the quiet argument. "I'll head out to pick up Francis now."

"I'm sorry," Dyson said, again.

Had I not been so distracted, the pain on my friend's face would have given me pause.

"I've got to get used to it, right?" David said. "I love you." He kissed her on the mouth and rushed out of the diner.

"You can't feed from him?" I asked.

"I can't," she said, wearily. "I'll tell you about it another time."

I nodded.

My watch buzzed telling me I'd received a text. Whatever it was wasn't as important as getting home.

"You and your brother only," Thav said to me. "We will ship your belongings."

"Not a problem," I said. "What do you need us to do?"

"Better we do this in the back," Thav instructed, eyeing the large windows.

We followed him through the kitchen and into a small office. Upon entering, he mumbled a word and raised his hand. The desk and chair slid to press against the back wall.

"Not much room in here, Pa," Ember said.

"It'll do," he responded. "Dyson, Ember, and I will hold hands with the boys in the centre. I will pull energy from the girls and fold space. When I do that, you," he nodded at me, "will push the image of where you want to go into my mind."

"Aye," I said, already picturing my living room.

"You'll know the moment. You'll feel it."

"Aye," I repeated. It all felt so rushed. Too rushed. When Magic was rushed, bad things happened.

"Dyson," I pulled her into a quick hug. "I'm sorry it's been so short."

"Don't worry," she said. "Make sure our friends are safe."

"I will," I promised.

Llowellyn and Ember exchanged a brief look before he came to stand next to me. The three clasped hands around us. The room stilled.

Thav started to chant. Gold light seemed to glow in a pattern beneath his shirt.

"Gods below," Llowellyn whispered.

The ankh mark all Ankhians were born with glowed through Thav's shirt. The size and placement of the symbol signified rank. Thavaindor was high in his order. High, even for those of the First Line.

A mist seemed to fill the room as the rhythmic chanting continued.

My feet left the ground. I thought hard of my living room, preparing to push the image into Thav's mind. I placed two fingers on his temple.

"Aiteal," I said, thinking of my mismatched couches and carpeted floor.

There was a tug in my gut. I spun around to face Llowellyn, gripped both his shoulders, and we were thrown into nothingness.

My feet slammed into my living room floor.

Llowellyn landed beside me.

A scream ripped through the air.

CHAPTER SIXTEEN
Lochlan

"Fanaidh," I said, freezing the popcorn in the air as Jenner continued to shriek. "Jenner, it's just me!" I shouted over him. "Stop screaming."

"¡Me cago en la hostia!" Jenner said, clutching the empty, upside down bowl to his chest. "Lochlan. You scared the absolute hell out of me, Dios . . ."

"I can see that," I said.

Jenner looked at the popcorn frozen in the air. Opening his mouth unnecessarily wide, he slowly moved his head forward, and closed his mouth around a hovering piece of popcorn. He began to chew.

"Do you mind?" I gestured at the bowl.

"Huh? Oh, right." He held it out, right way up. With a wave of my hand I directed the popcorn into the bowl. Jenner looked at it for a moment.

"What are you doing here?" he asked casually, popping a few more pieces of popcorn into his mouth.

"What?"

"You've been saying that a lot. I don't really know how to answer."

I narrowed my eyes at him.

"Zemila," I said with forced calm.

"Oh, you didn't read my text?" he asked.

"Your text?" I remembered my watch buzzing and ignoring it in all the commotion. "No, we just got here as fast as we could."

I gestured at Llowellyn. Jenner looked at him as if only just noticing he was there.

"Well, hello," he said. "You can sit next to me. Do you want some popcorn? I'm in the middle of the 2035 Terminator remake."

I looked down at my watch. The message was brief.

ZEMILA CALLED. EVERYTHING IS OKAY . . . KIND OF.

SHE WANTS YOU TO STOP BY HER PLACE WHEN YOU'RE BACK.

"Jenner," I said. "What does 'everything's okay, kind of' mean?"

"It means you don't have to rush back here, but when you get back, go see Zemila. I think you should wait until tomorrow, though. She made some kind of deal or something with Queen Anne. Cool that you can teleport! Weird that it took you an hour."

"A deal or something?" I asked. "An hour? What? Jenner, I spoke to you five minutes ago."

He wasn't listening. He was watching Llowellyn examining the living room.

"I could give you a tour?" Jenner said. "My bedroom is very nice."

"Sorry," Llowellyn turned to face my roommate. "You're a little lanky for my taste. When I'm with a man, I like to be the little spoon."

"Oh my god, you're gay! I was only joking! Lochlan, you didn't tell me your brother is gay! You can still be the little spoon," Jenner said to him. "I promise."

Llowellyn smirked.

"Can we please stay on task?" I wanted to know what was going on. I wanted to see Zemila.

Jenner looked at me like I had four eyeballs.

"You. Didn't. Tell. Me. He. Is. Gay." He emphasized each word with a clap.

"Standing right here." Llowellyn raised his hand.

"And you look great," Jenner said emphatically.

"He's not gay," I said. "He's an empath."

"So, he's gay," Jenner said.

"I'm still standing right here."

"Yes, beautiful, hang on." He waved his hand at Llowellyn.

"You think everyone's gay," I said. "What does it matter that I didn't tell you he sometimes sleeps with men?"

"Yes, everyone is gay. But if he actually sleeps with men, that's different," Jenner chattered on. "I think you're gay, but you don't sleep with men!"

"Ha!" Llowellyn barked out a laugh. "Lochlan doesn't sleep with men, yeah . . . right."

"WHAT?" Jenner screamed. The popcorn went flying again.

"Jenner please!" I ignored it this time. "What do you mean a deal, and what do you mean an hour?"

"I'm an hour into the movie." Jenner held the bowl in one hand. "I started it right after Zemila called me, which was right after you. We spoke an hour ago."

"What?" I whispered.

"Magic does funny things when its rushed," Llowellyn said.

I tapped at my watch. It was almost 3 a.m. Was that the correct time? Was my watch effected by the Magic too?

"What time is it?" I asked. Would Zemila be home? Would she be awake? How was Nemo?

"Amigo," Jenner said. "Zemila is at Heaven for the night. She made a deal with Queen Anne. It's almost four. Connect your watch to the home system and go to bed. See her tomorrow."

I nodded without realizing what I was agreeing to.

"I can go to Heaven now." I linked my watch to my system and the correct time set. "I can go and get them both now."

"Little One," I felt my brother's hands on my shoulders. I tried to pull away and move for the door. "Little One, think. You don't know the deal she made. You cannot go now. You do not know what danger that might put her in."

"I know she needs my help," I looked up at him.

"She needed your help, maybe. But she is safe for now."

"Safe?" I threw the word at Llowellyn.

"Sí, amigo," Jenner was hugging the empty bowl to his chest. "For now."

Jenner set Llowellyn up on a blow-up mattress in the office where Nemo should have been staying. He filled us in, as much as he could, on the Zemila and Nemo situation, then we watched the end of Terminator before sleeping for a few hours.

I woke up around nine. I performed a small cast to bring the three pieces of the stone back together. Holding the stones and the tangle of gold wires, in my hand, I closed my fingers around them and muttered a short incantation.

"That's it?" Jenner said, sipping his coffee.

His disappointment amused me.

"I guess so," I said, peering at the small sphere encased in gold strands.

"What were you expecting?" Llowellyn asked, snatching the chain from my hand and putting it around his neck. "Fireworks?"

"Sí, sí," Jenner said to Llowellyn as he headed out of the kitchen. "When a powerful magical artifact is unified, I expect fireworks. I expect you to deliver on that expectation next time."

We heard the office door close. My mind drifted to the conversation I didn't want to have with Zemila. Mayhap it wasn't the right time. Some of what I was thinking must have shown on my face because Jenner was staring at me.

"Oye, Carnal," he said. "¿Como te va?"

"What do I say to her?" I asked him. "Where do I even start? Do I just wait till this is all over? It's not like Balor is taking time off. He's still out there, likely as not creating more Famorians as we speak."

"Amigo," he sighed. "I don't know."

"I want her to be safe." I felt the invisible weight on my shoulders grow heavy. "People around me usually aren't safe."

"I'm doing okay," Jenner said.

"Two months ago, you were almost turned into a Famorian."

"Oh, yeah," he said casually, but his face went cold. "But I wasn't."

"And now Nemo."

"I'm pretty sure that's his fault."

"Even so, if I stay around her, if she stays around me . . . she's going to get hurt." I didn't like it, but it was the truth.

"I think that's a decision you need to let her make," he said. "If you don't want to be with her, that's one thing. But you can't decide whether or not she wants to be with you. Don't take her choice away. I have a feeling people have done that to her enough."

An hour later, I was out the door, and still unsure of what I wanted.

"Where are you off to lookin' so miserable?"

The unexpected voice made me jump. Mrs. Abernathy chuckled and stood with the help of her cane. Her gloved hands were covered in dirt, a bucket of pulled weeds at her side.

"I wasn't even able to sneak up on people when I was young," she said, pulling off the gloves. "And I'm an old woman now."

"Good morning, Mrs. Abernathy," I said, lowering my hand from my slowing heart. "Are you sure you weren't a spy in a former life?"

She chuckled. I tried to smile but couldn't manage it.

"Where are you going off looking like that?"

"Like what?" I asked.

"You look just like my Harvey when I said no the second time." She bent down to pick up the bucket of weeds.

"Said no to what?"

"Marriage," she told me with a smile.

My eyebrows popped up in surprise. "Really?"

"Oh, yes, I was a career woman. I wanted to get a job first, make it on my own. Then take a husband."

"That's so progressive of you," I said. Mrs. Abernathy had been born in the Deep South during the civil rights movement. Her parents had marched with Dr. Martin Luther King in Selma a few years before she'd been born. I shouldn't have been surprised.

"I am a progressive woman," she said, giving me an indignant look. "Now enough about me. Where are you goin' lookin' like my Harvey?"

Her dark brown eyes looked expectantly at me. I tried to formulate a response, but my heart's weight was too heavy.

"Uh huh," she said before I spoke. She walked over to me, waving me closer to her. I took a step forward and she reached up over the dividing fence, separating our walkways, to pat my cheek.

She did that often.

"Whatever you are working up to tell that beautiful girl," she said, hand still cupping my face, "don't worry about it. Love will find a way."

"I'm not—" I started, but she cut me off.

"Me and my Harvey, we were married for fifty-four years. This year would have been our sixtieth." She gave me a sad smile shrouded in memory. Then she let out a bark of laughter and slapped my cheek.

"My Harvey woulda liked you," she said turning away, laughing again. "Oh, yes, you two would have been fast friends."

φ

Love will find a way, I thought as I got off the bus a block away from Zemila's apartment. Wishful thinking. Despite Mrs. Abernathy's assurances, I knew this time it couldn't. The reality of my life was that the people around me weren't safe.

I needed Zemila to be safe. She'd already died once. Standing outside Zemila's door, I took a deep breath, and rang the bell. Oriole announced my presence on the other side of the door.

"Ori! Go to your bed," I heard, and then she was in front of me. "Lochlan," she said. "Jenner told me you were on your way."

She pulled me into a warm embrace.

"Hey, you," I said, wrapping my arms around her. I felt my resolve weaken. She smelled as she always did, of sweet earth and something else. "How's Nemo?"

"She moved him to one of the suites in the Heaven Hotel," Zemila said, releasing me. I looked at her for the first time.

My eyes took in her wounds. Heat and anger flared in my chest. Her jaw was slightly swollen and there was a bruise under her left eye. Her face was scratched and scabbed, and she pressed a hand to her side like she'd been hurt there too.

"He's doing okay," Zemila continued. "Come on up. I'll explain. I'll apologize."

"Apologize?" My surprise brought my eyes from the scabbed cut on her shoulder under the strap of her tank top to her bright brown eyes.

"Yeah," she said, putting her hand in mine and leading me up the stairs. "Apologize."

The staircase opened up into a bachelor apartment that was exactly as it had been the last time I'd been there. White walls and white couches with a slanted ceiling, large windows, and a growling dog in the corner.

"Hello, Oriole," I said, meeting the dog's gaze.

If possible, the animal's ears flattened further. My eyes went back to examining Zemila's scrapes and bruises.

"It's not as bad as it looks," she said, touching her hand to her black eye.

"It looks painful." I thought of offering to heal her, but didn't think she'd accept.

"Then it's exactly how it looks." She smiled at me. My heart beat faster. "Can I get you anything?" she asked, walking around her kitchen island. "I made some tea."

"No thanks, Mila. I can't stay."

"Your brother," she said, her long ponytail swayed as she shook her

170

head. "Of course. You two just got back."

"No, it's not that, it's—"

"Let me tell you about Queen Anne," she interrupted. "I need to get it all out to somebody."

"Okay," I said.

Zemila rested her elbows on the counter. I fought to keep my eyes on her face and my mind on her words as she started to talk. My shock seemed to increase with every new piece of information—getting in, the fight, the bargain with Queen Anne. I was impressed at how Zemila had handled herself.

"Of course," I said, as she apologized again. "Of course, I will meet Queen Anne with you."

"Thank you," she said, moving around the island towards me.

I thought she might hug me again. But she paused. I wanted to tell her I would do this favour and get out of her life. I'd make sure she was safe. I'd leave.

"There is something else too," she said. "Not Nemo-related, if that's okay?"

No! my brain shouted.

"Sure," I said aloud.

"Lochlan, I don't think I ever thanked you for saving my life."

I wanted to take a step back. My brain yelled at me to interrupt her, to start talking, to get out of there. I did none of those things.

I'd forgotten how beautiful she was, the grace with which she moved. I'd forgotten how much I loved it when she said my name. My eyes settled on her lips.

"I didn't understand how much of a risk it was for you. Casting that spell." She touched her neck. The movement brought my attention back to what she was saying. I struggled to keep it there as she closed the distance between us.

Zemila reached out and took one of my hands in hers. "I wanted to say, for that, I'm sorry too."

"Sorry?" I said, surprised.

"It's taken me so long to realize—"

"You couldn't have known—"

"Let me finish," she said. She took a steadying breath. "You were always just there . . . at Erroin, I mean. Not someone I really saw, you know? You were just my brother's friend. Before I really realized what I was feeling, you were gone."

"Zemila, I—"

"Then it happened again." She spoke over me, tracing the lines on my palm with a finger, and not meeting my eyes. "Not in the same way, but that night at the gala, and when we were at the karaoke bar. Then everything happened with Simmons and I got scared. But I'm not scared anymore." She squeezed my hand and released it. "I'm sorry it's taken me this long." She took a step back and looked up at me. "Would you like to go out with me sometime? On a date."

"Oh," I said, elation and dread warring inside of me. "Oh," I said, when dread won out. "I really think I should have gone first."

"Oh?" she questioned with a raised eyebrow.

"I came over to tell you that whatever I had felt, whatever I thought had been between us," I paused collecting my thoughts. "I shouldn't have told you about the spell, about any of it."

"You shouldn't have told me that you loved me?" she asked, her expression stony.

"I don't think that's what I said," I lied.

"You said the spell that saved my life only works if you love the person you are attempting to save." She crossed her arms.

"There are many types of love," I said, grasping at straws. "Varying degrees."

"So, you don't love me," she stated.

"I didn't say that." I felt like I was drowning. "I care for you very much, Zemila. I always have, I always will, but . . . but, I don't think a romantic relationship is right for us."

Silence stretched between us. I felt her eyes on me. I couldn't meet them.

"Run that by me again?" Her tone was ice.

"Just look at what's happening with Nemo," I said.

"What does that have to do with us?"

"People around me get hurt, Zemila." My voice was rising.

"I've already been hurt!" she threw back.

"And who knows what this Queen Anne wants with me," I continued, chancing a glance at her then looking away. "If she knows we're together—"

"I didn't ask to exchange promise rings, Lochlan, I asked for a few hours of your time."

"And I'm saying no."

Gods, I thought. This hurts.

She stared at me, blinked once, and turned to look out the window.

I waited for a response, then realized I didn't need one. I turned to leave.

"This is a side of you I haven't seen before." Her voice was cold and flat. She didn't sound like herself. I turned back to face her.

"I'm sorry I gave you the wrong—"

"No, no," she interrupted, taking a few steps backward and leaning against the island. "Don't apologize. If this is part of who you are, I want to know." Her eyes met mine. "Lochlan the Coward."

"Excuse me?"

"I guess I shouldn't be too surprised," she continued. "How many years were we at school together? You never so much as asked to share a milkshake. Lochlan the Coward who runs from his problems instead of facing them."

Her words were like a slap in the face.

"Hey," I said taking a step forwards, my anger rising. "It's not like I wanted to leave."

"Didn't you?" she said. "Isn't that what you do? Big brother dies, you run."

"That's not fair."

"Grandpa comes a knockin', you run."

"I didn't run!"

"Now I tell you that I want to be with you and you can't deal, so like a coward, you run!"

"Zemila!" I yelled, grabbing her by the shoulders. She winced in pain. Before I could release her, she shoved me with two hands on my chest.

"What?" she said, hitting me in the chest again. "What, Lochlan?"

I groaned in frustration. Did she think I wanted it to happen like this? Did she think I didn't care? I ran my hand through my hair.

"What is that?" she said, catching my wrist.

"It's nothing," I answered, trying to pull away.

"Do not lie to me," she said. "Ever again."

She pulled my wrist towards her. I stood still.

"When did you get a tattoo?" she asked, pushing my shirt up. "It's a sleeve?" She examined the twisted knots on my wrist.

"I got it a couple months ago," I said, not really lying.

Her hands lightly traced the lines on my forearm. She forced my sleeve higher.

"Take off your shirt," she said when the material bunched above my elbow.

"What? No."

"Lochlan." She grabbed two fistfuls of my shirt to emphasize her point. "Either you take it off or you're going to need a new one,"

"Okay, okay," I said. "I like this shirt."

I saw the corner of her mouth twitch up, and the heat of the argument turned into something else. A current of need ran through me. I tried to ignore it.

Stepping back, I pulled my sleeve down over my arm, grabbed my shirt at the base of my neck and pulled it over my head. Straightening, I looked at her.

Zemila's eyes followed the dark lines up my arm.

"Undershirt too," she commanded.

I watched her as she watched me. I took off my undershirt.

She stepped forward and lay her hands on my arm. I sucked in a breath when her fingers traced the lines over my inner forearm, over my bicep, then to my shoulder.

Heat seemed to rise everywhere she touched. My heart raced. I could feel her breath on my chest.

"You went to a tattoo parlour and got this?" she asked, her hand resting over my heart. The place the tattoo was most intricate.

"Yes," I whispered, trying to keep my breathing steady. Trying to keep my desire in check.

She looked up at me with the eyes of a journalist.

"This is a normal tattoo?"

"Yes," I repeated, cursing myself for the waver in my voice.

"What did I tell you about lying to me?" She lightly pressed her nails into my chest. I sucked in a breath. It was an effort to keep my hands at my sides. I wanted to hold her, to feel her, to run my hands through her hair and press my body into hers.

"I'm not," I lied again. It didn't even sound convincing to me.

"If this is a normal tattoo, why can I feel it?"

"Feel it?" I echoed. The haze of need lifted as my mind tried to make sense of what she'd said. "What do you mean feel it?"

Her breathing was heavy too. Her cheeks were flushed. She looked like she was glowing.

"I feel heat. Light." She took her hand off my chest and tapped her heart. "Right here."

The room seemed to dim with the loss of her touch. No sooner had the thought crossed my mind did her hand returned to my chest. The world brightened. She slid her hand up onto my shoulder and placed her other on my hip, pulling me close.

Heat and light, I thought. I could feel it too. It was building.

I couldn't keep myself from touching her now. With one hand tangled in her hair, I looped my other arm around her waist. I closed my eyes.

She ran her nose along my throat, then lifted her head until her lips grazed my ear. I shivered and stifled a groan.

Dipping my head to the crook of her neck, I breathed her in. Sweet earth and something else.

"Maybe," Zemila whispered. "Maybe that's part of, part of how Queen Anne knew about you, about the spell. She said it was her spell." She pressed her hips into mine. My exhale was harsh. "She talked about marks of . . . of . . ."

I lifted my eyes to meet hers. Brighter than usual brown eyes stared at me. I was getting lost in them.

With great effort, I dropped my hands and took a step back. Her hands fell too. We were both breathing heavily, gazes locked. She blinked once and looked away. I dropped my eyes too, as the world seemed to dim.

"What do you mean 'her spell?' " I asked.

"What the hell was that?" Zemila said, ignoring my question. "I felt like, I almost . . . and we were barely—"

She moved on shaky legs, over to the couch.

"Me too," I said, bending to retrieve my clothes. Zemila sunk onto the couch. The moment she landed, she shot back to her feet with a gasp.

"Oh my God!" she said, pressing a hand to her side.

"Did I hurt you?" I rushed towards her, the undershirt forgotten. "Are you okay?"

She lifted her shirt to show me a square of gauze and tape. It was stained with dried blood.

"Gods, did it open up again?" I asked.

She peeled off the bandage. The skin beneath was smooth.

"I got stabbed here yesterday," she said, running her fingers over her skin. She pulled off the gauze and dropped it on a side table. "I jumped behind a couch, crashed into a coffee table, and part of it stabbed me."

"How did you heal?"

"You," she said, looking up at me. Her black eye and swollen chin were gone. "It must have been you."

She pulled her shirt back into place and showed me her shoulder.

"I was grazed by a bullet here." She looked from where the mark should have been to me. "Now I don't even have a scar."

I ran my hand over her bare shoulder and pressed my lips to the place where there would be no scar. She let out a small sound that had nothing to do with pain. Before we could get tangled up in each other again, Zemila gently laid her hands on my chest and eased me back.

"If we're going to talk, you're going to have to put your clothes back on . . . and maybe stand on the other side of the room."

I let out a low chuckle. Her hands moved slowly down my chest.

"We don't have to talk," I said, not wanting to move. With a look of reluctance, Zemila dropped her hands. I took the few steps back to where I'd left my shirt and dressed unsteadily.

"Can you imagine if we actually—" Laughter cut off Zemila's words. She sunk back onto the couch. "Really, Lochlan, no lies. What was that?"

I sighed and leaned up against the stairs' big banister.

"I don't know. I can give you my best guess."

"I'll take your best guess," she said. "And my tea, if you wouldn't mind."

"Sure." I walked over to the marble island to retrieve her mug. "Ignis," I said, heating the cooled tea.

"Hmmm," she smiled at me.

I handed her the mug and her fingers brushed mine. Heat ran through me again.

"I, umm," Zemila said, catching her breath. She'd felt it too. "I like that you're not hiding from me anymore."

"Not much point, is there."

"I guess not," she said. "Thank you."

"For the tea or for not hiding?"

"For both," she said, her eyes brightening. "And for your best guess."

"Right," I said. "Do you remember what I told you about the spell?"

"Yes," she answered. "The one that doesn't have a name. The one that's dangerous because it needs both Light and Dark Magic to power it."

"Yeah." My voice came out a little dreamier than I'd meant it to. I stopped staring at her and redoubled my efforts to focus.

"You told me that the spell was Dark because it used Blood Magic," she continued. "But Light because it used Love Magic too. You told me the spell only worked because you loved me."

"Yes," I said, looking at the floor instead of her. The next part was tough to say. "That wasn't the whole truth. The spell worked because you love me too. I didn't want to tell you that before. I didn't think it was . . ." I took in a deep breath. "It just felt wrong to say that to you."

"Okay," she said, calmer than I'd expected. She took a sip of her tea. "And the tattoo?"

"I didn't know that would happen. I'd only heard rumors of marks and bindings."

"Queen Anne said I have marks of the spell." She put her hand to her chest. "But on my spirit, or something."

"Powerful spells will mark a Caster. I've seen spell marks, but nothing of this size." I glanced at my arm. "Sometimes when a spell is cast by two people, together, it binds them. We didn't cast together so I'm not sure why you could feel the mark, but mayhap . . ."

I stopped pacing. Pieces were starting to fall into place.

"What?" she asked.

I sat down on the couch beside her, careful not to make contact.

"The Blood Magic," I said, resting my elbow on the back of the couch. "You have to understand, I'd never seen the spell done. The stories I heard were all second- and third- and fourth-hand accounts. Three cast, two failed."

"But it worked once," she said.

"Yes." I stood and started to pace again. "I think the difference in that occasion was love. They loved each other. They were bound before the spell happened."

"Are we bound?" she asked.

I looked at her.

"I don't know. I can tell you it wasn't my intention."

"I believe you," she said, nodding.

"But perhaps . . ." I paused, fearful of her response. "Perhaps that's why your wounds healed . . . I don't know."

"I'm grateful," she said, touching the eye that was no longer black.

"As for the mark," I went on. "And why you can feel it. I had cut my hand to cast—to break a cast really." I showed her a scar on my left palm, now faded to a thin line. "When I cast, I needed your blood. I used my left hand in the blood from when Simmons . . ."

She shuddered at the memory.

"The spell worked its way through me, and it healed your wounds."

"And the tattoo is what's left?" she asked. "The mark of the spell."

"That is the only thing that makes sense to me."

"And now you're pretending you don't want to be with me because what?" she asked. "You think it will make me safer? You think I'll be out of danger?"

"Everyone around me is in danger, Zemila," I said as her brown eyes searched my face. "The further away you are from me, the better."

"You don't think that I'll be in danger where ever I go?" she asked. "Balor knew you well enough ten years ago to use me against you. What makes you think distance will stop him now?"

"I don't know, I just—"

"Queen Anne knows there's a powerful Caster in my life. What would happen if I went back to her without you? Or didn't go back at all?"

I opened my mouth to respond, but she continued.

"I don't think it matters one bit what we do. If Balor's going to send someone for me—or, God forbid, come for me himself—do you really think our relationship status will stop him?"

"Well, when you put it like that," I said with a weak smile.

"This is what's going to happen." She set down her mug of tea and caught my hand to cease my pacing. She laced her fingers with mine. I looked down at her. "We are going to deal with this Queen Anne situation tomorrow, then you are going to take me out. We'll take things slow— we've got time to see where this leads. Agreed?"

"Agreed," I said.

"Okay," she breathed. Very deliberately, she dropped my hand. "I'd hug you goodbye, but honestly if I get any closer, you'll need a new shirt."

"I hate this shirt."

She smiled and looked at me through her lashes.

I melted.

If I just went to her now, just sat down next to her on the couch. If I took the tea out of her hands and lost my fingers in her hair . . .

"We've got time," Zemila said, breaking my train of thought.

"I'm going to go," I said, pulling myself together. "Call me when

Queen Anne contacts you." I walked towards the staircase.

"I will," she said. "Hey, Lochlan?"

I turned, my foot already on the top step.

"I'm happy you came by."

"Me too," I said. "I'm . . ." I wasn't sure how to tell her what I was feeling. "I . . ."

"Me too," she said.

CHAPTER SEVENTEEN
Zemila

When the door shut behind Lochlan, Oriole rose to her feet. The dog covered the distance between her bed and the stairs in a few quick strides. A low growl filled the room.

"Give it a rest, Ori." Zemila held her tea in both hands. She liked the feeling of heat it gave her.

The dog looked at Zemila, narrowing her eyes as if to say, "Are you stupid? He's dangerous."

Zemila ignored her dog and organized her thoughts. Nemo was safe for the moment, but who knows how long that would last. When she'd left him yesterday, he'd been resting comfortably in a luxurious suite.

But luxury and safety were not the same.

All Zemila could do was hope Queen Anne kept her word and Nemo didn't do anything stupid.

She looked down at her watch. Her wrist was bare.

Right, she thought, standing. Washroom. She'd taken it off when she'd showered this morning. She hated how it tangled in her hair.

And thinking of showers, she thought as she headed into the

bathroom, I need a cold one. What the hell was that with Lochlan?

The intensity of their connection was something she'd never felt before. Just the thought made her ache for his touch.

Heat and light, she thought. Wild forests and quiet nights.

"Pull yourself together," she told her reflection. Taking her watch from the small shelf above the sink, she put it on before going back to her tea.

She had a few missed calls and messages. Tyler, Dyson, Cam and—

"Professor Adley." She changed directions from couch to desk. "Keyboard and screen," she said, after placing her watch on the projection stand.

"*Opening keyboard and screen,*" her system responded.

A blue keyboard projected itself in front of the watch, at the same time as her list of notifications was projected onto the whiteboard backing of the stand. With a few quick taps, she'd opened both the video message from Professor Adley and the file that came with it. She hit play.

A portly man with a large moustache appeared. "Hello, my dear."

Zemila had met Professor Adley at a conference on race relations in education reform. He was a history professor at the University of London in England. They'd hit it off and had lunch every time he came to the capital.

"I hope you're doing well, lovey. I've done a little digging for you," Professor Adley's bushy eye brows moved frantically up and down. A sure sign of his enthusiasm. Zemila smiled.

"You know how I enjoy a good side project. So I put together some objects that you may find interesting for this, ahhh, article you're writing. A little off your beat, isn't it? All the same, here we go. There is a brief summary of about twenty artifacts, all of which are either ancient or have a mythical history, per your request. I wanted to make a little video to tell you about the few I found most interesting."

Zemila felt a guilty twist in her gut. She'd told Lochlan "no more lies," but hadn't told him about her research. Shaking off the feeling, she turned her attention back to the video.

"There are three weapons claiming to be the Holy Lance or the Spear of Destiny. I personally believe that the one in Turkey has the highest likelihood of being authentic."

Zemila paused the video message and opened the document titled "Ancient and/or Mythical Spears."

The Holy Lance in Rome, she read, is preserved under the dome of Saint Peter's Basilica. The Catholic Church makes no claims at its legitimacy. Formerly housed in the Hofburg Palace, the Lance is a spear made of steel, gold, and leather. It was recently purchased by a wealthy collector and religious fanatic.

She scrolled down to find the one from Turkey.

Found in 1098 in Antakya, Turkey by a monk who'd had a vision from God. This spear of ash and iron was deemed fake by Roman Cardinal Prospero Lambertini in the eighteenth century.

"Hmmm," she said and hit play on the message.

"The Catholic Church never claimed their 'Holy Lance' was real, but somehow found the time to send a cardinal to denounce what I believe to be the true Spear of Destiny. But you know how I feel about the Catholic Church."

She smiled.

"Next I would like to draw your attention to the Clacton Spear. I don't think this is exactly what you're looking for. It is just a sharpened bit of wood, but it is quite remarkable. This one is on display at the National

History Museum here in London, where you always have a free place to stay, yet you never come to visit—"

She scoffed.

"— and it is 400,000 years old. Anyway . . ."

Zemila rolled her eyes at his jab. Work brought him to the capital. She had no reason to visit London.

"There is another, not nearly as old, made of the same wood as the Clacton, Taxus Baccata, or more commonly known as Yew. It rests in the hands of yet another collector, less fanatical but still a character. All the descriptions are in the file I sent you.

"Lastly, I wanted to draw your attention to a metal spear. A five-metal spear called a Vel, which is a Tamil psychic weapon. It has an exceptional mythological history. Quite fascinating.

"Anyway, my dear, lovely to hear from you as always. You have an open invite, and please let me know if you need anything else. Ta!"

The video ended.

Zemila had to talk to Lochlan about this. He would know which spear belonged to his brother better than she would. She scanned the document. She thought she could rule out the spears with a heavy connection to Eastern mythology, but who knew where Lugh originally got his Long Arm.

"Hmmm," she said again before beginning to draft her thank you email to Professor Adley.

The messages from Tyler, Cam, and Dyson blinked in the corner of her projection.

I can't ignore him forever, Zemila thought, reaching for the small box she kept on her desk.

She opened it.

The diamond was flawless. It shone with a near-blinding brilliance. She remembered that for the two days she'd worn it, it had reflected off nearly everything she'd walked past. The delicate platinum band encrusted with small diamonds was nearly invisible next to the five-carat gemstone that would make a skating rink jealous.

He didn't know me at all, she thought, looking at the small emeralds on either side of the cushion-cut diamond. It was the only part of the ring she liked. They reminded her of Lochlan's eyes.

That's what had made her realize she couldn't marry Tyler, as much as she loved him. As much as she'd thought she'd loved him. It was when she'd been explaining this, about to give back the ring, that he'd told her about the cheating.

She'd put the ring in her pocket, grabbed her bag, and left the hotel room.

Zemila hadn't seen him since, despite his best efforts. She put the box down and opened the message from Cam.

WHAT CAN I DO TO HELP?

Zemila smiled.

She quickly responded, telling Cam that Nemo was as safe as he could be—under the circumstances.

I WAS TALKING ABOUT YOU! Cam responded. YOUR ABILITIES, YOUR BROTHER, YOUR ROOMMATE, YOUR EX. IT'S A LOT. WHAT CAN I DO?

A BAD MOVIE NIGHT WOULD BE GREAT, Zemila sent back.

JENNER IS COOKING FOR MY BIRTHDAY TOMORROW, BUT NEXT WEEK FOR SURE, Cam sent.

THANKS, Zemila texted.

She thought of telling Cam about what just happened with Lochlan.

That electric feeling he gave her. The tattoo.

No, she thought. That was an in-person story, if it was a story at all.

She rubbed her fingers together. They still tingled with the sharp zing of Magic from Lochlan, or whatever that connection was.

Zemila tried to push Lochlan out of her mind and looked back down at her watch. Dyson had called. With the sun shining through her windows, it would be pointless to try and call back now.

"Local News," Zemila instructed her system. Four separate newspapers opened on her screen. "Top four."

"*JACE Co., The New York Times, The Protectorate, The Washington Post,*" her system answered.

She started with her own paper, JACE Co. Skimming over a few sections, she stopped and gritted her teeth at the piece titled, *Fires in Lowtown, Insurance Fraud?*

That should have been her story.

Lochlan would be going with her to Lowtown tomorrow . . . insurance fraud? Who wrote this?

She scrolled up to the byline after speed-reading the piece.

Dick Rabski.

She scoffed. If she'd known the self-important jerk was going to pick up her notes, she might have kept them.

Green eyes looked through thick black rims at her, heat rose in her chest . . .

"Close JACE Co.," Zemila told her computer. The New York Times took over her screen.

Arrests made in the Cartwrytte Murder. She read the article. It was light on details and heavy on anti-immigrant fear mongering.

Maggie Cartwrytte, she read, was survived by her husband William, prominent member of the Right Waters Party, and their eleven-year-old son, William Jr.

Did Lochlan have any children? she wondered. Could he have children?

The article discussed Mr. Cartwrytte's increased efforts for the party's new crime bill. She skimmed a sensationalized article in the Protectorate for the sheer ridiculousness of the title: *Skyview catches 3rdGens Killing Maggie Cartwrytte*.

Jenner would lose his mind, she thought.

Jenner was a 4thGen. Fourth Generation Immigrant. Zemila and Nemo were 1stGens who passed as 2ndGens. When they were children, they'd gotten American birth certificates. She was never sure why or how.

Does Lochlan have a passport? she wondered before going back to the article.

Skyview, the long-time unknown government project, Lochlan, has made its way into the public eye—Lochlan . . .

—after capturing the murder of Maggie Cartwrytte. Skyview saw— Lochlan . . .

—Mrs. Cartwrytte being followed by two then-unknown men on her way home from volunteering—Lochlan . . .

—at the local refugee centre. The men, both unidentified 3rdGens, followed her into a grocery store—Lochlan . . .

—near the church—Lochlan . . .

—then into the parking garage where the victim regularly parked— Lochlan. Lochlan. Lochlan.

She gave up, stood, and went to run herself a bath.

CHAPTER EIGHTEEN
Lochlan

The electric feeling of light and heat lingered on my skin. I paused at the front door of Zemila's building and closed my eyes.

What in Danu's name was that? I thought.

I felt like I was walking on air, like I could take on the world, like the invisible weight I'd carried on my shoulders was gone.

I sighed happily and walked towards the bus stop.

We can handle Queen Anne, I told myself. My brother is here. His powers are returning. The Magic of the Tools will help him. Nemo will be all right. Thav was sure Queen Anne would honor her agreement. And I have a date with Zemila.

Optimistic, I realized. I'm feeling optimistic.

"I hear you met the Shannon," said an unfamiliar voice.

The Shannon, I thought, stopping dead in my tracks. The woman on the train.

"She won't talk to us," the voice said.

I turned to face the speaker.

"Did she tell you anything interesting?" His bland features made him instantly forgettable.

"What are you?" I asked, calling Magic.

"Ethinnson, let's not play dumb. It's boring." The man picked at something under a fingernail.

"What are you?" I repeated.

"Just a man, Lochlan." His dull brown eyes laughed at me. "Just a man. There's nothing special about me. I can't do any of the things you can do."

"And what can I do?" I cast a silent revealing spell.

A small amount of Magic left my body, returning quickly.

"Apart from bring people back from the brink of death?" he said, his eyes flicking up to Zemila's apartment.

He didn't notice my casting. And why would he? The spell told me he was as he said. Just a man.

"You leave her out of it," I hissed, taking a step towards him.

"So predictable," he said. "'Please, don't hurt her! Your quarrel is with me! She has nothing to do with it,'" he mocked. "As if we play fair."

"If you—"

"Empty threats, Lochlan," he said. "You will do nothing to me here, on this street." He gestured at their surroundings.

A group of giggling teenagers walked by, emphasizing the public setting. I pulled in Magic. Fear gripped me. I wanted to be ready to cast if I had to.

"Naughty, naughty," he said, looking at my hands.

Small red and blue sparks flew between my fingers. I shoved my hands in my pockets.

"No doubt you will try to find me," he went on. "You and your little friends—the computer wiz with the stupid name."

My fear increased. Who was this man? How did he know me?

"But you won't find me, because," he sang the next part, "I've got friends in low places."

"Who are you?" I asked this time.

"No one of consequence," he answered, taking a few steps back.

Did he intentionally quote Jenner's favorite movie to goad me? How much does he know about us?

"I'm a stand-in, a messenger really." He smiled. "Just your local errand boy."

The smile did nothing to improve his features. If anything, it made him look less interesting.

"What do you want from me?" I asked.

Another group of people pushed past me.

"Your service," he said with a flourish of his arm, and he disappeared into the crowd.

I threw a tracking spell at him, but it bounced back. I tried the revealing cast again, but he was already lost to the crowd. I tapped on my watch and waited for the call to connect.

"Jenner," I said, when his face appeared on my watch screen, "we have a problem."

φ

"What have you got?" I asked, rushing into my living room.

"Whoever this guy is," Jenner said, "he's good."

Jenner's accent got stronger when he was angry, excited, or frustrated.

His voice was thick with frustration

I looked up at the many surveillance camera feeds covering the white wall. A blue keyboard shone under Jenner's frantically tapping fingers.

"You see," he said, pulling up video of me and the generic-looking man. "Here you are, but you could be talking to anyone."

The man was half-blocked from view by an electrical pole.

"And here again," Jenner showed a different angle. "Here's you, and you can only see his feet!"

"You couldn't get an image of his face at all?" I asked.

"Of course I did." Jenner hit me with a look. "But when I said this guy was good, I didn't just mean avoiding surveillance cameras. Is this the guy?"

An image of a man with pink-cream skin and sandy blonde hair appeared on the screen. His eyes were a dull brown and his features bland.

"Yes?" I searched back into my memory, trying to pull up an image of the man's face. All I saw was the image Jenner found. The man was so forgettable.

"That sounds convincing," Jenner mocked. "I assure you, this is the guy."

"How do you know?"

"He was waiting outside the apartment before you arrived. I caught his reflection in a window. It was a fluke."

"This looks like a DMV picture," I said.

"It is. I was able to find a match. Well, I found about fifty matches. But this one . . . this one was different."

"How so?" I asked, sitting on the couch next to Jenner.

"I could find records on everyone else. But not this guy. His records have been erased."

"Erased?"

"You won't find this picture anymore," Jenner said. "His file was being deleted as I found it. This was all I could get. I don't even know his name."

"He said he was a stand-in. A messenger. He said he was an errand boy."

"For who?" Jenner asked, fear creeping into his eyes. "Balor? Queen Anne? Someone else?"

"Balor," I said. "I'm sure of it."

"How?" Jenner's eyes went wide.

"He asked about the Shannon."

"Who's the—" The home system interrupted him.

"*Identification: Llowellyn MacEthan.*"

"Jenner?" called Llowellyn's deep baritone.

"In here, Llow," Jenner said. Llowellyn came into view and leaned against the doorframe.

"You were right," he told Jenner. "The tea was excellent."

I looked back and forth between them, confused.

"Where were you?" I asked.

"Little one, you ran right past us," he said with a nervous smile. "Jenner suggested I introduced myself to your neighbour. We had sweet tea."

I nodded.

"Is everything all right?"

"No. Everything is not all right," I said. "Sit down."

"The Shannon?" Llowellyn said, after I'd explained the strange encounter. "Interesting."

"Who the hell is the Shannon?" Jenner asked.

"She's a river," Llowellyn said.

"I'm sorry," Jenner said, turning the sass up to eleven. "She's a river? In your mind, does that answer my question? Because in my mind, it creates more questions."

"She is . . ." I tried to figure out how to explain it. "Complicated."

"Again, not an answer," Jenner said.

"Connla's Well is a doorway to the Otherworld," I told him. "There were five streams that led from Connla's Well throughout the Old World—the Shannon, the Bhanna, and the Three Sisters. The Shannon is the largest of those streams. She sees things. Sometimes she shares what she sees."

Jenner squinted at me.

"What is she?" he asked. Then he answered himself with a lilting accent I could only assume was supposed to be me. " 'A mythical being who sees the future.' Madre de Dios," he said, his accent returned to normal. "Not everything has to be an epic tale! You are so dramatic."

"This man knew of the Shannon," Llowellyn spoke over Jenner.

"He knew a lot more than that," I said.

"And he is a proxy," Llowellyn stated. "A proxy for Balor while he searches for a way to become corporeal."

"I think so," I said.

"The Proxy," Jenner repeated it as if it were a title. "That doesn't sound ominous at all. And he's human?"

"Yes," I told them. "Totally human."

"Is he brainwashed like Simmons was?" Jenner asked.

"I don't know. He could be." But for some reason, I didn't think so.

There was a ding from Jenner's watch, and something popped up on the screen.

"Ahh," Jenner said. He opened the program. "I set up a program to search the image I found of the Proxy. Thank you for the nightmares with that charming nickname." He threw a look at Llowellyn. "It just finished."

We spent the next few hours scrolling through picture after picture, trying to determine if it was, in fact, the Proxy, or another equally generic-looking man. Two hours in, Cam joined us. She brought Chinese.

"You are a goddess," Jenner said to her, his mouth full of noodles.

"And don't you forget it," she said. Then to me, "How did things go with Zemila?"

"Well, I think," I hoped. "We'll go to see Queen Anne about Nemo tomorrow. She seems to think he is out of harm's way for now."

"All right," she said. But the stress she carried didn't leave her.

When all the pictures started to look the same, we took a break. Cam and I went for a walk, needing some space from Llowellyn and Jenner's budding bromance.

"How are you?" I asked her. "How are you dealing with all this?"

"I think I should be asking you that." But she indulged me with an answer. "I'm stressed. Work has been busy. There was another police shooting. I'll be put on it."

"Those cases are tough," I said.

"This kid was a 2ndGen. He was flagged a couple months ago for shoplifting from a grocery store. So, now, he sets off all these alarm bells because the system doesn't discriminate between violent offenders and hungry kids. The police get jumpy."

"Sounds like a mess," I said.

"You have no idea," she groaned. "There's talk that some kids are being flagged as 3rd- and 4thGens because their parents took DNA tests."

"DNA tests?" I asked.

"Spit in a cup and track your heritage, you know?"

"Oh, right," I said, remembering the craze from a few decades ago.

"They never thought bad people would use the information against them, but here we are." We walked slowly up the street. She snaked her arm through mine and leaned her head on my shoulder.

"I feel guilty about Nemo," she confessed.

"You too, huh?"

She lifted her head and looked at me.

"Why do you feel guilty?" she asked.

I shrugged.

I hadn't given it an overabundance of thought. There had been so much going on. Everything with my brother, with Simmons, with how I had left Erroin five years ago. How I had torn his sister's life apart. How all I had to offer him was a pull-out couch in my living room he thought he had to pay for.

"Because I did something that made him feel like he couldn't come to me," I said. "I don't know what it was. Probably lots of things . . . but I did something that made me untrustworthy in his eyes. That eats at me."

She sighed and turned us around.

"I feel exactly the same," she said.

As soon as we got back to the house, we started again. Some 1,500 images were whittled down to 200 before we took another break. With thirty left to look through, and twenty we had confirmed were the Proxy, Cam spotted something.

"Jenny," Cam said, standing up and pointing one out. It was just as bland as the others. The small frame showed the face of a man who was probably the Proxy, standing in front of a bush or a tree.

What makes this one any different? I wondered.

"Can you make this one bigger," she asked.

"Like, zoom in?" Jenner looked at his sister.

"No, like a wider look." Cam spread her arms apart to illustrate what she wanted. "I want to see what's around him."

"Okay," Jenner said. He sounded skeptical, but he did it.

Now the Proxy stood a few feet away from a small grouping of people. There were trees, a fence, and a lawn behind him. He could have been anywhere, a park maybe? Were those stairs in the far-left corner?

"Again," Cam said. "I want to see what he's looking at."

After a few clicks on the keyboard, the imaged changed.

"Madre de Dios," Jenner said.

The Proxy, who had been in the center of the frame, was now in the bottom right-hand corner.

"Gods," I said, standing too. I'd seen this picture before, months ago. Save Llowellyn, we all had.

The small group of people in front of the Proxy were watching an interview.

"Isn't that—" Llowellyn started to ask.

"Aye," I said, staring at the image. "It is."

Zemila stood speaking with Redford Justal. Simmons watched her hungrily from the small group of spectators. And not ten steps behind Simmons, was the Proxy.

CHAPTER NINETEEN
Lochlan

My alarm went off at 5 a.m. I needed the water more than I could say. I waved my hand over the clock, and the high-pitched beeping stopped.

Cam had left around nine the night before. Though I'd wished her a happy birthday yesterday, it wasn't her real birthday then.

Camile, I wrote in a text message to her. You are an amazingly strong and compassionate person. I am so lucky to call you my friend. Happy Birthday.

I hit send, then swung my legs out of bed

φ

I spent a moment at the edge of the community centre pool watching Tim's progress, then I dove in. It was bliss.

The familiar panic that rose up in me pushed away the stress of the Shannon, the Proxy, and Queen Anne. I was fortunate my body had never grown accustomed to the water. I didn't know what I would do if I didn't have this release. This distraction.

For thirty minutes, I had the fast lane to myself. When it got crowded, I left to stretch in the sauna, humming all the while.

On my way home, I detoured to pass my thinking spot and sang as I walked the empty streets. The old oak tree reminded me so much of the old days. Of Lugh.

I should bring Llowellyn here, I thought as I sang an old hymn.

I checked the time. 7:30 a.m. A message from Cam popped up. We texted back and forth about menial things as I leaned against my tree. Then I asked a question that had been weighing on my mind, only leaving me when I was in the water.

WHEN DO I TELL ZEMILA ABOUT THE PROXY?

I saw the bubble that indicated she was typing appear for a few seconds, before it vanished.

I DON'T KNOW, she finally answered. AS SOON AS POSSIBLE, BUT MAYBE ONE CRISIS AT A TIME.

I WAS THINKING ON THE WAY TO HEAVEN, I replied.

ONE CRISIS AT A TIME. NEMO IS MORE IMPORTANT.

YOU'RE RIGHT. I'LL WAIT.

KEEP ME UP TO DATE, she wrote. TELL ME IF THERE'S ANYTHING I CAN DO.

My stomach grumbled as I responded.

I WILL. I HOPE YOU HAVE A GREAT BIRTHDAY.

She sent back an emoji from a sci-fi TV show I'd never seen, then with the "live long and prosper" hand gesture.

I smiled, pushed off my tree, and started in the direction of home.

φ

I crept in as quietly as possible, not sure of who was awake. I glanced at the pull-out couch. It was neatly tucked away.

Nemo's not here, the couch seemed to say. Your friends are not safe.

I'd offered to convert the office to a bedroom for Nemo, but he'd insisted he wouldn't be here long enough for that.

And he was right, a dark corner of my mind said.

"We'll get you back," I whispered to the vacant living room.

I went upstairs to hang up my towel and swimsuit before heading into the kitchen.

Llowellyn sat doing a puzzle at the kitchen table.

"You're up," I said.

"It's nearly eight," he answered.

"You're doing a puzzle."

"Jenner said it's Cam's. She left it here when you were sick."

I never really put much thought into what my friends had been doing while I'd been unconscious.

A little self-absorbed, I thought.

Jenner had said it had been four days; they must have been doing something in that time. I was grateful they'd taken care of me.

"Breakfast?" I asked, holding up the bag of oatmeal I pulled from the cabinet and pushing the memory out of my mind.

"Better make enough for three," he said, trying to fit a piece into several places before abandoning it. "Jenner is going to be up soon . . . and frantic because he's late."

"Why haven't you woken him up?" I asked.

"He's hit snooze about eight times. I think he was up pretty late."

"Speaking of up late." I scooped oats into a pot and added water. "Who were you up late talking to last night?"

"That is none of your concern." He found a home for the piece in his hand.

"How did you even get a phone? I didn't think you knew how to use one?" I started to make coffee.

"How to use a phone?" he said. Green eyes searching for a piece.

"You know what I mean," I said, exasperated. "Tech has changed in the last thirty years."

"I'm used to change." He picked up a blue piece with a white corner. "You're the one who is bad with change."

"I'm just surprised, is all," I said, ignoring his jab.

"Jenner gave me his old watch," Llowellyn said. "Taught me how to add a contact and make a call. It's not so different from what we used to use."

"And pray tell," I said, turning away from the oatmeal to get a few bowls from a high shelf, "who did you add as your first contact?"

"I'm not listening to you anymore." He started humming in an attempt to ignore me.

That song, I thought—and smiled. He'd pulled it from my mind.

That sounds familiar, I thought to him. What are you humming?

"Oh, nothing," he said. "I just—"

He froze.

His eyes locked on mine.

"Gods below," he said.

"Gods below, indeed," I said with an honest laugh. I turned to the French press and poured three cups of coffee.

He was getting stronger.

"¡Dios mio!" We heard from upstairs. The cry was followed by hurried footfalls and a stream of Spanish curse words. The bathroom door slammed and the shower turned on.

"Full marks to you this morning." I slid the mug to Llowellyn before raising mine in a salute. He grinned and clinked his mug against mine before drinking.

A thoughtful expression took over his face. He put the mug down and looked at me. "I had a dream last night. More of a feeling, really."

He paused.

I waited.

"I should come with you today. With you and Zemila."

"I don't know," I gave him a wary look.

I should come with you and Zemila, he thought at me.

My eyebrows popped up in surprise.

So did his.

"I didn't actually think that would work." He looked pleased with himself.

"A few shared thoughts does not a Caster make," I said.

"The stone is helping." He touched the chain at his neck. "And we are stronger together, Little One."

When I didn't respond, he went on.

"Bad things happen when we split up."

I couldn't argue with that.

"Stronger together," he repeated.

"Not alone," I said, giving him the answer he wanted

φ

"That is a very small car," Llowellyn said, stepping out of Zemila's hatchback.

Heaven loomed over us.

"You spent the last thirty years in a jail cell," Zemila told him. "How bad could a thirty-minute car ride be?"

"Time is a social construct," he said, shaking one leg then the other. "Have you spent time in France?"

"Lochlan made it seem like you were a bit of a downer," she smirked.

I looked at her sharply.

"I did no such thing," I said.

"It's because he thinks he's the funny one."

"I never said—"

"And my humor goes over Lochlan's head," Llowellyn finished.

"You're funny," she said to Llowellyn. "He's funny," she said, nudging me in the ribs with her elbow. "I like him."

I knew my brother liked her too. Zemila and Llowellyn had known each other for all of half an hour and already they were ganging up on me.

"It's always nice to be appreciated," Llowellyn said.

We approached the entrance. The flashing lights of the building fought against the bright sun. The sun was winning.

"Eight-pointed star," Llowellyn said. He paused at a pair of stone lions.

"Hmmm," I said, and continued inside.

The automatic doors slid open. The air conditioning inside had no regard for the unseasonably cool day. Zemila rubbed her arms as we walked through the lobby.

I was following her brisk pace, but stopped at the fountain. Zemila backtracked to stand beside me. I gazed up at the figure riding a lion.

"It's a woman," Llowellyn said from behind us.

"On the lion?" Zemila questioned.

"We'll it's not the one with the beard," I nodded to the head under the lion's forepaw.

"I've seen women with beards," Llowellyn noted.

I glared at him.

Zemila smiled.

"Yes, I think it is a woman riding the lion," I agreed.

"Eight-pointed star," Llowellyn said again.

Queen Anne . . . Heaven. The thought worked its way through my mind.

Queen Anne of Heaven, I thought at Llowellyn. Queen of Heaven. Llowellyn frowned.

"I bet you're happy I came along now," he said.

We passed through the cream linen hangings at the end of the lobby. Immediately, we were joined by four security guards.

"Ms. Alkevic," the shortest of the group said. "Please come with us."

She nodded and we followed without resistance.

We were weaved through the casino and through a back door and eventually what looked like an apartment. A few doors later, we stood in a small library.

"Please sit," the short guard said. "Queen Anne will be with you shortly."

Zemila and I took the chairs in front of the desk. Llowellyn perused the bookshelves.

"What were you two ho-humming about upstairs?" Zemila asked.

"What are the odds that she isn't listening to us right now?" I responded.

"I'm sure she is," Zemila said.

I looked at her. Her words were playful. They lit something inside me I had to fight very hard to control.

"Could you two please stop flirting until after we're out of this godforsaken place," Llowellyn said, turning from the bookshelf.

"Godforsaken?" said a woman of medium height and build. She entered through a door behind her desk. Entirely covered with books, the door blended seamlessly with the shelves surrounding it. "I doubt that."

"I don't think my brother would agree," Zemila said dryly.

"He's quite comfortable, I assure you," the woman said. She extended her hand to me. "And you must be the Caster?"

I looked at the offered hand and cast a quick protection spell reaching only to the edge of my skin before I shook it.

"I'm a friend of Zemila's," I said.

She accepted that.

"And I see you've brought an uninvited guest."

"We're something of a package deal," Llowellyn said in his deep baritone voice.

"I didn't think you'd mind," Zemila said. "I'm assuming this favor can be done by two just as well as it can be done by one."

"And, if not, I'll complete it alone." I knew Llowellyn wouldn't openly object. The only displeasure he showed was a slight tilt of his head.

"Now pray tell," I asked. "What must I do to secure the release of my friend?"

"Right to business I see," she said, eyeing me and my brother.

"How else should it be when we've captured the attention of the Queen of Heaven?" Llowellyn asked. "It's been a long time, Inanna."

Shock at her true name covered her face. Her mud brown eyes met my green ones, then my brother's.

"Ethinnsons," she hissed. Then she threw back her head and laughed. "Gods! It has been lifetimes!"

"At the very least," I said, less amused.

"What do you go by these days?" she asked.

"Funnily enough, true names," Llowellyn told her.

"Llowellyn and Lochlan. Ethinnson, Balorson, Cianson," she seemed to chant. "Where is your brother," she asked with a manic glint in her eye. "He was always my favorite."

"I bet he was," Llowellyn said, "but I'm afraid he has long left the world of the living."

His tone was so matter-of-fact. I could never manage that when speaking of Lugh.

"Ahh, pity," she said. "You were always so grumpy," she pointed at me, "And you never wanted to play," she pouted at Llowellyn. "I'm sorry for the both of you. He was . . . a good King."

"You're sorry for the loss of a good lay," my brother said.

"Llowellyn!" I was shocked he spoke of Lugh so casually. So disrespectfully.

"He wasn't the sharpest but he sure had a big—"

"Inanna!" I said, outraged.

"Inanna . . ." Zemila repeated, drawing the attention of the room. "God, it's you riding the lion in the statue."

"Smart cookie you've got there," Inanna said to me with a wink.

"She's not—"

"Don't bother." She waved away my interjection. "I may not be the god I once was, but I still see. There was a time I was the most recognized goddess of love and desire."

"And war," I said. "Let's not forget war."

"Details." She waved the accusation away. "Now it's all Venus this and Aphrodite that. Have you ever met a more vain and petulant pair of deities? You know, Venus had the nerve to tell me—" She huffed out a breath. "Never mind."

"I never met Venus," Llowellyn said. "I thought Aphrodite was . . . interesting."

Inanna's eyes widened.

"I bet you did," she said.

"Hermes was more my speed then," he corrected her.

"Oh, I would have killed a thousand virgins to see the look on her face when she learned that."

"It was interesting," Llowellyn said.

"Well, as interesting as this is," Zemila interrupted. "Can we discuss the soap opera of the gods after my brother is home?"

"Yes," I agreed, giving Llowellyn a sharp look.

"You always were the killjoy," Inanna said to me.

And you were always self-involved, I thought.

Inanna rubbed me the wrong way. We hadn't gotten along in the Old World and I couldn't see it being different now. Llowellyn was another story. Truth be told, I think she would have preferred him over Lugh. But Llowellyn wasn't interested. He just got along with everyone.

"What are you doing here?" I asked Inanna.

"Talking to you?" she responded dryly.

"Little One," Llowellyn said, realizing my meaning. "Cleverest of us all."

"You've lost me," Queen Anne said.

"If only," I muttered.

She hissed at me like an angry cat.

"He's thinking about the odds," my brother explained. "How did we all end up here?"

"We all?" Inanna repeated. "Is there another deity I should know about?"

The look she sent us told me she had no need of an answer from me.

"You already know," I accused.

"I knew a heavy hitter showed up a while back. But with you two here, it could only be that bastard of a grandfather you have."

I looked over at Zemila, trying to game how she was taking everything. She looked confused and frustrated.

"What are you guys talking about?" Zemila asked.

"You never thought it odd," Llowellyn walked to the side of the table and leaned against the near wall, "that you and my brother both left Erroin and came here."

"He didn't come straight here," Zemila said. "But, yeah, I guess it's a little coincidental."

"There is no such thing as coincidence," he said. Zemila nodded like she agreed.

"The capital is a door," Inanna explained. "Of sorts. That is why we are all here."

"A door," Zemila repeated.

"Yes, little Luman girl, a door."

"A door to what?" Zemila asked.

"That is the real question, isn't it?" Inanna leaned forward conspiratorially.

I looked between the two women, unsure of what I was seeing. There was some connection there.

Curiosity from Zemila, I thought. Hunger from Inanna.

I didn't like it. Zemila didn't know her as I did. Zemila didn't know that when Inanna looked at someone like that, with hunger in her eyes, she wanted them.

Inanna was ruthless when it came to getting what she wanted.

"There are doors everywhere," Llowellyn said. "What does that have to do with anything?"

"Not like this one," Inanna told him, tearing her eyes away from Zemila.

"There are only a few doors like this one, Nanjing, China has one. There was one in Kigali. A witch was able to close it with no small cost to himself. There is one in Syria, Russia, the Vatican, of course," she said with a wicked smile. "And here. I'm missing a couple, but—"

"I still don't understand," Zemila said.

"We're basically in Sunnydale," Inanna leered.

"Hey," Llowellyn smiled. "I get that reference. I liked that show."

"You were always my favorite." She winked at him. Then to Zemila she said, "There are a few places in the world where power accumulates. Not good or evil, just power. And where there lies power, there lies potential. Not good or evil," she repeated. "Just potential. You think the government of this country was put here by accident?"

"You came here for the power?" I asked.

"The power drew me here, as it drew you, as it drew her." Inanna nodded at Zemila. "As it drew . . . other things."

Again, I got the sense that she knew more than she was letting on. It made me uneasy. I wanted to leave.

"Tell me what this favor is," I asked her.

"Killjoy," Inanna said. "So grumpy."

I gave her a cold stare.

"Zemila made a promise on your behalf," she said.

"I am aware." She knew I hated that Zemila had come to Heaven alone, without me. But I would not rise to her bait, nor would I refuse what she asked of me. There would be no war between us. The world hadn't seen a true battle of gods in a long time.

The might of Sumeria against the Magic of the Celts.

Few would survive.

"I don't need much from you," said the Love Goddess.

"I'll believe that," I answered, "when I hear the extent of the favor."

CHAPTER TWENTY
Zemila

"Killjoy," Queen Anne said to Lochlan. "So grumpy."

Zemila looked between them, her journalist's mask firmly in place.

Gods, she thought. I'm sitting in a room with actual gods.

Not only was Queen Anne, the boogie man of Lowtown, actually real, she was a god. The ancient Sumerian goddess of love and war. And she was talking to Lochlan like they were old . . . well, not friends.

Zemila eyed Llowellyn.

His big body leaned up against one of the many bookshelves lining the wall. He liked Queen Anne. She could tell. She could also tell how much that frustrated Lochlan.

"Zemila made a promise on your behalf," the Queen said.

"I am aware," Lochlan told her.

Zemila's gut twisted in guilt.

"I don't need much from you," Queen Anne continued.

"I'll believe that when I hear the extent of the favor," Lochlan said.

"I've recently learned that the Ruiz cartel is selling in my territory. They also set fire to a few of my buildings."

"Interesting," Zemila whispered, a headline popping into her mind. "The fires have been exclusively in your buildings?"

"Oh no, you don't," the Queen said. "Not part of our deal—"

"Our deal is that your face stays off my boss's desk. You didn't say anything about your name."

"I still have your brother, little Luman girl. Watch your step." She turned her attention back to Lochlan. "They're moving in slowly. Club drugs, right now. The old school stuff—MDMA and Special K—but they have this new drug. People are calling it Candle."

"I've heard of this," Zemila said, thinking of a piece she'd read not long ago. "A couple of girls died a few weeks back. It's synthetic cocaine cut with something else."

"One of those girls was the daughter of an employee," Queen Anne said.

"Ever the protector," Lochlan muttered.

"When it suits me," the Queen nodded. "It suits me now."

"What would you have me do?" he asked.

"I've been informed of a meeting tomorrow night."

"What kind of meeting?"

"The kind no one's supposed to know about. You will go, unseen, and gather information. That's all."

"Why do you need a Caster for that?" Llowellyn asked from his spot against the wall.

"When I felt my spell on this little Luman girl here," she pointed a short finger at Zemila, "I was curious. That spell is no small feat. There is power behind that spell. If I could get my hands on such a Caster, well . . ."

Her gaze drifted to Lochlan.

"All that was bargained for was a favor," Lochlan said, narrowing his eyes at her. "Nothing more."

"Your glasses are stupid," she said, her tone flat.

Zemila snorted. Lochlan glared at her.

"Sorry," she muttered.

"Age has taught me to adapt," the Queen said. "Had you been anyone else, I would have held my favor for a time of greater need. But an Ethinnson? I will use you to protect my people. Right now, that is what I value most."

"Package deal," Llowellyn said.

Zemila noticed Lochlan's shoulders tighten. His dark eyebrows knit together. He didn't want Llowellyn here, she realized.

"You," the Queen said, still pointing at Lochlan, "can magically keep my people out of sight. If, for any reason, things go south, I trust the pair of you—since you're a package deal." She sneered the words, "package deal," and shot a look at Llowellyn. "You two can make it as though you were never there. Change what people see," she waved a hand through the air like she was casting a spell, "if you're seen."

"I'll just be the driver, then," Llowellyn said.

"Something I should know?" the Queen asked.

"Apart from the fact that changing memories is Blood Magic?" Lochlan added.

Blood Magic. Zemila knew that wasn't good. Lochlan had told her Blood Magic was addictive. It ate at your soul.

"I will be of little use, Magically speaking." Llowellyn tapped his temple. "The last spell I cast was a wall. But like I said—"

"—we're a package deal," Lochlan added.

"—and I will go with my brother regardless of your wishes."

"I see." Queen Anne drummed gold nails on the table, thinking.

"And why can't you take care of that?" she asked Lochlan.

"Me?" Lochlan pointed a finger to his own chest. "I did, in part. I reconnected his body. But his soul . . . it's not an easy spell to break."

"I see," she said again. She stood and walked over to Llowellyn. "Since you are more use to me at full strength, this one's on the house. An olive branch," she said over her shoulder to Lochlan.

She raised her hands to either side of Llowellyn's head, and closed her eyes. Her thumb and index fingers rubbed together as though twisting an invisible needle running straight through his skull. Her hands moved slowly, always exactly diagonal to each other.

Her eyes snapped open and her hands froze in place.

"Look at me," she hissed. "Think of the wall."

When their eyes met, Queen Anne snapped her fingers and Llowellyn jerked back.

Zemila felt a wave of power wash over the room—then dissipate.

The Queen's heels tapped loudly as she walked around her desk. Or was the room so quiet it just sounded that way?

"I felt what you did," she gestured to Lochlan. "You have your grandfather's power. But you are still young."

Lochlan scowled at her.

"I've reconnected his soul," she went on, before looking at Llowellyn. Zemila read sadness in the Queen's eyes. "The last piece, your mind . . . only you can connect that."

Llowellyn stared at the ground. He blinked away tears.

"You and a few of my men will go, gather information, and come back unseen." She pointed a short finger at Lochlan, back to business.

"Unseen," Llowellyn repeated. "That will somewhat depend on the intelligence of your men."

"You will make sure that no one knows you're there," she spoke over him.

"What's the location?" Lochlan asked, no doubt thinking he could give it to Jenner.

"You will learn that when you arrive tomorrow night. Qillian will give you a burner watch. You will be contacted."

"And my brother?" Zemila asked.

"He stays here." Her words were as cold as her look. "Until the job is done."

"Can I—"

"No," the Queen answered. "You've seen he's fine. I'm a goddess of my word. Isn't that right, Lochlan?"

"Some stories say she cannot lie," Lochlan said. "Others say she chooses not to." He looked up at the Queen. "What do you say?"

"I say what I mean." Queen Anne's tone was flat. "Now I mean for you to leave."

She waved at the door behind them. It opened. Two men walked in. They couldn't have been more opposite. One had a short army-cut hairstyle, pale skin, and a stern expression. The other had smooth hazelnut skin and dreadlocks falling to his shoulders. He handed Lochlan a small black rectangle. A burner watch.

The first man roughly grabbed Zemila's upper arm and pulled her onto her feet. She shook him off. As he reached for her again, Llowellyn stepped between them.

"Zemila will see Nemo. Llowellyn and I go with your men," Lochlan said.

Hope flared in Zemila's chest. All she wanted was to see her brother.

To see that he was all right.

"Will she now?" Queen Anne said.

Zemila caught the Queen's humorless smile. She turned to watch the gods negotiate.

"Yes," Lochlan said. "She will."

"And why would I allow that?"

"Because you would have an Ethinnson in your debt if you do." He glared at her.

The mere fact that Queen Anne paused to consider this made Zemila uneasy.

Who are you, Lochlan Ellyll? she thought. Thousands upon thousands of years old. Countless lifetimes. Countless people he has loved before me. How could I think I know you? How could I ever truly know you?

Doubt crept into her mind. Yet there he stood. She watched him trade another favor, the currency of the gods, to help her.

She knew he would always help her. She knew that he made her feel special and unique just by being herself. She didn't need to be Zemila Alkevic, the journalist, with him, as she had with so many people. She didn't need to be Zemila Alkevic, the ditz, with him, as she had with so many men.

No, he didn't love the masks she wore. He wasn't threatened by her job or her willfulness. He loved it. He loved her.

I know him a little, she thought. For now, a little is enough. We've got time.

"A favor of my choosing?" the Queen asked.

"The gratitude of the third Balorson, gifted by the Druids and cursed by the gods."

Something happened when Lochlan spoke. His accent seemed to thicken and the air, though still, seemed to be sucked towards him. Like he was gathering power.

"How many Casters do you know who can call the Light and the Dark?" he said to her. "How many cast your spells and live?"

The Queen's eyes flicked to Zemila. They lingered on her. Zemila squirmed under the scrutiny.

The Queen smirked.

"Your grandfather was a son of a bitch." She ran her tongue across her white teeth. "He intrigued me. As do you. She can go there now and will be brought home tomorrow morning."

Lochlan gave the Queen a small bow.

"You have my gratitude."

A guard took Zemila's elbow outside the door of Queen Anne's office. He held her more gently than the man with the army haircut had. She was uncomfortable anyway.

He didn't release it until he'd pressed his thumb to the lock outside Nemo's room.

"I will be back for you at 8 a.m. tomorrow morning, Ms. Alkevic. If there is anything else you need, just pick up the receiver and dial star eight."

"Thank you," Zemila said with a nod.

She walked into the suite, past the empty trays of eaten room service and into the bedroom. Nemo sat at the desk by the window. Head down and working, he hadn't heard her come in.

Grunting angrily, he ripped a page out of his book, and tossed it over his shoulder. The floor was littered with half-finished drawings of the same face over and over again.

Zemila's heart hurt, seeing him like this.

"Nemo," she said softly.

He jumped and turned.

"Mila, hey," he said. "I didn't hear them let you—wow, your bruises. They're gone."

"Lochlan helped."

"Oh," Nemo said. He turned to start cleaning up the mess of strewn papers. Pain flashed across his face. He clutched his ribs.

"Let me do that," Zemila rushed forward.

"No," he protested. "I don't want you to see them. They're horrible."

She bent down and picked up the one closes to her. Flattening it from the ball Nemo had crushed it into, she looked down at a rough sketch of Cam. "They're not so bad. Not bad at all."

He huffed and slumped back in his seat.

"You were pretty out of it when they brought you up here the first night," Zemila said, picking up another piece of paper. This one was better, more detailed. But still unfinished.

"Yeah." Nemo ran his hands through his hair. "I don't remember much, apart from the mess your face was."

"Thanks."

"Did I say anything incriminating?" He tried for a smile but at the expression Zemila wore it faltered. "Mila, I'm sorry."

He didn't meet her eyes.

Zemila looked away from her brother. She knelt down to collect more of the strewn pages.

"I didn't want to be any more of a burden than I already was," Nemo said.

"You've never been a burden."

"I've always been a burden," he said. "Ever since you grew up enough to take care of yourself, I've been a burden. Asking for money, crashing at your place. I did the same thing to Lochlan."

"Lochlan loved having you," she insisted.

"Oh, yeah?" Nemo said. "How would you know? You're too scared to talk to him."

"Harsh," she said, sitting back on her heels and wrapping her arms around her chest. "I did talk to him. And even if I didn't, that's a little pot and kettle, don't you think?"

"You talked to him about your gift acting up?" His tone was accusing. He knew she hadn't. "Besides, it wasn't fear stopping me from asking for help."

"Then what was it?"

"Shame." He stared at his feet, toes digging into the plush carpet. "It was shame."

Zemila finished collecting the sheets of paper.

"Shame drove you to use your gift at the craps table of the most dangerous casino in the country?" She shook her head. Her chest ached with uncertainty. She had to remind herself, he was safe, if only for now. "Nemo, please don't do something like this again. I never want to feel this way again."

She looked up at him, trying to blink back the tears. His eyes were glossy. He blinked and a tear rolled down his cheek. He nodded and wiped his face.

"Where did you get the art supplies?" Zemila asked.

"One of the guards, George, he saw a sketch I did on the little notepad in the room. The next day I had pencils and proper sketch paper."

"That was very kind of him."

"Yeah, George is all right." He rubbed his jaw. "He's got a mean right hook though."

"He was one of the ones—"

"No," Nemo said quickly. "But he brought me into the basement. I resisted. He did his job."

"Okay," Zemila said, not wanting to get into it.

"Good guy, though." Nemo had always been quick to forgive.

She turned her attention down to the smooth lines that crossed the pages in her hands. The same face gazed up off of every one. He'd been drawing Cam a lot lately.

"These are good," she said. "Really good."

His cheeks turned pink.

"I was trying to get one right for her birthday," he said. "I wanted her to know how I see her. But I can't put it on the page. Not yet, anyway."

"Does she know you think about her this much?" Zemila asked.

"Yes . . . no . . . I don't know."

She scoffed a laugh and rolled her eyes.

"No, don't laugh," he said. "It's hard. You know I'm not good at that stuff. I kept messing up. I was supposed to have dinner with her, but I got that black eye, so I canceled. Then this. Mila. I think I ruined it."

"I think you won't know until you talk to her," Zemila said.

"What should I say?"

Zemila laughed.

"You're coming to me for relationship advice? Are you kidding? Look at me. I can't tell Lochlan how I really feel any more than you can tell, Cam. What a pair we make."

She stood, put the pages on the desk, and hugged her brother.

"What's wrong with us?" Nemo asked, tucking his sister under his chin.

"Many, many things," Zemila said into his chest, careful not to squeeze his injured ribs. "But let's watch a movie, order room service on Queen Anne's dime, and not think about it."

"Deal," said Nemo.

CHAPTER TWENTY-ONE
Lochlan

"Could cut the tension in here with a knife," the driver chuckled.

An oncoming car lit his face. I'd been so lost in anger I hadn't noticed he was the same man who'd given me the burner watch.

"You don't look like you should be working for Queen Anne," I said. "What's your name?"

"Qillian," he told me. "Like Gillian but with a 'K' sound. What does someone who works for Queen Anne look like?"

"I don't know." Looking at him in the headlights of another car, I thought it was his eyes. They seemed awfully young.

"Stop talking to them," said the man in the passenger seat.

I leaned over to look at him. Greying close-cropped hair and gaunt pale skin.

"Yeah, him," I said. "He looks like he should be here."

"Shut up," the man said.

"Easy Frank," Qillian told him. "Nothing to get your panties in a twist about."

"Queen Anne doesn't like it when—"

"Inanna doesn't care," Llowellyn said.

I looked at him sharply. He rolled his eyes. I leaned back in my seat, and silence filled the vehicle for the rest of the way home.

φ

"What is your problem?" Llowellyn asked once Qillian had driven off.

"I don't have a problem," I said, walking through the gate surrounding my front yard.

"You're upset with me," he said. "I can feel it."

"Urgh," I groaned and stopped walking. We stood on the path in my front yard. No secrets. That's what a telepathic link meant. Unstoppable in battle, but no secrets in life. "I forgot how annoying this was."

I took in a deep breath to temper my reaction. It didn't work.

"How can you speak of him like that?" I spat, anger tainting my words. "How can you let her speak of him that way?"

"What— Lugh?"

I said nothing. He knew very well I spoke of Lugh.

"You're mad at me because I joked with an old friend?"

"Oh, you did more than joke!" I accused.

"What are you—"

"You mocked him!" I shouted. "So did she! What's worse is that you let her!"

I spun on my heel and headed up the stairs to my porch.

"She's an old friend," he said.

Trying to defend himself? I thought punching in the door code and walking inside. Shameful.

"Friend? In what world was Inanna ever our friend?"

"She and Lugh were together for a long time," Llowellyn followed me inside.

"They were hardly together. And that does not make her a friend," I said. "I wouldn't even call her an ally. Do you know how many times she tried to kill me?"

"Oh, come on," he groaned.

"And even if she was an ally, that doesn't give her the right to say such things."

I started up the stairs to my room. Llowellyn's hand on my arm spun me around.

"She was an ally when we had few," he hissed, frustration showing on his face, showing in his voice. "They found comfort together."

"And where was she when he needed her?!" I wrenched my arm out of his grip. "Where were you?"

I stared up into his eyes, my eyes . . . Lugh's eyes. I wanted to hit him. My fist balled at my side. I felt uncontrollable Magic spark around my fingers. His expression, a moment ago so cold and full of rage, softened.

Pity, I realized. My hand relaxed.

"Don't look at me like that," I said.

"Little One."

"Don't call me that."

"You need to stop this." His words were soft. "You need to stop carrying a weight that was his."

He might as well have slapped me in the face.

"Do not speak ill of him," I forced out through gritted teeth.

"Why?"

I turned away and started up the stairs, ignoring the question.

"Because he was perfect?" Llowellyn said. "Because he was a fair and just King?"

"He was!" I yelled, turning to face him.

"To his subjects, yes! To us, most of the time. To his children, always. But to his wives, almost never. He treated his lovers, Inanna among them, far better than any woman who bore his children."

"You dare speak of him this way."

"I do," Llowellyn didn't hesitate. "I do now. I did then. I told Lugh time and time again, he could not command the women who bore his children with disregard. He did not heed me. He did not respect them as he respected all others. He treated them like property."

"They were his property!" I shouted. "That's how it was then! They knew what they were signing up for, as did any man who attempted to court them. They all knew the punishment was death."

Llowellyn shook his head at me.

"You are smarter than that, Little One." He looked up at me. "You know better than to think the laws of man triumph over love."

"Love, please," I scoffed. "If that woman had loved her King a little more, mayhap we would still have our brother."

"Her name was Bauch—

"I don't care what her name was—"

"And she loved that man," Llowellyn said. "She asked for Lugh's blessing. Did you know that?"

No. I thought, stunned. No, that couldn't be.

"You didn't." Llowellyn nodded as if he'd suspected as much. "He left out that detail to you. I was there when she begged him. I was there when she pleaded at his feet, saying she would serve his every whim willingly, if she were just allowed to see this man who loved her a few times a week. That's all she wanted. To serve her King and see this man.

And Lugh told her no."

There was a long pause. I digested the information.

"And what of a son's love for his father?" Llowellyn continued, no doubt referring to the sons of the man my King had had killed.

No more than he deserved, I thought.

"What of it?" I demanded.

"You don't think that when those boys learned what Lugh had done to their father, they didn't feel the same rage you felt when you learned they had killed our King? Of course they did."

I said nothing.

"When does it end, Little Lochlan? How long do we kill each other for vengeance? It will last forever if we do not forgive."

"You want me to forgive them?" I asked.

"I want you to forgive yourself."

A long silence stretched between us. I worked hard to keep my mental walls up. I knew he didn't have full command of his Magic yet, but our link was coming back, and he was an empath.

"Which part do you think I need to forgive myself for?" My words were ice. "Killing those men? Or leading Balor's army?"

"For not being there when they came for our King," he said slowly. "For Lugh's death."

Tears filled my eyes. Shame hunched my shoulders.

"It was not your fault then. It is not your burden now. Lugh's death can be laid at the feet of the men who killed him, and with the choices he made that led him there."

My knees felt weak. I buried my head in my hands. Llowellyn walked up the few steps until he was on the one just below where I stood. We were almost the same height like this.

"Let it go," Llowellyn put a big hand on my shoulder. "Let him go."

I took in a deep breath.

"No," I whispered and turned up the stairs.

Anger battled sadness. I didn't know what to think, how to feel. I was confused and guilty and hurt. Then something froze me at the top of the stairs.

"Well!" I heard Jenner's voice ring out from the living room. "That sounded like something we weren't supposed to hear."

"Jenner!" Cam hissed at him.

Embarrassment washed over me.

"What?" he said. "They interrupt our tea party, I interrupt their argument."

"Dios Mio."

"Anyway, it's your party," he went on. "Ah, ah, ah! Not a chance, beautiful. No costume, no tea."

What? I thought, sitting down, my feet on the top step.

"Hi, Llow," Cam said. I heard a chair sliding. "How's it going?"

Llowellyn huffed.

"Nice outfit," he said instead of answering.

"Thanks," Cam said.

"You can have the rabbit ears or the cat ears," Jenner said. "But you don't get tea or cake without ears."

"This is a bit of a birthday tradition for me," Cam explained.

"Really?" I heard Llowellyn say.

"Our parents and sister used to come too," Jenner said. "They couldn't make it this year, which is good because they make their own outfits and they are always horrendous."

"They aren't that bad," Cam said. "Mamá called me this morning.

228

Mariana looked great with her crown and face paint."

Jenner huffed.

My eyebrows came together in confusion. I didn't know Cam had any birthday traditions.

"Yeah, a costume party," she went on. "I didn't really want to this year because of everything going on, but—"

"But I told her, 'You think your birthday is just about you?'" Jenner interrupted. "Oh, no! I want a costume party."

"Yeah," Cam agreed. "It was going pretty well until . . ."

"I'm sorry," Llowellyn said.

"Excellent choice," I could hear Jenner's wide smile in his voice. "Now, do sit down. You're late, you're—"

"Isn't that my line?" Llowellyn asked.

"It is," Cam said. Then, so quietly, I had to strain to hear, she asked, "Do you think he'll come down?"

"I don't know," my brother said, equally quiet.

The next exchange was too soft for me to hear.

"He'll come down. I'll get him—LOCHLAAAAAN!" Jenner screamed.

"Christ," Cam said. "You don't want to go get him?"

"That's what I'm doing." Jenner sounded genuinely confused. "The house isn't that big—LOCHLAAAAN!"

They'd heard my outburst. My admission. My shame. I was still angry at my brother. But none of this was Cam's fault. She should have her birthday costume party . . . or whatever it was.

I stood, and started down the stairs.

"Told you," I heard Jenner say. "His royal grumpiness is only moments away from disappearing into a shadowy corner right before your eyes."

"Ha ha," I said. "Very funny, Jen—"

But when I looked into the room, the words died on my lips.

In the center of the living room, a pink child-sized table replaced mine. Llowellyn sat in a toddler-sized chair, his knees up to his ears, holding a small cup of tea, and wearing white rabbit ears. A paper cut-out of a pocket watch was dangling off the side of his headband. It swayed as he looked up at me.

Cam looked beautifully put together in a blue dress and a white apron. Her hair was pulled out of her face with a navy ribbon so dark it was almost black.

Jenner grinned at me, tossing me a pair of pink cat ears. I caught them, but didn't put them on.

I took a moment to appreciate Jenner's outfit.

He wore a maroon velvet overcoat, white gloves, and a tall top hat with a note saying "10/6" tucked into the brim. His yellow and blue polka dot bowtie was almost as wide as his shoulders, and stripes of the same colors ran up and down his pants.

"Well, put them on and sit down," Cam gestured to the open space at the kiddy table.

"Don't worry, Lochlan," Jenner said, his lips curling into a satisfied smile. "We're all mad here."

CHAPTER TWENTY-TWO
Zemila

Zemila tapped the business card on the little window ledge of the SUV. She'd been surprised when one of the men standing outside Nemo's door had handed it to her.

WHEN YOU'RE READY TO LEARN, it said in the elegant scroll she could only assume belonged to the Queen. On the other side of the sand-colored card were the words, "Queen of Heaven," followed by a number. Lochlan's obvious distain for the Queen made Zemila wary of accepting anything from Queen Anne, beyond seeing her brother, and getting him back.

The strange turn of events had left her head spinning. The phase "What the hell is going on?" had popped into her head more than a few times this morning.

Zemila sat in the back of a black SUV on her way to work. A suit, blouse, and shoes had been delivered to Nemo's room at 7:30 a.m., and a car was waiting to take her to work at eight.

"What's your angle?" Zemila whispered, sliding the card through her fingers.

"I think she likes you," the driver said. She thought his name was Qillian.

Zemila looked up into the rear-view mirror.

"I'm sorry," she said.

"You shouldn't—" the man in the passenger seat said.

"Give it a rest, Frank. Did you see the security cam footage?" The driver raised his hand, fingers wide, and made a sucking sound.

Zemila's stomach turned at the memory of red mist called from the man's face to her finger tips.

"It. Was. Wicked."

Frank gave a reluctant nod.

"I heard some of the guys talking," the man she thought was Qillian said. He turned to her. "I think that's why she likes you."

"Because I nearly killed someone?" Zemila asked.

"Because you're powerful," he said. "Because you're not afraid to use that power to get what you want, no matter the cost."

Zemila felt sick.

"Qillian's right," Frank said. "She respects that."

"I don't know if I want that kind of respect," Zemila said.

"It might be the only thing keeping your brother alive," Frank told her.

She turned her eyes back to the card.

WHEN YOU'RE READY TO LEARN, she read again.

The SUV stopped outside the JACE Co. building. Qillian walked around the car to open Zemila's door.

"Thank you," she said, hopping out.

The man looked nervously over his shoulder. He closed the door behind her.

"It's also 'cause she's worried," he said, barely moving his lips.

"What?" Zemila asked.

"She's worried." He looked at Frank who was checking his watch. "She's worried there's a mole in her house. She needs friends on the outside."

"A great way to make me a friend would be to release my brother."

Qillian smiled. It was a beautiful smile. "She needs to save face. She lets one thief go free today, she'll have a hundred try—"

Frank rolled down the window.

"Qill, let's go," he said.

"Be right there." Qillian turned back to Zemila as if to speak again, but Frank didn't roll up his window. Qillian sighed once, inclined his head, and left.

Queen Anne, Zemila thought. Queen Anne is trying to recruit me.

She pushed it to the back of her mind, looking up at the tall skyscraper. She wanted in on the Cartwrytte story. Maybe bringing Ms. Jace a peace offering would butter her up.

Yeah right, Zemila told herself. But I guess it's worth a try.

Instead of walking up the concrete steps and into the building, she turned and headed to the nearest RidgeBean coffee, hoping there were two seven-layer squares left.

She wanted one too.

φ

Zemila reached for the RidgeBean door handle at the same time as a man with sandy hair and a bland expression.

"After you," he said with a smile.

"Thanks."

There's no reason to feel uneasy, Zemila told herself. He's just holding the door open for you. There's no reason to think that smile was . . . wrong.

Since the incident with Simmons, Zemila had been wary when strangers—male strangers—got close to her. She fought to ignore the hairs on the back of her neck rising each time she was walking the same direction or riding in an elevator with a stranger.

"Are you all right, miss?" the man holding the door asked. He placed a hand on her elbow. Her skin crawled. She flinched away.

"Sorry," she said looking up at him. "I'm a little jumpy today."

He smiled. There was definitely something wrong with that smile. It changed his face from ordinary to boring.

"Not a problem," he said.

He's not following you, he's not following you, he's not following you, Zemila mentally chanted. He's behind you in line. This is how lines work.

She looked at the glass display and was happy to see a full tray of the treat she and her boss loved. When she got to the front of the line, she ordered two coffees and two squares.

"I got it," the man behind her said when Zemila reached for the pay pad.

He brushed her hand as he leaned over. She gritted her teeth, but managed not to flinch away. After pressing his thumb to the pad, he retreated.

"Thank you," she said, her unease rising.

"You're welcome," he answered with the same boring smile.

Something's wrong, something's wrong! a small voice yelled at her from the back of her mind. Run, Run! it told her.

"Who are you?" she asked, not caring how rude the question might be.

"No one of consequence," he responded.

She squinted at him.

That answer sparked something in her memory. It made her think of Jenner. It made her fear increase.

"I must know," she said, brushing a strand of hair behind her ear.

At her words, his dull brown eyes seemed to brighten. Like she'd said the right thing.

"Get used to disappointment," he said, looking at her with an expression she couldn't read. Then he turned and walked out of the coffee shop without getting anything.

"Okay," she said, looking down at her watch.

The picture she'd taken as she'd brushed her hair behind her ear wasn't the best, but it would do. She sent it to Jenner.

The barista called her name. Her hands shook when she reached for the coffees. She battled to keep her body under control, to keep her nerves in check.

"Steady, Mila," she said under her breath.

She walked out of the coffee shop, though she wanted to run. She took deep breaths on the way to her office, though she wanted to scream. When she was the only woman in the crowded elevator, she closed her eyes and focused on breathing.

A sigh of relief escaped her when the last man exited three floors from the top and the doors slid closed behind him. Balancing the coffees in one hand, she looked at her watch to see if Jenner had responded yet. She had a notification but couldn't tap it with her hands full. She'd forgotten to turn her voice control back on this morning.

Too many nights she had been woken up by her emergency alarm. She'd turned her voice control off after she realized she was calling for help in her sleep. She'd check the message later. Right now, she had to sweet-talk her boss.

φ

"What's wrong?" Ms. Jace asked when Zemila entered her office. Zemila internally rolled her eyes. It seemed her plan to sweet-talk her way onto the Cartwrytte story was already ruined.

"What's wrong?" Ms. Jace repeated.

Zemila silently held out the coffee and square to her boss.

"Bribery?" Ms. Jace raised an eyebrow. Zemila nodded emphatically. "Sit down," Ms. Jace said. Zemila sat across the large Intelliglass desk.

"How was your vacation?"

"My vacation?" she asked dryly.

"Your time-out," Ms. Jace corrected.

"It was fine," Zemila lied. "I did some thinking on a couple of stories."

"Of course you did." Ms. Jace reached for the coffee. Zemila slid it across the desk. "Tell me about them."

"Some work on the fires in Lowtown. I can pass on my notes."

"Did you finish the Justal piece after your interview?"

"You read it yesterday."

Ms. Jace smiled. "You know me so well. It was good. You think he's looking for a higher office."

"I know he is."

"And you want to give your notes away on the Lowtown fires." It was a statement, not a question.

"I do," Zemila said.

"Why? What are you angling for?"

"Right Wat—"

"Absolutely not," Jace cut in. "We've been over this."

"Not the Cartwrytte murder," Zemila said, switching tactics. "The suspects. I want to do a piece about the suspects."

"Explain to me how that's not about the murder?" Ms. Jace asked.

"Isn't it convenient that two 1stGens were arrested for the murder of the wife of a Right Waters member just when the immigration registration bill was losing traction?"

Zemila paused, giving her boss a moment to think.

"Keep going," Ms. Jace said.

"I want to write about how the suspects are being written about," Zemila explained, passion evident in every word. "I want to turn the spotlight on the media who support the Right Waters Party. How they are perpetuating stereotypes in an attempt to bring back the political style of thirty years ago."

Zemila looked at her boss.

"Have you been reading what the other outlets are saying?" Zemila asked. "There is no way you're okay with this kind of coverage."

Adrienne Jace drummed her nails on the Intelliglass desk. Zemila knew she had her boss convinced.

"Don't smirk at me," Ms. Jace said, her fingers freezing mid-tap.

"I'm not smirking," Zemila lied.

"You're smirking and you know it," she said. "Fine! Write it! I want it by the end of the day. Dismissed!"

Zemila checked the message from Jenner the second she was out of Ms. Jace's office. There was one from Lochlan too.

She read his first.

I'M SORRY, it read. I SHOULD HAVE TOLD YOU. LET ME KNOW WHEN WE CAN TALK.

Her brows knit together in confusion.

What was he talking about? she thought. She moved on to the message from Jenner.

HERE'S WHAT WE HAVE ON HIM, it read.

There was a file attached titled "The Proxy."

"What we have on him?" Zemila said aloud.

"I'm sorry?" she heard from beside her. Zemila looked up to see Wendy, Ms. Jace's assistant, looking at her.

"Sorry, Wendy," Zemila said. "Talking to myself."

"Can I call you an elevator?" she asked. "You're going to your office?"

"Please," Zemila nodded.

The elevator was empty and went directly to Zemila's floor. She chewed her lower lip on the way down and wondered what Lochlan's message meant.

Here's what we have on him, she thought. Not here's what I found. Here's what we have.

The elevator dinged and opened to her floor.

Lochlan knew, she thought, walking to her office. He knew and he didn't tell me.

When Zemila settled behind her Intelliglass desk, she tapped her watch and sent the file from Jenner to her desktop. Tapping on the table twice, she skimmed the minimal information on the Proxy. Her fingers stilled when she saw a photo of her interviewing Redford Justal. Simmons was in the photo too.

She took in a deep breath and closed the file.

She took another deep breath, shoved everything she was feeling to the back of her mind, and threw herself into her new story.

When she left the office some seven hours later, she took the stairs down to the lobby. Once out on the street, she scanned the crowd for Billy.

But it didn't work like that. He found her, not the other way around.

Zemila gave Ida a pat on the dashboard when the car started without any problems and instantly connected to her phone. She drove home listening to classical music, trying to let everything outside her car melt away.

Oriole needed a walk. Zemila took her for a run. When they got back, Zemila opened the window over her bed and sat on the sill. She shifted a loose brick from under the sill and pulled out a pack of cigarettes.

She smoked three.

When she was done, Zemila went to the bathroom and turned on the shower. Without undressing, she sat under the hot jet of water and she screamed.

She screamed and screamed, until she couldn't scream anymore.

CHAPTER TWENTY-THREE
Lochlan

As soon as I woke up, I checked my phone.

No messages.

Of course no messages, I thought. Did I really expect Zemila to message me between 1 and 5 a.m.?

I lay in my bed staring at the ceiling. The water damage I'd noticed months ago was getting worse. I knew that the longer I left it, the worse it would get. I knew I needed to fix it.

That is a problem for another day, I thought, looking away.

I yawned, got up, and started to pack my gym bag.

φ

"You're late," Tim told me, pausing at the edge of the pool. His face was back in the water before I could respond.

It was 5:50.

I dove in and performed my usual ritual of breath and movement. It wasn't long before the thought of Zemila broke through the peace panic brought me.

Was she mad at me? I worried. I'd sworn I'd never lie to her again. I'd tried not to. I'd screwed up by not telling her about the Proxy.

Thinking over how things had gone, I thought of when I should have told her.

Before we got to Heaven? Before she went up to see Nemo? In a text? No . . . that didn't seem right either. There was so much going on. I'd hoped to spare her from even more stress. If only for a little while.

I switched to a leisurely breaststroke when the 6 a.m. crew joined my lane.

I should have told her. Instead, I'd made the decision for her. I'd decided how much she could handle. That wasn't fair and it wasn't right.

I hope she can forgive me, I thought. I hope I haven't ruined us before we've even had a chance.

φ

I ate breakfast with Jenner at the kitchen table when I got home. He filled me in on the latest in world news, and the many preparations going on around the city, and the country, for tomorrow's patriotic celebrations. He read me a piece Zemila had written about the prejudicial coverage of the Cartwrytte murder suspects.

"And the song stays the same," Llowellyn said, entering the kitchen.

"¿Que?" Jenner asked.

"Power, fear, humanity. That's the song. Hatred is the refrain. Every few decades, someone thinks isolation is a good idea. Nationalism. Cleansings."

"Good morning to you too," Jenner said. "Who were you up late talking to?"

"None of your business," Llowellyn said.

"It's my watch," Jenner said.

"Which you gifted to me," Llowellyn replied.

"I'd like to take you somewhere," I said, ignoring their banter. "Maybe we can work on our link today."

"Me?" Jenner asked. "But our link is already so strong?"

I rolled my eyes and waved his words away.

"All right," Llowellyn touched the stone at his neck, then tapped his temple. "I can work on bringing down the last wall."

The burner phone from Inanna started to ring.

"Her majesty will be expecting you at 8:30 p.m.," a voice said as soon as I'd answered.

"Frank?" I asked.

He scoffed and hung up.

I looked from my best friend to my brother.

"You're going in blind," Jenner said, clearly pissed. "This is happening too fast."

"What choice do we have?" Llowellyn asked.

Jenner considered, then nodded. "You call me when you get where you're going. I'll dig up what I can."

"That's a good idea," Llowellyn said.

"I am brilliant." Jenner gave him a mock bow. "I am also off to work."

"Don't work too hard," I smirked at him, knowing what his response would be.

"I never do," he said and left the kitchen.

I knew Llowellyn would feel the same thing I did when he saw my tree. As we crested a small hill and he saw it for the first time, I heard him suck in a sharp breath. I knew exactly what he was feeling.

When we stood under the full branches, he placed his hand on the trunk and whispered words in the old tongue. I fought back tears as I listened to my brother send prayers to Lugh.

We settled ourselves in the shade of the wise old oak and stayed there for a long time. Cross-legged, like children, we sent messages back and forth to one another. It was immediately clear that Llowellyn had no trouble receiving thoughts; projection was the problem.

For the next few hours, Llowellyn would meditate while I read. Every so often, when he was ready, we would try to communicate through thought. By the time the sun was sinking toward the horizon Llowellyn was able to send me full sentences. No images or fully developed ideas like we'd sent before, but it was a good start.

"I can feel the stone helping," he said after yet another semi-successful attempt. "It's like he's helping me."

"Maybe he is," I said, wishing I believed it. "Maybe he is."

φ

"This is so her," Llowellyn said, turning away from a lanky blond man. "She's making us wait here to watch us squirm."

I silently agreed.

Llowellyn and I had been patiently declining offers from the working men and women in the Heaven lobby for the last thirty minutes. My brother turned and looked for a camera. When he found one, he gave it a little wave.

After another ten minutes, we were escorted through the casino.

"No," I said, when we were brought out a back exit. I looked at the pair of SUVs we were guided to.

"I haven't said anything yet," Frank growled.

"You want us to split up and it's not happening."

"I—"

"No," I repeated.

Llowellyn and I moved to the second SUV. In sync with each other, I walked to the passenger side, and he to the driver's side. We simultaneously opened the doors and pulled out the men occupying the seats. Once comfortably inside, I rolled down the passenger window. Frank wore a slack-jawed expression. Qillian hid a smile.

"Told you it wouldn't work," Qillian said.

"Shut up," Frank shot back.

"Waiting on you, now," I said, giving the side of the car a pat.

Frank glared at me and went to the first vehicle.

The guy who used to be sitting shotgun gave a half-hearted look to the back door of the SUV we'd commandeered, thought better of it, and joined the first car.

We followed the lead car past the outskirts of Lowtown. Jenner started tracking us as soon as we called him. Twenty-five minutes later, we pulled over.

"This neighbourhood has scheduled brownouts," one of the men informed me. "There is a section that never comes back on. We think they have some new wave jammers and their own power source. The Queen suggests we go by foot from here." He gave me a shifty look. "Ummm, under the cover of your Magic."

"Right," I said. "How far are we going?"

"Under ten minutes at a light jog, sir," Qillian said. "And we are to leave all trackable tech here."

The "sir" surprised me.

That's about the edge of our range, Llowellyn thought to me. Any further and we won't be able to communicate.

I gave him a half-shrug and took off my watch.

Not much we can do about that now, I thought back. I'll let you know where we end up. You pass it along to Jenner.

The way Llowellyn and I communicated was more covert than an open call anyway.

He nodded.

"My brother is staying here," I said. "I suggest one of you stay with him. It wouldn't be a good idea for me to exhaust myself covering a third person. What's your name?" I asked the man I didn't know.

"Yacob," he said.

"You'll stay," Frank said to him. "The three of us will go. Let's get a move on."

I nodded to my brother, then to Yacob. Taking in a deep breath, I called for Magic. It answered. I placed a hand on Qillian's shoulder.

"Dorcha tothaim," I said.

"Holy shit," Frank whispered.

"Well, I'll be goddamned," Yacob muttered.

"What?" Qillian looked down at himself. "Ha!" he laughed, looking at his hands.

"You next." I gestured to Frank. He seemed nervous, but stepped towards me all the same. When I repeated the words, darkness closed around him, wrapping him up as though he were in a blanket of shadow.

I could barely make out either Frank or Qillian in the half-darkness. It was like I was only seeing them out of the corner of my eye.

"You too?" Qillian asked me.

"Soon enough," I said.

I turned to my brother and we clasped wrists as we had done in the old days before heading to battle.

Be safe, Little One, he thought to me. Get what we need and get out.

I will. Keep me informed on anything interesting from Jen.

"Stronger together," he said aloud.

"Not alone," I answered.

As three shadows, Qillian, Frank, and I jogged through the low-income neighbourhood to the small industrial one behind it. Every hundred yards, Llowellyn and I checked in. Our link was holding. I was grateful.

Right before the stretch of abandoned factories stood a small building with an eerie glow to it. The light source wasn't normal.

I sent Llowellyn the address.

Be safe, he sent back.

The light hum coming from the solar-panelled cylinder at the side of the building explained the power. The battery was actually a Tjart Tech product. It was created to simultaneously work as a power source and a jammer.

Jenner could crack Tjart Tech in his sleep.

"Easy," I warned, looking the building over. There were slate grey boxes mounted on the brick walls every few meters. I had no idea what they were, but I didn't like it.

"Why?" Frank asked.

That battery isn't enough to power this whole building, I thought. Not unless— I saw the booster attached.

The old school booster worked off the grid and was unhackable. It's connection to the battery had nothing to do with the internet and was an independent power source. We couldn't externally cut their power.

Hopefully, we wouldn't need to.

I quickly filled Llowellyn in on what I was seeing and he voiced my growing concern.

That sounds a little more permanent than a meeting location, he told me.

"Yeah," I agreed aloud.

"What?" asked Frank

"He's talking to his brother," Qillian told him.

"We said no trackable tech," Frank looked annoyed. "You're endangering the mission by using coms."

"They talk up here." Qillian tapped his temple.

Frank looked back and forth between me and Qillian.

"That's impossible," he said, dismissing the idea.

I looked at Qillian. My opinion of him grew.

"This looks more permanent than a meeting location," I said, repeating Llowellyn's words. "We should go, come back when we have more intel."

The suggestion meant staying indebted to Inanna. It meant Nemo staying captive for who knew how much longer. But what was the alternative? Go into a place that was heavily guarded?

"Are you crazy?" Frank said. "We are here to gain information."

"Aye," I kept my eyes on the building. "But the likelihood of us getting caught has gone up, and part of the mission is stealth."

Jenner's working on getting in, Llowellyn thought to me.

"That's why you're here," Frank growled. "To prevent exactly that."

I looked at Qillian. He shrugged at me.

"I have orders and he's the boss."

"Let's move," Frank said and he started for the square two-story building.

"Mair adh," I said, casting a quick spell of silence over his footsteps and ours as Qillian and I followed him.

My skin started to crawl. Something wasn't right.

"I've got a bad feeling," Qillian voiced my concerns.

He's in, Llowellyn told me. Says they've been there a while. About six months.

"Get over here," Frank said, approaching a side window.

"Just don't touch anything," I said. "This operation has been here for six months. We have no idea what security they may—"

The words died on my lips as I looked through the window.

The building didn't have a first floor. We could see right down into the basement. Old stoves and broken refrigerators covered one end. The other had a row of tables with tall piles of brightly colored powder.

"Candle," Qillian said. "They're packaging Candle."

Each of the six mountains of powder were a different color. Someone with a mask over their mouth and nose sat on either side of every pile.

"What are they doing?" Frank asked.

"They're filling capsules with powder," Qillian said. "See the little buckets off to the side."

It looked like candy, I thought, as the workers continued to toss filled capsules into the buckets.

Lochlan, get out of there, Llowellyn's voice was frantic. I'm on my way.

"We have to go," I said.

Why? I thought back.

"Jesus, the Queen is going to love this," Frank said. He leaned

248

forward with excitement.

Jenner says the place has motion sensors, Llowellyn answered. And—

A loud siren went off and Frank moved away from the window.

"Shit," he said. "Fix this!" he yelled at me.

I started to pull Magic to me with the intention of casting a disabling spell. A pulse would emanate from my body and knock out the security system.

A loud clacking sound made me open my eyes.

"Get down!" Qillian yelled, diving towards me.

The slate grey boxes along the walls opened to reveal mounted machine guns, all swinging in our direction.

I felt Qillian shake with the impact of bullets as he protected my body with his.

"Gada," I cried from the ground.

I threw the gathered Magic at the side wall. The spell took out two of the four mounted guns.

No sooner had I mentally reached out for my brother did I hear a squeal of tires.

Thank the gods, I thought.

"Ditiun," I said, raising my hand. A shimmer of protection surrounded me and Qillian. Frank was already sprinting for the SUV.

"I . . . I . . ." Blood bubbled up over Qillian's lips.

"I've got you." I stood and hoisting him up. "Nartha," I pressed the strength spell into his chest.

He found his feet and I half-dragged, half-carried him to the SUV.

Llowellyn rushed out to help.

"Where is Yacob?" I asked as we lay Qillian across the back seats. I got in beside him.

"Took the other van back," Llowellyn answered in a rush.

Frank was in the passenger seat, pointing at the men flooding out of the building.

"Go, go, go, Jesus Christ!" he yelled.

Llowellyn threw himself into the driver's seat and floored it.

"Why the hell did we even bring you two?!" Frank was frantic.

Tires screeched. Bullets ricocheted off the SUV.

"You were supposed to make sure this didn't happen!"

"Call Heaven," Llowellyn said to the vehicle. Frank continued to berate me. "Call Heaven," he repeated when the system got confused by the multiple voices.

"—useless demigods with no fu—"

I tried to turn Qillian onto his side. He groaned in pain.

"Call Heaven!" Llowellyn yelled for a third time.

"Did . . . Did you get hit?" Qillian asked me.

"—supposed to be these powerful beings that could—"

There was a blur of motion in the front seat. Frank's voice cut off.

If I hadn't looked up, intending to do the same thing, I wouldn't have seen Llowellyn's fist flying through the air.

"Call Heaven," Llowellyn said into the silence.

"*Calling Heaven*," the angelic voice said.

"I didn't get hit," I cradled Qillian's head in one hand. I placed the other under him, rolling him onto his back.

"G–good," Qillian spat blood.

"Why did you do that?" I asked, calling Magic to me.

"We're twenty minutes out and we have one unconscious, one shot," Llowellyn said when someone at Heaven answered.

"Boss said . . . keep you safe . . . prophecy," Qillian told me.

"Try to stay still for a second, okay?" I told him.

"Kay."

I took in a deep breath and moved my hand from under his neck to over his chest. "Aire cagair-gada," I chanted. "Beannachd nartha. Aire cagair-gada, beannachd nartha."

Over and over again I chanted. I heard Llowellyn join in and, together, slowly, we pushed the bullets out of Qillian's body. The holes in his lungs began to knit back together. The gurgling sound, when he breathed, went away.

It was forever and a moment that we cast together. Llowellyn's power was weak but present. He had always been the better healer. His empathic abilities allowed him to find just the right spot to push the Magic, to guide the spell.

"Chaidil," I said with a hand on Qillian's forehead.

He fell asleep.

"He's lost a lot of blood," I told Llowellyn.

"There'll be someone waiting to treat him when we get there," he assured me. "Yeah, okay." Llowellyn said and took a sharp right down a side street.

I could only assume that last part was to Jenner. No doubt he was in the city traffic system giving us green lights.

"I see it," Llowellyn made another hairpin turn. "Yeah, almost there. Thanks."

The bright lights of Heaven shone ahead of us. I looked down at the man sprawled across my lap.

"You don't belong here," I said to him, brushing my hand across his dreadlocked hair. "I'm going to get you out of this."

"Don't make promises you can't keep, brother," Llowellyn said. "Where does all this leave your friend?"

I thought of Nemo and a whisper of fear moved through me.

"I don't know, Llowellyn," I said. "Gods. . . I don't know."

CHAPTER TWENTY-FOUR
Lochlan

Paramedics were waiting at the entrance of Heaven.

When Qillian and Frank are out, I thought to Llowellyn. Take the van and go

"We were told only one was unconscious," a paramedic said, lifting Qillian's sleeping form out of the SUV.

I took a step over towards them. Snapping my fingers over Qillian's face, I removed the sleeping spell. His eyes fluttered open.

"Jesus," the paramedic said. "He's one of them."

One of them, I thought. Don't know they work for a god, do they.

"The bullets are out," I told the medical staff. "His lungs are healed but he's lost a lot of blood. He still has the surface wounds. I'm not sure what else."

The paramedic looked confused, but she seemed to trust my words.

"Understood," she said and started yelling instructions at the others.

I moved around to the passenger side door and opened it. Frank, still out cold, slumped sideways. I grabbed him by his collar and pulled. His head hit the concrete side walk.

"Lochlan!" my brother shouted.

"Get home," I said.

"You could kill him like that," he scolded.

"You're the one who knocked him out."

"I know but, just . . ." Llowellyn stumbled on his words. "Get someone to take a look at him. Make sure he doesn't have any brain damage."

I nodded.

"I don't like that look," he said.

Turning my face down, I closed my eyes, trying to block the emotion wafting off my brother. Worry. Fear.

I understood his meaning.

"You're afraid of me." I stated, my rage rising.

"Afraid you will succumb to what he wants you to be," he said calmly. "Not of you. Never of you."

I nodded, still not looking at him.

"Hey," he said, aloud and in my mind.

My eyes snapped up to his.

"Never of you."

He looked at me. He waited. I knew what he wanted me to say. The words stuck in the back of my throat.

"Stronger together," I reached out my arm.

"Not alone," he said. We clasped wrists.

The familiar action dampened my rage. But it wasn't gone.

I glared up at the statue of Inanna conquering Hammurabi.

Though Babylonia had no law against women owning property, women too were owned, and became the property of their husband's father as soon as they were married. The restrictions on female sexuality legislated in the Hammurabi code became social norms around the world that still exist today. This subtle display of female empowerment in Inanna's lobby was a warning to all men who came looking to restrict her.

I reign here, it said. I am War. I am Love. This place is mine, and caution is required in my dominion.

I walked past it with the intention of entering the casino floor. The notion was halted by a pair of hands grabbing my arms.

"I seek an audience with the Queen," I said, shaking the two guards off me.

"I seek a queen myself, you know," said one. "But we were told to stop you at the door."

"By whom?" I asked coldly. Inanna was not foolish enough to deny seeing me.

"Don't you worry about that—"

"Obey-ordu." I barely had to call Magic. It was waiting to be used. Crackling under my fingertips. The men stilled.

"Take me to Queen Anne," I commanded.

I wiped my hands on my pants, trying to get some of Qillian's blood off them. It was no use. Like the rage slowly building inside me, the blood on my hands wasn't going anywhere.

Inanna looked up from her book when I walked in. Slowly, she put down her steaming mug of tea.

"Release my men," she said, placing a bookmark in her thick paperback. "And, please, sit."

She gestured to the chairs Zemila and I had occupied on our last visit.

I waved my hand to loose my hold on her men. They swayed on the spot, looking around like they didn't know how they'd gotten here.

"They were blocking my entrance," I told Inanna.

"You asked them to see me?" she asked. When I didn't sit, she gestured at the chair again

"They said they had orders to keep me away."

Her eyes narrowed at me, then at her men.

"Dismissed," she waved the men away.

They left quickly. We were alone in the room. Inanna settled herself behind her desk.

"He talked about you all the time, you know," she said. "Both of you. But you more."

I stared blankly at her.

"He loved you so much. I was jealous. Of you. Of him . . . that's why I always hated you." She reached over to the table beside her reading chair and took her tea. "I'd never loved anything that much. I'd never been loved that much."

"It wasn't a meeting," I said, ignoring her words.

"Yes," she said. "I've heard."

"That operation has been there for months."

"Had," she corrected. "The place has burned to the ground."

"What?" I was shocked. Not an hour had passed since we'd been there. "That wasn't—"

"I'm well aware it wasn't you," she said calmly. "Please sit."

She had done it, I realized. After learning the operation had gone south, she'd sent someone to clean up the mess.

"They were making Candle." I continued to ignore her request.

"Yes," she repeated. "Yacob told me some. Frank filled in a bit more."

"Frank's awake?"

"Despite your better efforts." A small smiled played at the corners of her lips. "He is. You aren't the only one who can heal. He would have been out for weeks otherwise . . . The severity of his concussion . . ." She trailed off.

"And Qillian?" I asked.

"He's also fine. Getting a blood transfusion as we speak."

"Nemo," I said.

"Fine."

"Fine?" I repeated.

"Yes, he is still fine," annoyance tainted her words. "Though he will be staying here as you did not do as I asked."

I'd expected this. That didn't make it easier to hear.

"Release him," I demanded, calling Magic to me. "Give me back my friend."

"Don't test me, boy," she placed her mug down and rose to her feet.

"Release him," I pulled in power.

I pulled so hard that the old flavor of Dark Magic touched the edges of my awareness. I hadn't tasted that raw power in centuries. It felt good. Different than when I'd saved Zemila. Half-dead as I was, that part of Magic hadn't tempted me then.

It tempted me now.

Here, facing Inanna, I could pull just a little harder and she would bend to my will. Nemo would be safe. Zemila would have her brother.

All I had to do was pull.

"This is my house." Inanna raised her arms, interrupting my thoughts. She seemed to bring light and power into herself. "You and the

Northern gods may have power. But we from the East existed long before your world."

I felt the Magic I'd called drain out of me. The sweet seducing darkness being taken from my grasp. Pulled out of me and into her. All the air in the room was sucked away. The lights flickered. I couldn't breathe.

This was the Queen of Heaven. Goddess of love and war. The Venus. The Lion. Ishtar. Inanna.

"Though our followers may be gone," she continued, power glowing around her like the sun. "All those who step into my house, who seek riches here, love here, desire here. All those prayers come to me, little brother of a dead god."

The Lion clenched her fists at her sides.

I tried fruitlessly to breathe.

"All those prayers give me the power of the Old World. My Old World. A world that was old when yours was born. Do not test me, child. You know not what you do."

I fell forward, wide-eyed and gasping. I was empty of Magic. I was useless. A failure. Again.

The lights came back on. I could breathe. Inanna returned Magic to my body. But it didn't feel the same. It didn't feel safe. I had no power here and she knew it. How would I ever save my brother?

My friend, a small voice in my head corrected. Nemo . . . not Lugh. Lugh was long dead.

"Sit." Inanna bit out the word.

I sat.

"I am a goddess of my word," she said. "No harm has come to your friend in your failure. He will be released upon the destruction of this particular branch of the Ruiz cartel. You will do this for me."

"I want all the information beforehand," I said. "Your people don't have the access mine do. I want to know what I'm getting into this time."

"Acceptable," she said. "If everything you learn also comes to me."

"Yes," I agreed. "And I want to see Nemo."

"You know," Inanna picked up her tea. "You make a lot of demands."

"A request," I begged. "Please, can I see my friend? He is a brother to me."

Her eyes snapped up to mine. She stared intently at me—I felt self-conscious. She had never looked at me like that before.

Then the look was gone.

"Since his sister is already with him," she said, and my heart did a summersault. "I will permit this."

"Thank you, Inanna." I felt a mixture of elation at seeing Zemila and fear she'd reject me when she learned I'd failed.

"He knew this would happen," Inanna said with a heavy sigh. "Your brother. Did he have the gift of sight?" She looked at me with a warmth I'd never seen in her eyes before.

"Not that I was aware of," I said. "And we shared everything."

"Not everything," she countered. "Not this . . ."

I looked at her, brows knit together.

What did she know? I wondered.

"A prophecy," she said.

Qillian's words echoed in my mind. "Boss said keep you safe . . . prophecy."

"I already know about the prophecy."

"Not this one," she shook her head. "I've heard of the prophecy you speak of. The death of your grandfather, that one." She paused. Considered. "That one doesn't trouble me. Not as much as the other."

When gods like Inanna felt troubled by a prophecy, there was cause to panic.

"Oh, don't worry just yet," she said, reading the horror in my face. "You have a couple lifetimes before this one plays out. You're just a cameo, in any case, but an important one. I don't really understand it myself. Lugh told me to tell you. He said I'd know the moment."

"He told you?" I said in disbelief. "When?"

"Look, kid, I didn't believe him either. I didn't believe him when he said a brother of his brother would be in my possession."

"A brother of his brother," I repeated, confused.

"He told me in that moment I would be a messenger of the past and future. That my deliverance of this prophecy would change the course of the world. He said when I held the brother of his brother, there were three lifetimes left."

"Left?" I asked. "Brother of his brother? What does that mean? You don't have Llowellyn, you have . . ." I trailed off.

"Since when does brotherhood only mean blood?" she asked. She was right. Nemo had become a brother when we'd lived together at Erroin. He was my confidant and friend, my family.

"Three lifetimes left," I repeated. "Left in what?"

"I don't know," she said. I believed her. "But he said that was the time to tell you."

"I am so sick of riddles," I said. "First the Shannon, then the Proxy, now you! Why can't anyone speak plainly? Why does it have to be so hard?"

Inanna laughed.

"The Shannon is a right bitch, I'll tell you that," she said. "I saw them once, a few millennia ago. Started spouting something about a vampire, a new god, and invaders like never before. Then, boom," she snapped her fingers. "Christianity. Colonization. Was I supposed to stop it or just get out of the way, I still don't know. I hate them," she muttered. Then her eyes flicked up to mine. "What did she tell you?"

"Now you want to help?" I asked, still skeptical.

She didn't speak. But I knew the value of an Ancient, and so did she. Perhaps Llowellyn was right and she was an ally after all. Mayhap she wanted to be.

"The Lady of the Lake has your answer, and you will be found with the Virtuous Collector. Trust him with truth. You will not be the one," I recited.

"Trust the collector?" she asked.

"I assume so."

"Don't." She pointed a finger at me. The nail at the end of it was long and gold.

"Don't trust him?"

"Don't assume," she said. "If there is one thing I know about the Shannon, it's that they are as easy to understand as the sea. Everything moves in unexpected ways because of unseen forces."

She paused, then held up a finger.

"One," she said, "the Lady of the Lake has your answer. Two," she put up another finger, "you will be found with the Virtuous Collector. Three," she raised a third finger, "trust him with truth. Don't assume that those three phrases are linked."

"Why are you helping me?" I asked.

"You are needed in a great war," she said. "You must survive this so you can end that. Or so your brother told me." She seemed to want to say something else, but struggled to find the words. "He told me you needed to make sure the vampire was there."

She paused.

"Where?" I asked. "What vampire?"

"Where it happens," she said. "Where it can all be lost or won. When hope is gone, find her. You'll be the only one who can."

CHAPTER TWENTY-FIVE
Zemila

Her eyes were wide. She stared at her brother, willing him to make the right decision.

You can do this, she thought. You can do this.

"Nemo," she said aloud. "Not everything rides on this . . . but—"

"Everything rides on this," he said.

"Yeah . . . sorry."

"That's okay." His hand drifted up. He paused. Considered.

Zemila held her breath. Nemo picked the red five and discarded it.

"Nooooo!" Zemila cried throwing herself onto the neatly arranged cards. "I told you that was a five—why would you discard it?"

"Well," Nemo said defensively. He put a circular blue chip back in the square tin. "You discarded the last yellow four! I don't know what you're complaining about."

"You didn't tell me it was yellow."

"We'll get it next time," he smiled. "You only have ones left."

There was a knock on the door.

"And you only have white," she said, tossing down her cards.

"Ms. Alkevic." A guard appeared in the doorway.

"It hasn't been two hours yet," Nemo protested. "George, please."

The anxiety in her brother's eyes wrenched at her. She hated seeing him here, like this.

"I just need a word with her outside," he promised. "I'll bring her right back in."

"Okay," Nemo nodded, brows knit together.

Did something go wrong? Zemila worried. Is Lochlan okay?

She followed George out of the room. She looked over her shoulder as she went. She tried to give Nemo an encouraging smile, but his worried expression didn't change

"Ma'am." George closed the door behind her.

She looked up at him. He was a tall, broad-shouldered man with wide features. Nemo had been right. He was a good guy.

George pointed his chin over her shoulder. She turned.

"Lochlan," she said. For a moment, warmth spread through her. It was soon replaced by worry and fear. He was covered in blood. "God, Lochlan. Are you all right?"

She rushed to him.

He cringed away.

The motion stopped Zemila in her tracks.

"Mila, I–I—" He struggled to get the words out.

"It's okay," she said, moving towards him slowly, taking in his bloody hands, his bowed head, his hunched shoulders.

He'd stood like this when he'd told her the worst of his past. This was what shame looked like when Lochlan wore it.

"It wasn't just a meeting," he said, not looking at her. "It was so well-protected. One of the guys tripped an alarm—"

"Is this your blood?" she asked, reaching for his hands. He pulled them back, not allowing her to touch him. His brow furrowed. He shrunk in on himself. "Is this your blood?" she asked again.

"No," he told her. "A guard, Qillian. He pushed me down. He protected me. Why did he do that?" He shook his head. "She told him to do that, but she knows bullets can't hurt us, can't hurt me. I don't know why she told him to do that—"

He was rambling and staring at the blood on his hands.

Zemila didn't know where his mind had gone, but she didn't like it. "Is Qillian okay?"

Lochlan didn't respond. She slowly reached up to touch his cheek.

"Hey," she said when her skin made contact with his. A current of heat zinged through her. Green eyes met her brown ones. "Hey, right here. You're right here with me. Talk to me."

"He can't leave yet," Lochlan said, pain in his voice. "She won't let him leave yet."

"I know." She'd known that the moment she'd seen him.

"She won't let him leave until I complete another favor. Something to do with the Ruiz cartel." Then he spoke in a language Zemila didn't understand. It sounded like a curse.

"When does she want you to do it?" Zemila asked calmly.

His eyes were back on his hands. On the blood on his hands. Zemila didn't like that either. She cupped his face and forced him to look at her.

"This is not your fault," she said. He tried to look away. She held him, repeating her words. "This is not your fault."

"I'm so sorry," he whispered.

She pulled his forehead to hers and slid her fingers to tangle in his hair.

"I know," she said. "That doesn't make it your responsibility."

The same connection she'd felt with him before flooded back. It was more emotional, less physical. The world seemed to brighten, but only a little this time.

She took in a deep breath and let it out slowly. Lochlan did the same. He relaxed against her. She pulled back, letting her hands drop.

"Is Qillian—"

"He's fine," Lochlan said, looking less like the shrunken ball of failure he'd been a moment ago. He pushed his glasses up his nose.

Adorable, she thought.

"Llowellyn and I healed him on the way back."

"Llowellyn did?" she said, shocked.

"Yes, his connection to Magic is getting stronger."

"That's good, right?"

"Very good." He nodded.

"When do you have to do whatever it is the Queen wants?"

"She'll let us know, but in the next couple of days, I think . . . I hope."

"Okay." Zemila took in a breath. "Come inside."

She turned back to the door. Lochlan hesitated.

"I—"

"What?"

"Why don't you make sure he wants to see me," Lochlan suggested.

"What?"

"I just mean . . ."

"Of course he wants to see you," she said, exasperated. She turned back to look at him.

"Can you just check?" he pleaded.

"Fine." She scoffed. George opened the door. She went back in the room. Nemo was anxiously shuffling the Hanabi deck and watching an infomercial.

"Everything okay?" he asked.

"Not really," Zemila answered.

"Off," Nemo said to the TV. The wall flickered blank. Nemo stood and turned to her. "What's going on?"

"You can't come home tonight," Zemila said.

"Oh my god, is Lochlan okay?"

"He's okay." Zemila's heart warmed at her brother's reaction. "He's outside. He wanted me to ask if you would see him."

Men are remarkable, Zemila thought as her brother shrunk into the mirror image of failure Lochlan had been.

"Does he want to see me?" Nemo asked in a small voice.

"Oh my god!" She threw her hands in the air. "Lochlan!"

The door opened. Lochlan walked in. Zemila looked back and forth between the two men. They stared at each other, then spoke at the same time.

"I'm sorry," said Lochlan.

"I was an idiot," said Nemo.

They grinned shyly. Zemila shook her head.

"I've got to pee." She stalked off to the master bedroom's en suite.

The sound of the tap drowned out the "I'm sorrys" and the "my faults" passing between the two men. Zemila washed off the blood that had been transferred to her skin when she'd held Lochlan. He'd been so careful not to touch her.

What a mess, she thought, splashing cool water on her face. After drying off with a fluffy white towel, she left the washroom to find Nemo alone on the couch.

"Where's Lochlan?" Zemila asked.

"George got him a change of clothes," Nemo said. "He's taking a shower and changing."

"Oh." Zemila sat on the floor across from Nemo.

"He is," Nemo paused. "He thinks everything and everyone is his responsibility," Nemo finished.

"Peas in a pod," Zemila smirked.

"Oh, come on," he protested. "I'm not that bad."

"I mean, I love you for it, but you're not much better."

"I love you too, you know that?"

"Yeah. I know that." She smiled.

"And him?" Nemo asked.

"Him what?"

Nemo looked at her expectantly.

"What?" she repeated.

"You know exactly what."

"I really don't—"

"Don't play dumb with me, little sister. You're too smart for that." He shook a finger at her. "I was there, remember?"

Zemila leaned back, propping herself up on her arms.

"I was there after he left," he went on. "I knew there was something going on between you two, even then. Your long walks around the school, your 'study sessions.'" He put air quotes around the words.

"We were studying," Zemila said. "Nothing ever happened between us."

"Nothing physical, maybe," Nemo agreed. "But the way you two would look at each other sometimes . . . it was like the rest of us weren't there."

She remembered.

"Then he left and you were crushed."

She remembered that too.

"You weren't much better," she accused.

"I never said I was. I'd lost my best friend and had no idea why. But you . . . It was like a piece of your soul left with him. You changed after that. You got cold. Hard."

"I'm sorry," she said. Zemila hadn't realized she'd been that way. "I never meant to make you feel—"

"You misunderstand me," he cut her off. "With me, you were just sad. I understood that. I was sad too. But then you became so driven. Left school the next year, moved to Baltimore, started your website, got hired at JACE Co., met Tyler. It all seemed so fast."

"Yeah," she agreed. "Yeah, I guess it was."

"You were so focused, so busy. Like you were trying not to think about him. Like if you stopped for one single second, it would all become real."

"I'm happy he's back in our lives," Zemila said.

"Me too," Nemo agreed.

They heard the shower in the second bathroom turn off.

"Do we have time for another game?" she asked.

"Does Lochlan know how to play?"

"He's a smart guy," Zemila said. "He'll figure it out."

He did not figure it out. Twenty-five minutes later, the best they'd got was eighteen. Lochlan kept discarding cards they needed and giving hints that had already been given.

"You are so smart," Nemo said as they were saying goodbye. "How is it possible you're so bad at this game?"

"I do not know, my friend," Lochlan said as they hugged. "Next time at my place. I'm going to get you out of here."

Zemila hugged her brother next.

"Talk to him," Nemo whispered in her ear. "I love you."

"I love you too," Zemila said.

George escorted Lochlan and Zemila back to her car. It was nearly one in the morning and the roads were empty.

"I'm dropping you off at home?" Zemila asked Lochlan.

"Yeah," he said. "Will you stay over?"

"Yeah," she told him.

Zemila parked the car up the street from Lochlan's house.

"Can we walk for a bit?" she asked, looking up at the clear sky. She could almost see the stars past the street lamps.

"Sure," Lochlan said. "A long walk or a short walk?"

"I want to talk to you about a couple things." Zemila thought about what Nemo had said. He'd been right. She needed to talk to Lochlan.

"I know just the spot," he said and started up the street. "But before we get there, I want to apologize for something."

Zemila looked up at him. Her brows knit together. She walked silently at his side while he found his words. She thought she knew what this was about.

"I should have told you about the Proxy right away." He sagged under the weight of his confession. "I didn't want to add to everything happening to you. I didn't want—"

He cut himself off.

She took one of his hands in hers, pulling him to a stop. He took a breath, not looking at her. When he finally met her eyes, he said, "I didn't want to add to everything going on for you. I didn't want to bring more of my problems to your doorstep. But I was wrong to do that. I should have told you. I'm sorry."

Zemila hadn't spent much time thinking about Lochlan not telling her. She'd been so in her own head, terrified that she was being followed again. But now that she heard these words from him, she realized she'd needed it.

"Thank you," she said. "I wish you'd told me right away, but I understand your reason for keeping it from me." She put a finger under his chin and forced his eyes to meet hers. "After tonight, no more secrets, okay?"

He nodded.

"If this is going to work"—and she really wanted it to work—"we have to be honest with each other. Even when it's uncomfortable."

"Even when it's uncomfortable," he echoed.

"Now," she said, dropping his hand. "Where are you taking me?"

"Not far from here," he said, putting his hands in his pockets.

Zemila didn't know why she'd dropped his hand. She regretted it.

Their pace was slow. Silence surrounded them. Zemila knew he was waiting for her to break it. When she was ready—and aching to touch him again—she linked her arm in his. He took his hand out of his pocket and she entwined their fingers.

"I've been having trouble sleeping," she said.

There was a long pause. He brought their fingers to his lips and kissed the back of her hand. She sighed and relaxed a little.

"I'm having trouble sleeping," she said again. "And I'm having trouble controlling my abilities."

"How so?" he asked.

"Do you remember that night, a couple months ago," she said. "At Once More With Feeling?"

"Am I about to learn what really happened to the pepper shaker?"

"It's not just that," she said. "It's happened a few times. I keep breaking things by mistake. That pepper shaker, the countertop at my place, car windows, I even pulled some concrete up out of the sidewalk when I was scared. All by accident."

"How long has this been happening?" he asked.

"About a year," she confessed.

"And you've just been keeping it to yourself? That must have felt really lonely."

"You have no id—" she broke off. "Actually, I guess you do." She looked over at him. His smile was sad. "I guess you know exactly how that feels."

"Unfortunately, yes." His eyes were turned down. "But this sounds like an extension of your Earth Driver abilities. Marble, glass, salt—those are all things of the earth."

"Last week, I pulled Nemo's plastic sunglasses off his face," she said. "And when I went into Heaven to get him, I . . ."

She remembered the red dots that appeared on the man's face—and the blood mist that followed.

"I don't know what I did," she said into the darkness. "It was like I was pulling the blood out of this man. Like I was pulling out his life."

Zemila expected Lochlan to drop her hand, to recoil. He did neither. Instead, he pointed to an oak tree a few blocks in front of them.

"That's where we're headed," he told her. "I call it my Thinking

Spot."

The old oak tree stood at the top of a little hill not far from where they were.

"It reminds me of my brother Lugh. It reminds me of old times."

"Better times?" she asked.

"Different times." He gave a heavy sigh.

She knew something weighed on him too. Just like he'd done for her, she waited for him to organize his thoughts.

"I had a fight with Llowellyn," he admitted.

"Siblings fight," she said.

"It was about Lugh."

"Oh."

Though she'd given it a lot of thought recently, Zemila had no idea what it would be like to lose a sibling.

Lochlan told her about the argument. When he'd finished, they were sitting with their backs against the oak tree. His arm was wrapped around her. Her head rested on his shoulder.

"Sometimes I think of those men I killed," Lochlan said. "The Magic I'd used was so powerful, so all-consuming. Like the spell was making the decisions, not me."

"I felt that when I . . ." She took a breath. "When I killed Simmons. I was so angry, so scared. I didn't mean to do what I did. I didn't mean to kill him that way."

"Neither did I."

"Turns out neither of us is perfect, huh?" she tried to joke, tried to break the tension.

Zemila felt his lips on her temple and she closed her eyes.

"You're pretty close," he whispered.

Warmth and softness gave way to the cold spray of waves crashing against the shore. Rough stone stretched around her. Salt water sprayed into the cavern.

Zemila held up a hand. The water stopped. Though she could still hear it crashing against the rocks, the sea no longer sprayed her face. It seemed to hit an invisible barrier projected by her hand.

Where am I? she thought.

Light shone in from above. She looked up. Through a circle in the stone, she saw a clear blue sky.

Where's Lochlan? she thought.

She closed her eyes. Zemila could still feel the large oak at her back and Lochlan's chest under her cheek. She was with him, but she was here too . . . and her feet felt wet.

She looked down. She was standing in water.

No. She was standing on water.

No sooner had she realized this did it give way. She plummeted. Sinking like a stone into the icy depth. Shock opened her mouth in a silent scream. Cold salty liquid poured into her. It flooded her lungs.

No, she thought, trying not to panic. This is my dream. I control this.

She brought her arms down beside her like she was climbing out of a swimming pool. The motion propelled her upward. Her body, seconds ago fully submerged, hovered in the air above the water's surface.

She wanted up. She wanted out. She wanted to see where she was.

Lifting her eyes to the blue sky above, she flew out of the cavern. Water stretched in every direction she looked. She'd had enough of this. She closed her eyes again and reached for Lochlan, hoping to pull herself out of the dream.

He was there. She felt him. But that was all. She couldn't reach him. She couldn't pull herself back to reality.

When she opened her eyes, she wasn't alone.

The sea quieted. The waves stopped. A woman with almond-shaped eyes and a long braid smiled.

"There aren't many who help raise the dead." The woman reached out a slender hand. She touched Zemila's cheek, then let her hand fall. "Viviane sees something in you."

"Who is Viviane?" Zemila asked.

The woman turned as if someone behind her had spoken. When Zemila looked, a speaker appeared. Another woman with a long braid. Her skin was dark and her hair thick.

"Yes," the first woman said. "Yes, Nineve always chose very carefully."

"Nineve?" Zemila repeated.

A third woman appeared. She had a broad face and terracotta skin. She wore her hair in the same long braid as the others.

"Are you Nineve?" Zemila asked.

"That is more than enough, I think," said the second woman. "She doesn't get more time."

"More than enough," said the third. "A shift is coming."

The first woman reached out for Zemila's face again.

"Yes," she said, stroking her cheek. "Enough."

CHAPTER TWENTY-SIX
Lochlan

I woke to the cawing of a crow. Blinking my eyes open, I righted my glasses. The iridescent black bird seemed to scream only at me. Zemila was still fast asleep. When I looked at it, the crow quieted. We stared at each other for a moment. Then the bird spread its wings and took flight.

I ignored the omen.

Instead, my eyes fell to the woman asleep on my shoulder. My arm was numb. My back hurt from leaning against the tree. I barely felt it when I looked at Zemila. I wanted to stay in this moment forever.

I knew I couldn't.

I looked at my watch. There was a message from Jenner, responding to my text from last night saying we were going for a walk.

Be safe. Use protection.

But seriously, amigo, be safe.

I rolled my eyes. It was 5:32 a.m. The newborn sun was slowly lighting the sky.

We should get back, I thought.

"Zemila," I whispered, pressing a kiss on her head. "Wake up."

Her eyes snapped open and frantically looked around.

"Are you all right?"

I shifted so we were both sitting up.

"Yes," she said. "Urgh . . . no. Why did we sleep under a tree?"

"I think it was an accident. But it isn't the first time I've slept here," I admitted.

She gave me a strange look. I smiled and stood. My body ached.

"I'll tell you about it some other time." I extended a hand to Zemila. "We should walk back."

"Okay," she said, taking my hand and standing. She looked stressed, confused.

"Are you all right?" I asked again.

"I just had the weirdest dream," she said.

"The Shannon," I told Zemila. She had laced her fingers in mine as we walked. "The Shannon and her sisters."

Zemila's confused look kept me talking.

"There is an Irish legend of a creature wiser than man. The Salmon of Knowledge."

"A fish?" She seemed shocked.

"Yes, a fish. A fish that fed upon acorns that fell from the Tree of Knowledge," I told her. "It was said whoever first ate this salmon would have its wisdom and foresight. A young boy named Fionn MacCool had great success after his claims of doing just that."

"You don't sound convinced," she said.

We turned down a side street into my neighbourhood.

"It was said that the Tree of Knowledge was planted on the banks of the River Shannon, the longest river in Ireland. Some say the Salmon ate the acorns produced by the tree. Others say the river herself took them in, and as she flowed into her sisters, they grew strong and wise. The Shannon and her sisters are known to lend aid when they see things going awry."

"She's a guide," Zemila said.

"In a manner of speaking."

"Why is she talking to me?"

"Do you feel you need guidance?" I asked.

"I think everyone needs guidance," she said.

"She visited me too."

I explained my own encounter.

It wasn't until I'd finished my story, and we were inside my front hall, that Zemila released my hand. We had fallen into a thoughtful silence after my tale of the Shannon. But now, with the loss of contact, all I thought of was her.

"Coffee?" she whispered, walking up a few steps and bending over the railing. "Will you make me some coffee, please?"

I had to crane my neck to look up at her. Even after only a few hours' sleep, she was stunning. I reached up a hand and cupped her cheek.

"I want nothing more than to kiss you right now," I said.

She grinned, her brown eyes big and warm.

"Breakfast first," she said, pressing her lips into my palm.

I stood motionless as she pulled away from me. Only with the sound of the washroom door closing behind her did I lower my arm.

She is beguiling, I thought.

I wanted to follow her up the stairs. I wanted her in my room, in my bed. I wanted to press my lips to her skin.

But she was right. We had time. I turned to the kitchen.

Jenner was always an early riser, but when he stumbled into the kitchen at 6:15 on a day he didn't have to be up, I was surprised.

"The she-devil woke me up when she started the shower," he said, stumbling over to the cupboard and pulling down a bright pink mug that read "Bad Hombre."

I think he had it custom-made.

"Coffee's on the counter." I gestured to the French press and continued to stir the oatmeal.

He poured the remainder of the coffee into his cup, then raised it to me. "Happy Independence Day," he toasted before drinking.

"I fought for the British," I said, and he nearly spit out his coffee.

"Dios Mio, you did not!"

"No," I smirked, "I didn't. I was on the other side of the world, but I wanted to take your mind of the... she-devil?"

"That woman frightens me," he said from behind his bright pink mug. "Maybe more than el diablo himself because she's actually here!"

"You're being dramatic." I moved to fill the kettle.

He gave me a dark look, then sat at the small kitchen table. I remembered him telling me how Zemila had killed Simmons. I'd seen so much death and destruction over my lifetimes. I'd been the cause of some of it. It made me forget it wasn't normal.

"She sent me a file yesterday to look at with you," he told me. "Did she mention it?"

"No." My brows drew together. "We talked about . . . other things."

"Naked things?"

"Jenner!" I dumped the coffee grinds into the compost and rinsed the glass cylinder.

279

"What? What?" he said, cradling his bright pink mug. "I'm curious! I have no one else to live vicariously through. Llowellyn and Ember are so boring."

"Llowellyn and Ember?" I nearly dropped the coffee.

"Whoopsies," Jenner flicked his fingers over his watch and found the file Zemila had sent him.

"So that's who he's been up late talking to," I whispered. I heard the shower go off upstairs and light footsteps leave the bathroom.

Jenner's eyes flicked to the ceiling, following the progress of steps. We were silent as we heard a door open and close.

"She's in your room," he raised his eyebrows several times in quick succession.

"Jenner, come on."

"Wanna go join her?" he asked with a wicked grin. The kettle started to whistle.

Did I want to join her? I thought, taking the kettle off the burner. Hell yeah, I did. Was I going to? No. She wanted to take things slow. I could give her that.

"I can play some music really loud. I'm considerate that way," Jenner said.

"Tell me about Llowellyn and Ember," I asked.

"Urgh, you're boring. They're boring too. Not much to tell," Jenner said turning his eyes back to the file. "They just talk and talk and—whoa."

"What?" I asked, moving over to the table and reading the file over his shoulder. Jenner was scrolling fast. "Slow down. How do you even read anything at that speed?"

"I'm just skimming, old man." He elbowed me in the gut.

I grunted in mock pain.

"Tell me what it says." I went back to the stove, pouring the water on fresh coffee grounds, and dishing up two bowls of oatmeal.

"She's been doing research for you." He was still skimming through the file.

"For me?"

"For you, amigo," he said. I slid him a bowl of oatmeal. "Gracias."

"What do you mean for me?" I sat down across from him with my own bowl at the same time as Zemila walked into the kitchen.

"Hey, Jenner," she said, drying her hair with a towel. "Oh, you're reading the file I sent you. Great! I can give you the highlights."

She was wearing my clothes.

A t-shirt that fit her loosely but still seemed to cling in the right places. A pair of sweatpants she rolled twice at the waist so they'd be the right length. I had never seen her look so sexy.

I wanted to pull the towel out of her hand, pick her up, and carry her to my room, Jenner and his considerately loud music be damned. The image of her sprawled on my bed filled my mind. I imagined dragging my mouth down her body, taking my clothes off of her, pulling her close to me . . .

"Lochlan. Lochlan?"

Vaguely, I realized someone was talking to me.

"Dios mio, this one is hopeless. Lochlan!"

"Huh?" I looked at Jenner.

"Stop staring at her. You're embarrassing yourself."

Danu, I swore. I had to pull myself together.

"Zemila is going to tell us what she's been doing," he said very slowly. "Then after we are done listening," he pointed at his ears, "you can go back to staring." He pointed at his eyes, then at Zemila.

I showed him a rude hand gesture. He pretended to snatch it out of the air and put it in his pocket.

"I'll save that for later," he said.

I snuck a look at Zemila before returning to my oatmeal. She didn't meet my eyes but smiled and walked over to the French press.

"My Lady," Jenner said. "If you would take over."

"It's about the Tools," she started. "Is Llowellyn here? Maybe he should hear all of this too."

Llowellyn, I thought to my brother. Wake up.

It was Lugh who first realized we could wake each other this way. He did it by accident the first time. We were teenagers. Once he figured out how to do it consistently, he did it when he was annoyed. He would scream in our mind while we slept.

At first, we thought we were waking up from nightmares or someone actually screaming outside our room. Lugh would always pretend to be asleep.

His favored time to wake me, was three in the morning after I'd won the evening's sparring matches. He would still be awake trying to figure out how I'd beaten him and would wake me up just to annoy me. Finally, I got so frustrated, I stopped sleeping in our room. I came back when I'd learned how to do it too.

It didn't take long.

Llowellyn, I thought again.

Wow, Llowellyn thought back. Didn't miss that.

I smiled.

"If the party gets bigger," Jenner said. "We move to the bat cave."

"Bat cave?" Zemila asked.

"Living room," Jenner explained. "Where we do our best

superheroing."

Give me a minute, Llowellyn sent to me.

"He's awake," I said. "Let's relocate while he's getting dressed."

After Llowellyn joined us in the living room, Zemila took us through the file.

"You two would be a better judge than I," she said, nodding at me and my brother. "But I think if it was any of these, it would be one of these four."

She pulled up the images of the Holy Lance found in Turkey, the Holy Lance in Rome, the Clacton, and the Vel.

"But I have no way to narrow them down. Do you?"

"It's not the Vel." I said. "The Vel is metal. Lugh's spear was wood, all wood, or mostly wood, wasn't it?"

"I think it was wood," Llowellyn said. "Didn't it have a metal head? Lugh never told me where he got it."

Jenner got rid of the profile of the Vel.

"I assumed he made it," Zemila said. "Lugh, Master of Arts and all."

"You would think that, wouldn't you?" Llowellyn said dryly.

I snorted.

"What?" Zemila asked.

"We all had our skills," I explained. "Llowellyn, here, was the blacksmith in the family. If the weapon was made by one of us, it would have been him." I nodded at my brother. "It worked better if the people thought Lugh was doing everything and we didn't exist."

"Well, that sucks," Jenner said.

"It kept us alive," Llowellyn responded. "Didn't it, Lochlan . . . Lochlan?"

I was staring at the profile.

"You will be found with the Virtuous Collector," I whispered.

"¿Que?" Jenner asked.

"Can you pull this one up, Jen?" I asked, pointing at a side tab that wasn't opened.

I ran over the words of the Shannon in my mind.

"What do you see, Little One?" my brother asked.

"This is it," I pointed at the profile of the collector, Kennedy Virtue. "Zemila, why wasn't this one on your list?"

"I don't know," she said. "There wasn't much information on it. More history to the others and I thought—"

"You thought that," Jenner interrupted. "Because they are superhero gods, everything to do with them is impressive?" He paused. Zemila gave him a half shrug. "Well, I hate to burst your bubble, but sometimes they are just super boring."

She hid a laugh behind her hand.

"I think this is the one," I said.

"How do you know?" Jenner pulled up the image and profile of a simple wood spear with a metal head, and the profile of the owner. Kennedy Virtue.

"The Shannon," I said.

"The Virtuous Collector," Llowellyn and Zemila spoke at the same time.

"Of course," my brother said. "Kennedy Virtue. The Virtuous Collector."

"But this can't be the only collector in the world named Virtue," Jenner said. "What if the Shannon meant he was actually virtuous, not that his last name was Virtue? This could just be a coincidence."

"There is no such thing." My tone was dark.

"I'm not convinced," Jenner said.

"It is a bit of a stretch," Llowellyn agreed. "But worth looking into farther."

"No, no, Lochlan, you're right. I'm sure you are." Zemila stood and walked towards the profile filling the wall of my living room. "You will be found with the Virtuous Collector."

She pointed to a particular line in the profile.

"This spear is made from taxus baccata," she said.

We looked at her blankly.

Was that supposed to mean something? I thought. Then it clicked.

"What's the common word for taxus baccata?" I asked.

"How the hell would I know that?" Jenner said.

But Zemila knew, and answered.

"Yew."

CHAPTER TWENTY-SEVEN
Zemila

For a little while, Zemila forgot how messy and overwhelming her life had become. Sitting there with Lochlan, Llowellyn, and Jenner had made the rest of the world melt away. She felt accomplished and proud that she'd figured out the Shannon's riddle.

Well, one riddle, she told herself.

Zemila had no idea what that dream had meant, who Viviane or Nineve were, or why the Shannon was directly communicating with her. But that was for another day.

"Paleolithic!" Jenner said. He'd hacked into Kennedy Virtue's home system. It turned out the collector had run a multitude of tests on the spear. One dated it to the Paleolithic era. "You're that old?"

Lochlan looked over at his brother, who shrugged at him.

"Unlikely," Llowellyn said.

"Dios, you don't remember either!"

"It was a long time ago," Llowellyn sounded defensive. "But I would put us at late Neolithic Age, not Paleolithic . . . I don't remember an Ice Age, do you?"

"Mayhap it was while we were away," Lochlan replied.

"Away where?" Jenner asked. "Where were you that you missed the Ice Age?" Then his eyes went wide as he realized what he was saying. "Dios mio," he crossed himself. "Where were you that you missed the Ice Age?"

"Time moves differently there too," Llowellyn said, half-ignoring Jenner's question. "That's part of why it's hard to know how old we are."

"Where?" Jenner asked again.

"Jen," Zemila said, changing the subject. "It's just a piece that's Paleolithic." She pointed at the screen. "See there? There is a piece of stone in the head. Why would he have done that?"

"There is power in age," Lochlan said. "Wisdom and strength. Using something old would have given the spear more power?"

He looked at Llowellyn for confirmation.

"It's possible," Llowellyn said.

The spear was kept in Kennedy Virtue's private collection. There were no records of how he'd acquired it. Jenner was able to find proof of sale in the mid-1970s, but it wasn't to Virtue.

"How do we get it?" Llowellyn asked.

"It belongs to us," Lochlan said. "We take it back."

"Somehow, I don't think Virtue believes it's ours."

"You could make a copy?" Jenner suggested to Llowellyn. "Swap it out."

"Could you do that?" Zemila asked.

"Perhaps," Llowellyn responded.

"Where is the spear?" Zemila turned to Jenner.

"It would be too easy if Virtue was in the city," Lochlan said, almost hopefully.

"It would," Jenner said. "He lives in Austria."

Llowellyn swore.

"That's okay," Lochlan said. "We know where it is."

"Aye," Llowellyn agreed. "We know where it is. That's not nothing."

An alert popped up in the top right corner of Jenner's projection.

"Where is the burner watch?" Jenner asked. The mood in the room immediately shifted.

"It's in the kitchen," Lochlan answered.

"Go get it," Jenner ordered. "You're about to get a call."

"Tonight." The voice echoed through the room. Lochlan had put the call on speaker. "9:30 p.m., for a meeting to discuss the terms of your friend's release."

"How's Qillian?" Lochlan asked.

Qillian, Zemila thought. The image of the man who had warned her about a mole in Queen Anne's operation came to her.

"He's surviving, no thanks to you," said the voice.

"No thanks to you, you mean," Lochlan muttered.

"What did you say to me?" the voice questioned.

"Nothing, Frank," Lochlan yawned. "See you tonight."

"Bring your stupid brother," he said.

"Stupid?" Llowellyn questioned, mock pain in his eyes. "That really hurts." The line went dead.

This could all be over soon, Zemila thought.

Who knows what would happen tonight, what Queen Anne would want, but Zemila had faith Lochlan would get her brother back.

"Do you think you'll be going out on a mission tonight?" Jenner asked, bringing Zemila's attention back to the group.

"No," Lochlan said. "But I'll still try to get Nemo back." He looked over at Zemila. "I will do everything I can."

"I know you will."

"I need a nap," said Llowellyn. When Lochlan yawned, he said, "And so do you."

"I didn't sleep under a tree," Jenner looked at Lochlan. "Or stay up until two in the morning talking to a fire Gifter," he looked at Llowellyn.

Lochlan rolled his eyes. Zemila grinned. Llowellyn looked embarrassed.

"So, I'm going to keep working," Jenner said.

"When do I get to—" Lochlan started.

"Never," Llowellyn said, and he left the room.

"Get out of here, you two," Jenner said. "But remember the walls are thin."

"Tactless," Zemila shook her head.

"Will you stay with me?" Lochlan asked.

The apprehension in his eyes made Zemila's heart break.

Forever, she thought. I'll stay with you forever.

"I'm going to grab a couple files from my car," she told him. "Then I'll come up."

He nodded, still looking worried. It hurt her that he didn't believe how much she—but then, how could he believe it? How could he know? She'd never told him. She'd barely admitted it to herself.

That needed to change.

Lochlan stood, left the room, and headed upstairs. She watched him go.

"You need to tell him," Jenner said. "Also, I can't believe you carry paper files."

"Tell him what?" Zemila asked, tearing her gaze away from the spot where Lochlan had disappeared.

Jenner hit her with a look.

"It's not so easy."

"I never said it was easy," Jenner said. "Just that you need to tell him, because as much as that spell working told him how you feel, he doesn't believe it. Not really. You need to tell him."

"I will," she said, and headed out to her car.

By the time Zemila got up to Lochlan's room, he was curled on his side, his breath even and steady. She smiled and put her book bag down on the chair in the corner.

Kneeling down in front of him, she removed the glasses he didn't need and placed them on the bedside table.

Must just be habit now, she thought, running her fingers lightly through his hair.

"I want nothing more than to kiss you right now," she whispered.

She wasn't playing fair, but she couldn't help it. Bending low, she pressed her lips to the corner of his mouth. He sighed like a happy puppy, but didn't wake.

Zemila crawled into bed behind him and curled her body around his. He shifted, leaning into her. He moved his arm over hers where she'd laid it on his chest. She smiled as he snuggled into his place of little spoon. Her nose grazed the back of his neck.

"I love you, you know that," she whispered, too quiet for him to hear.

His body relaxed. So did hers. And it was seconds, not minutes, before she joined him in sleep.

CHAPTER TWENTY-EIGHT
Lochlan

"A guy could get used to this," I said, waking up from what might have been the best nap of my life. Zemila was sitting, typing on her old-school laptop. Early afternoon sun bounced off her screen.

"Get used to being woken up by the sound of a keyboard?" She smiled down at me. Her hair fell in loose curls around her face. She spared me only a glance before returning to her work.

"Waking up to you," I said.

"Take me to dinner first," she said in mock outrage.

"If I remember correctly," I told her, "you asked me out."

I looked around for my glasses. They were on the bedside table. She must have taken them off for me. I left them there.

"That's true," she said, still not looking at me.

"As soon as we get Nemo back," I said, taking her chin between my first finger and thumb, forcing her to pause in her furious typing. "I'm going to hold you to that."

Her hands stopped and her eyes met mine. She bit her bottom lip. Her eyes moved down to my mouth.

"Thin walls," she said.

I smiled and dropped my hand.

"Right," I answered.

In the back of my mind, I heard the echo of a cawing crow.

Cam came over for an early dinner. Jenner ordered in. The five of us slowly made our way through the grilled meat and fish as we watched the news. At the same time as Jenner cursed at a poorly wrapped pita that landed tzatziki in his lap, Cam cursed at the news station.

"And for the fourth time in as many years," the reporter said. "The Senate will vote on the Immigration Safety Act. Supporters hope the tragic death of Maggie Cartwrytte will spur a different result."

The shot changed to a gaunt-looking man standing in front of a podium. Behind him, with a woman who looked like his grandmother, was a ten-year-old boy.

"My wife was senselessly murdered by two criminal 2ndGens. Had this bill been passed, those men wouldn't have had the opportunity to take my Maggie away from me."

Zemila scoffed.

Cam swore. "They can't even make up their mind on what generation they are."

Jenner scrubbed at the tzatziki on his pants, muttering about yellow stars on armbands and in shop windows.

"Had they been registered and watched by local authorities, my son—" The man's voice broke. The child was pulled from the arms of the old woman. A man with sandy hair and bland features shoved him toward his father. The child stumbled forward.

I squinted at the screen.

The child hugged his father. The sandy-haired man stepped back and out of the frame.

"You've got to be kidding me," I said.

Everyone in the room turned away from the boy now awkwardly hugging his father and looked at me.

"What is it, Loch?" Cam asked.

"Jenner," I said. "Can we get a look at the man who pushed the child to his father?"

"Sí, amigo." His fingers flicked over his watch.

The image froze, rewound, and froze again. We were all looking at the profile of a man in a baseball cap. His face was angled down, but it didn't matter. I recognized him.

"The Proxy," Zemila said.

"It can't be him," Jenner shook his head. "He was so careful. Avoided all cameras. Why would he be careless now?"

"I don't know," I said.

"Is he making another Famorian?" Camile asked.

For the first time in a long time, I remembered she too had nearly been turned. The wave of self-loathing at my selfishness was pushed aside by her next words.

"The man or the boy?" she asked.

"Well, that's a terrifying thought," Jenner said.

"He wouldn't turn children," but Llowellyn didn't sound sure.

"Wouldn't he?" I asked.

I would, I thought. If the goal was to terrorize the masses, to rule by fear. Creating immortal demonic children who the public feared to hurt and feared to help? I wouldn't put it past him.

"It may not be him," Cam said. "And, even if it is, I know this sounds horrible and maybe a little selfish but . . . Nemo is more important than that kid and his dad, right? Nemo is—"

"The priority right now," Zemila finished. "And I don't care if that's selfish."

Zemila clasped Cam's hand reassuringly and the two women exchanged a look.

"I wish I was more help," Cam spoke softly. "I've barely been able to do anything for you."

"The information you got us on Heaven was invaluable." Zemila squeezed Cam's hand.

"It's the only reason I'm in their system," Jenner said.

"Stop lying." Cam glared at her brother. "You're just trying to make me feel better. I bet you hacked into their system before I even got you that information."

Llowellyn snorted.

"I will have you know," Jenner's tone was imperious. "I was not in before you gave me that information."

"But . . ." she asked.

"But you are right, I didn't need it to get in. It was helpful though, hermana menor, I promise."

"We'd better start getting ready," Llowellyn looked at his watch. "We don't want to be late."

I looked up at Zemila from my cross-legged position on the floor.

"Is there any way I can—"

"No," she cut me off. "I'm coming with you. No discussion."

"Aye," I said. "It was worth a shot."

φ

When a pair of guards met us at the entrance to Heaven, Zemila seemed to shrink in on herself. She kept sneaking furtive glances at one of the guards. I tried to catch her eye, but she avoided my gaze.

Mayhap he was the man she'd almost killed, I thought, as we were guided through the casino.

Inanna was standing when we entered her office. Her expression was grave. Dark circles sagged under her eyes.

"Inanna," Llowellyn said. There was a concern in his voice I didn't share. "What's happened?"

She sighed deeply and waved us further into the small office. "Come in. Can I get any of you anything?"

"My brother," Zemila said.

Inanna rolled her eyes. "George, Otto, wait outside please?"

The two men left.

"How's Qillian?" I asked.

"What is it with you and this kid?" She squinted at me.

"What's it to you?" I responded.

"He's a good kid," Llowellyn said. "Respectful, seems like a hard worker."

"He is," Inanna confirmed.

"How did he end up here?" I asked.

"How did you?" she countered. "How does anyone end up here?" I understood her to mean here, metaphorically, not here at Heaven. "Life," she went on. "It screws us all and we do the best we can with what we have. Life takes and takes and takes and when we have nothing left to give, when we are at the end of our rope, we end up here. And we do the best we can. Don't judge him for that."

"What happened?" Llowellyn asked again. He stepped forward and took one of Inanna's small hands in both of his. "Inanna. I see you are troubled. Let us be allies once more. Let us help one another as we did so many years ago."

Inanna looked up at the ceiling and shook her head as if to curse the gods.

"All right," she gave in. "All right."

Zemila stepped forward and opened her mouth. No doubt to ask that if we were allies, could she kindly have her brother back. I stopped her advance with a hand on her wrist. She looked at me accusingly, but this was the moment for patience.

Llowellyn, an empath, was better equipped to manage Inanna than either of us. I didn't know if Zemila understood that, but she stepped back. My shoulders sagged in relief when she took my hand in hers.

"I have been betrayed," Inanna stated. "Someone in my home has been feeding me false information. Someone has been working for outside forces. My buildings are being burned, Candle is flooding my casino, and my people are dying. I cannot protect my people." She looked up at Llowellyn. A tear slid down her face. "What kind of Queen cannot protect her own people?"

She gasped and shook loose Llowellyn's hand.

"Urgh!" she screamed. "Don't pull that empathic hoopla with me, Balorson." She threw the last word at Llowellyn like the insult it was. "Don't think you know me. Don't think this means anything."

"No more of this, Inanna," Llowellyn said calmly. "You know us, you know me. You know I am as true to my word as you are to yours. We are allies here. Let us help each other."

"Help each other?" She spat.

"Yes," he said. "Help each other."

"I need help finding a leak in my organization and you need help conquering the most powerful Demon King to plague this earth. Doesn't seem like a fair trade to me."

Zemila and I watched the argument, our heads turning from one to the other.

"You know very well how bad things can get. A leak is never just a leak. Like water, the damage is always worse than what you see."

"Worse?" She threw her hands in the air and stalked back around her desk. "I'm not sure how things could get much worse."

A deep boom answered her challenge.

"What the—" Zemila said, dropping my hand and turning to face the wall.

Another boom sounded, this one was closer. Behind us, the door crashed open. The two guards, Otto and George, burst in.

"My Quee—" His words were cut off.

The bookshelf seemed to explode. My feet left the ground. Zemila's body was thrown through the air.

And Heaven started to fall.

CHAPTER TWENTY-NINE
Lochlan

Zemila seemed to turn in slow motion. She looked from me to the wall of plaster, wood, and metal bars flying towards us. Throwing up her hands in the direction of the explosion, she landed on me. Hard.

My ears rang, my eyes cleared, and some twelve inches above our heads, Zemila held steady pieces of the wall, books, and debris with her gift.

"Thanks," I said.

The sounds of the world returned. Alarms screamed. Guards cursed. Zemila stood and tossed the debris through the hole the explosion had made.

"No problem," she gasped and pulled me to my feet. "What the hell was that?"

"I don't know." I looked around the once-tidy office. The disarray of smouldering books and broken furniture made it unrecognizable.

Llow, where are you? I thought.

"Here," said a voice from under a pile of rubble and singed pages.

"Let me," Zemila said, raising her hands and sending the rubble soaring through the hole in the wall.

When had she gotten a handle on her gift like this? I thought, looking at her in amazement.

Llowellyn stood. He'd tried to use his body to shield Inanna. It had half-worked. She didn't look hurt, but she was out cold.

"Can you wake her up?" Zemila asked, just as we heard a groan from under another pile of rubble.

"I can try," I said.

"I'll help," Llowellyn said. He lifted her and moved her onto a bare bit of ground. We bent over Inanna's limp form, and Zemila went to work freeing the security guards from a collapsed beam.

Inanna woke with a start.

"Ruiz," she said, after looking around. I helped her to her feet. "This is the Ruiz cartel."

"My Queen," said one of the guards, trying to get to her. He was limping badly.

Zemila helped the other one—George, I thought—to his feet.

"Otto, stop. You'll hurt yourself even more," Inanna said. She turned to me. "Can you heal him?"

"Yes," I said. "But healing is not a natural gift. It will drain me."

"I'm okay for now," Otto said. "We need to get you out of here."

"How did this happen?" Llowellyn asked. "How did they get in?"

"Shhh," Zemila raised a hand to quiet him. "I think I hear footsteps coming."

Llowellyn tilted his head.

"Mór-amharc," he said. He waited a moment for the spell to come back to him. "At least ten coming here, more than that upstairs. This wasn't the only blast."

"Bastards," Inanna swore.

Zemila walked through the hole in the wall and looked up and down the hallway on the other side.

"Which way are they coming from?" she asked Llowellyn.

"The right," he said.

"Can I get to Nemo going left? Can we get out that way?"

"Yes," Inanna nodded.

With her back to us, Zemila took in a deep breath and raised her hands. The rubble, broken furniture, books, and bookshelves lifted off the ground. With a smooth motion, Zemila created a barricade, blocking the tunnel we'd just come down.

"I'll be goddamned," George said.

I ducked as a chair flew over my shoulder.

"Not bad," Inanna walked over the now-cleared floor to Zemila's side.

"It's the adrenaline, I think," Zemila said. "I don't know how long this control will last."

Inanna nodded, then said something in a version of Sumerian few spoke. A shimmering gold light covered the barricade, then vanished. "Just a little something extra," she explained. "We should move."

The five of us started down the hallway, alarms blaring. Zemila moved to my side and took my hand. Inanna quietly spoke to George.

"We're okay," I whispered to her. The fear in her eyes said she didn't believe me. But there was determination there too.

"We were supposed to have so much time," Zemila squeezed my hand.

"And we will," I told her.

When we came to the next place, the hallway split. George sprinted

300

off in one direction, and Inanna led us down another.

"What the hell is going on?" Zemila's voice was stronger than it had been a moment ago.

"I don't know," Inanna replied.

I scoffed "Since when does the Queen of Heaven not have control over her house?"

"Since now." Inanna stopped at the next junction in the hallway. "I told you there was a leak."

"Qillian warned me," Zemila said. "The day he drove me to work. He told me there was a problem."

"This is a bit more than a leak, Inanna," Llowellyn said.

"You don't think I know that?" she shot back at him. "There was an overdose six months ago. Since then I've been on alert and have—"

Another explosion rocked the ground we stood on. Otto fell with a cry of pain. Llowellyn took off his shirt and tore it into strips. Finding a suitable piece of wood from a broken chair nearby, he started to splint Otto's leg.

"We have to get Nemo," Zemila said. "Will your people lead him out?"

"I don't know," Inanna admitted with a truthfulness I didn't expect. "I don't know who's with him or what they'll do if they aren't one of mine."

Zemila looked at me. "We have to get him."

"We will."

"We have to get out of here," she said.

I wiped a line of blood from her forehead with my thumb. She'd been hit with something. She winced at my touch. Did she have more wounds I didn't see? Was she putting on a brave face like Otto had been?

Otto groaned in pain behind us.

"Almost done," Llowellyn said, tightening a strap.

I ran my hands over Zemila's shoulders and back, looking for wounds. She stopped me, with a hand on my cheek.

"We should have had more time." She looked up into my eyes. I felt heat rise in my chest. My breaths grew shorter. "We should have gotten here a long time ago."

Even in this chaos, my heart skipped at her touch. I knew she wasn't talking about Heaven. She wasn't talking about the mess we were in, here and now. She was talking about us. She was right.

"I shouldn't have left," I tucked a strand of hair behind her ear.

"I shouldn't have waited." She dropped her gaze. "God, what if we got lucky last time? How are we all going to get—"

"Don't talk like that," I said. Her eyes bore into mine. I tried to convey my truth in a look. "We'll all survive this. I'm not going anywhere."

I'm not running anymore. I'm right here, I wanted to tell her. I'm here facing whatever comes at us. I tried to say it aloud but the words got stuck. I wanted her to know I'd fight for this. For us. For the people we loved.

"I—" I started.

"I know," she said, and she pressed her lips against mine.

It was soft at first, chaste even. Then the kiss deepened as she parted my lips with her tongue.

Was it the building that shook or my very soul as I tangled a hand in her hair? The feeling of her mouth on mine lit my whole being with sensation. She pressed her body against me, every curve of her fitting perfectly.

A soft moan escaped her lips. My world brightened. Ecstasy. Electricity. That same heat I'd felt before, radiated through me. Could she feel it too?

One of her hands went to the back of my neck, the other to my waist. She pulled me closer. The world glowed gold. I breathed her in. I memorized her scent, her taste, every detail of her mouth, every curve of her body.

The building shook.

We broke apart.

Breathing heavily, my eyes roved over her face. I didn't want to let her go.

I ran my thumb over her forehead. My brows knit together. It happened again. Her wounds had healed.

"What the—" Otto looked down at his splinted leg. He shifted his weight from one side to the other. Pulling a switch blade from his pocket, Otto cut the straps holding the splint.

"What the hell was that?" he looked between us, his Queen, and his healed leg.

"I'll explain it later," Inanna said, looking just as shocked as Otto.

"Ummm, okay," he said. Then he looked at Zemila. "We're even now, in case you decided you wanted to make eye contact with me."

"I'm sorry," she looked at him. "I didn't mean—"

"Queen Anne explained it was instinctual. That's good. Hopefully those instincts will get us out of here."

"We'll get out of here," I told Zemila, only half-following the exchange.

"Up the stairs to the left," Inanna instructed. "There is a staircase that will get you onto the casino floor. Can you find Nemo from there?"

Zemila nodded then looked at me.

"Come with me." She gave my hand a small tug.

"Of course," I said. "Llowellyn, let's—"

Llowellyn jerked strangely and clutched his leg.

"Llow!" I yelled, realizing what was happening a moment too late. I pulled Zemila to me and turned my back to the hailstorm of bullets headed toward us.

Zemila screamed. My body jerked against hers. Pain erupted in my back. My whole body seemed to scream with it. Inanna turned and threw up her arms. The same shimmering gold light that had secured Zemila's barricade now protected us from the four shooters who'd just turned the corner at the other end of the hall.

I groaned in pain, releasing Zemila and almost collapsing. She caught me, half-dragged me to the nearest wall.

"You okay?" I said. It hurt to breathe.

"You pull that hero garbage with me again and I'll kill you myself." Zemila examined my chest and back. She gave the shimmering wall a nervous look. "We aren't safe here. How long will that hold?"

"We need to leave." Inanna's voice was cold. "Now."

"There will be more of them soon," Otto said. "These halls are all interconnected. We have to beat them to the exit."

Another explosion sounded in the distance and the building shook again.

"Heaven is falling," Inanna said in a mournful voice.

"My Queen." Otto took her hand then took a knee in front of her. "We will rebuild. We will take our revenge. But now, we must leave."

"Yes," the usual fierceness back in her eyes.

"Nemo," Zemila looked between me and Inanna.

"I would only slow you down," I said. I tried to hide how much I hurt. I tasted blood. One of the bullets had punctured a lung.

"I need you," she said.

"You don't," I tried to give her a smile.

"There is an office three doors down the hall," Inanna said. "Go in there, heal. I will take your little Luman girl to get her brother. I will get them out."

I didn't trust Inanna.

"She needs allies. Right now, so do you, Little One," Llowellyn said.

"But can't we just—" Zemila started, looking over at Inanna.

"Make out and heal him?" Llowellyn cut in.

I tried to laugh. It turned into a cough. Before I knew it, I was spitting up blood. I slid down the wall, my legs too weak to hold me.

"Oh God," Zemila knelt in front of me, linking her fingers with mine and pulling the back of my hand to her lips. "Come on," she pressed her lips to mine. They came away red with blood. "Come on, come on."

She kissed the back of my hand and pressed it to her forehead. Rocking back and forth, she cursed under her breath. Blackness crowded the edges of my vision and pain ricocheted through me with every movement.

"Why isn't this working?!" she yelled at Inanna. "We were just holding each other the first time—this should be working!"

I tried to breathe. I coughed up more blood. I was too weak to move. Too weak to wipe it away as blood trickled out of my mouth.

"I hear footsteps," Llowellyn tilted his head. "They're closing in."

"Come on, come on," Zemila pressed her lips to mine again and again. "Please, please, please," she said, squeezing her eyes shut. She brought my forehead to hers, still rocking back and forth. When nothing happened, she let out a scream of frustration.

"It's not reliable Magic when it's new," Inanna said. "And we don't have the time."

"She's right," I managed to say, pushing Zemila away. She had my blood on her lips. I lifted my hand to wipe it away. "Bullets can't kill me. Go get Nemo. I'll see you soon."

"Zemila," Llowellyn pulled her off me and threw her in the direction of Inanna and Otto. They were already halfway down the hall. "Go now. I've got him."

My brother lifted me off the ground. Zemila was backing away, her eyes full of tears.

"We've got time," I said to her over Llowellyn's shoulder. I didn't know if she heard me. "We've got time," I repeated as loud as I could.

She turned away and ran off to save her brother.

After kicking down the door and barricading it with a desk, a couple chairs and a shelf, Llowellyn came over to where he'd left me in an armchair.

"This . . . sucks . . ." My breathing was laboured. I spat blood.

"We can heal you," he said. "I have enough Magic for that. Then we get out of here."

I nodded.

"I hope I've enough," he muttered, so quietly I didn't think he meant me to hear.

He squatted down, his big shoulders filling my darkening vision. I extended my arm. It felt like it weighed two hundred pounds. He grasped my wrist, and I his. Behind him I saw the door shake.

Someone was trying to get in.

"Aire cagair-gada," Llowellyn started to chant. "Beannachd nartha."

I tried to join in.

"Aire cagair-gada," we said together. "Beannachd nartha."

Llowellyn broke off and looked over his shoulder at the door. It took another loud hit. It would come down soon.

He knew it. I knew it. I needed to be healed when it did.

"You can do this," I said through the blood, hoping against hope his Magic would surge under pressure. That, like Zemila, the adrenaline would focus him. "Aire cagair-gada," I stammered.

We chanted.

The door shook.

My wounds did not heal.

I could feel the bullets slowly moving out of my body, but it wasn't enough. That was my Magic alone. And, right now, it was weak.

The door opened an inch. Whoever was on the other side threw their weight against the pile of office furniture.

"Curse you, Danu and the gods below," Llowellyn growled, defeated. His Magic refused to come to his call.

The door was two inches open now.

"I am sorry, Little One," Llowellyn said, tears of frustration in his eyes. "I cannot. I don't have—"

"It's okay." My vision had cleared slightly, but my body still ached.

Three inches open.

I was surprised no one had pointed a gun in and started shooting.

"We have survived worse than this," I said. "Help me stand. I can fight. Stronger together?"

With our linked hands, Llowellyn pulled me to my feet.

"Not alone," he said.

With those words, Magic surged through his body. I heard the roar of triumph in his mind. But at that moment, the door burst open.

CHAPTER THIRTY
Zemila

Zemila sprinted off after Otto and Queen Anne, her mind still on Lochlan. She wanted to heal him as Otto had been healed. But she knew there was no chance for that now. Nemo had to be her priority. Llowellyn could take care of Lochlan . . . she hoped.

Up flights of stairs and down damaged hallways, around corners and over collapsed walls, Zemila ran. Otto took the lead, easily dispatching three men on the casino floor. The Queen threw up a glistening gold shield to protect them from the shooters in the balconies as they crossed through the gaming tables and slot machines.

Zemila did her best to use the rubble as projectiles. She was only able to take down one of the two shooters before they passed into the safety of the stairwell that joined the casino to the hotel.

"Not far now," Queen Anne said, passing the twenty-fourth floor.

Zemila's hands were shaking. Her legs were screaming. Finally, Otto and Queen Anne stopped. Otto pressed his ear to the door, then opened it a crack and peered through.

Whatever he saw had him sprinting into action.

Queen Anne called for him to wait, but he was gone.

Zemila followed the Queen through the door. The hotel hallway was destroyed. There was a hole in one wall that looked like someone had been thrown out of their room. Broken shards of a decorative vase mingled with pieces of the large mirror on the floor. At the end of the hall, Nemo was fighting against three men, alongside a man with a short crewcut and a hard, military expression.

Frank, Zemila thought.

She watched the two fight. Otto rushed in to join them.

"On your left!" Otto yelled.

Nemo ducked. Frank hit the oncomer with a round-house kick over Nemo's hunched form. Nemo reached for the splintered pottery and glass. Directing them with his gift, he threw the barrage of shrapnel at his attacker.

Otto slammed one of the intruders to the ground. It was three-on-three, now. Zemila and Anne approached slowly, not knowing how to help. With Otto, the fight ended quickly.

The attackers lay face down on the ground, one on top of Frank. Nemo kicked the limp form off of him and helped Frank to his feet.

"Thanks," Frank told him. "You're all right for a freak, you know that."

Nemo smiled. "I guess you're all right for a prick."

"Hey!" Queen Anne said. "I'm a freak."

Frank's demeanour immediately changed. He stood straighter, then inclined his head to her.

"I meant no offence, my Queen," he said.

"You fought well together," she said, by way of accepting his unspoken apology.

"Never fought alongside a Gifter before," he said. "I saw the video footage of you," he gestured to Zemila, "but . . ."

"It's different when you have a common enemy," Zemila said.

"Yes," Frank nodded.

He knelt down, turned over one of the bodies and emptied the man's pockets. Otto did the same to the other two. Zemila weaved around the debris and bodies.

"I was so worried," she buried her face in Nemo's chest when she got to him. "I thought I might never see you again."

He kissed the top of her head, wrapping her in a tight hug.

"Can't get rid of me that easy," he said. "Where's Lochlan?"

Zemila looked up at him. She could feel tears stinging her eyes.

"We had to leave Lochlan behind."

Nemo's face went pale.

"He's not—"

"No," Zemila said. "And he's with his brother, Llowellyn. He was shot and needed to heal." She stepped back from Nemo. Now that he was safe, panic for Lochlan flared in her chest. "He said he would slow us down. He made us leave. Made me leave."

Her breathing picked up, and she started to cry. It all became too real. The explosion, the fight, the many times her life had been in danger in the past three months.

It all hit her.

"I shouldn't have left him." She tried and failed to stop the tears rolling down her face. "He needed help, protection. He would have never left me. I abandoned him."

"No," Nemo said.

"I abandoned him!" she nearly screamed.

"No," Queen Anne echoed, and there was a push to her words, truth Zemila hadn't heard when Nemo had said it. There was a strength that made Zemila look up, take a breath. In that moment, Zemila understood why they bowed down before this woman.

This Queen.

This goddess.

"It was the right thing to do. He's resilient. He and that brother of his. You forget, I've known them a lot longer than you have and I've tried to kill him a fair number of times. Lochlan will be fine."

"Ruiz cartel," Otto said, looking at a tattoo on one of the man's forearms.

"I thought as much," Queen Anne nodded. "Well, let's get out of here before—"

Zemila saw it happen in slow motion. Two men with machine guns sprinted through the stairwell door.

No, she thought, remembering the feel of Lochlan's body jerking in her arms.

NO! she yelled in her mind as Nemo spun his body around to protect hers.

Frank and Otto were moving to protect the Queen as she raised her hands to throw up another shield. But the guns weren't pointed at Queen Anne.

They're pointed at me, Zemila thought. Why are they pointed at me?

Otto raised a gun he'd stripped off one of the bodies. He fired at their attackers. His aim was true. But late.

Zemila, protected by Nemo's body, heard rather than saw a burst from one of the machine guns. Otto fired once, twice, and it was over.

"NO!" Nemo yelled, releasing Zemila and flinging himself to the ground.

Frank had thrown himself between the spray of bullets and Nemo.

"No," Nemo felt for a pulse and tried to stop the bleeding.

One of the bullets had gone through his neck. Another through his chest. He wasn't moving.

"Frank," Queen Anne said. She knelt over her fallen soldier, placing her hand on his forehead. "Frank." A tear rolled down her cheek and landed on his face. "Go in peace." She kissed his forehead.

When she rose, her voice was stern.

"We need to leave."

Zemila's heart sank when she saw her crushed hatchback. Sirens rang out in the distance. Help was always slow to come to Lowtown.

"Ida," she whispered. The once brightly lit "V" of "Heaven" now flattened the front half of her car. It must have been thrown off the building in one of the blasts.

Zemila quickly grabbed a few things from her trunk as the sirens grew louder. They all piled into a surviving SUV as quickly as possible. Queen Anne had no interest in being caught up in emergency services.

She also refused to wait for Lochlan.

"He could already be gone," she said.

He would have waited for me, Zemila thought. He would have waited for Nemo.

"He could be at the house," Nemo said. It looked like he didn't believe his own words. Queen Anne didn't give them an option. They left.

Thirty minutes later, they pulled up in front of Lochlan's house. Zemila's desire for a cigarette and her own bed was overridden by the hope she'd see Lochlan.

There was a light on in the living room, but the second floor was dark. Her heart sank.

He didn't have a car, she told herself. He had to find his way out, away from the Ruiz cartel, then a way to get back here.

She barely contained her panic as she scanned her palm and knocked on the door. Nemo was a calming presence behind her, his arm around her shoulders as they waited.

The door flew open. Cam stood in the light now flooding the porch.

"You're back," she said to Zemila. "You're safe," she said to Nemo.

There was a moment of indecision where it looked like Cam was trying to decide who she wanted to hug first. Zemila jerked her head towards her brother in a "go for it" gesture, and Cam launched herself into Nemo's arms.

Zemila walked inside.

"Do you have anything?" Zemila asked, correctly interpreting why Jenner hadn't left the living room.

"I can't find them anywhere," he said. "I was following the three of you, waiting to open a line. Then the first blast hit. Heaven's systems went down. I can't hack a system that isn't there. What happened?" He stopped the frantic motion of his fingers and turned to her.

She sighed, sat down, and started to talk. Part way through, Nemo and Cam joined them. Nemo was able to fill in parts Zemila didn't know.

He told them he'd overheard a few guards talking about a mole in Heaven. How there were only a few that were trusted. Qillian, Otto, George, and a couple other names Zemila didn't know.

"They suspected Frank," Nemo said sadly. "I guess he proved them wrong tonight. He was spectacular. There were a few cartel guys roughing me up, asking me questions about Lochlan, about you." He nodded at Zemila.

"Why?" Zemila asked. "Why me?"

"No idea," Nemo shrugged. "Frank snuck into the room, so quiet. God, he could have been a Gifter. He snuck up on one guy and took him down almost before the other two noticed he was there. He got up so quick, and threw another one through the wall. Dove through the hole the guy made in the wall after him. Wasn't long after that, a couple more guys showed up, then you."

"You two fought well together," Zemila said.

"He fought well. I barely did anything. I owe him my life . . . twice."

Zemila didn't know what she would've done if her brother had died tonight. She owed Frank too. A debt neither of them could ever repay.

"Then what happened?" Jenner asked.

Nemo kept talking. Zemila wasn't paying attention. She was too worried about Lochlan. Jenner had a program searching security cams and home systems around the city, but no hits yet.

"I'm going to go lie down," she said. Everyone looked up at her. She stood. "Wake me up the second Lochlan's back."

"Of course," said Nemo.

"I'm sure he'll be here soon," Cam reassured her.

"Yeah," Zemila nodded, slowly making her way out of the room. "Yeah."

She went up the creaky stairs and into Lochlan's room. She curled up in his bed. His scent was stronger in his pillow now. He'd been there just a few hours ago.

He'll be here soon, she told herself. We're supposed to have so much time. He'll be here.

She shoved the worry she felt to the back of her mind and went to sleep.

Early morning sun woke her. It took a moment for Zemila to remember why she felt so tense. She half-rolled over, but hit something on the way. Hit someone.

"A guy could get used to this," Lochlan said. "Waking up to you."

"Take me to dinner first," she said, relief spreading through her body. She rolled over to look at him.

"If I remember correctly," he brushed a lock of hair out of her face and behind her ear. "You asked me out."

"That's true," she leaned in close. "But we've got—"

CAW! CAW!

Zemila and Lochlan both whipped around. A crow was flying repeatedly into the window.

"Oh my God," said Zemila.

The bird scratched and pecked at the glass.

"What's wrong with it?" Zemila asked, eyes transfixed on the frantic bird.

"I would only slow you down."

"What?" Zemila turned. "Oh God!"

Lochlan's white sheets were stained red with blood. He clutched the bullet wounds in his chest.

"No, no, no," she cried. "Not again, I need you."

"You don't," he told her with a feeble smile.

The crow cawed louder.

Lochlan went still.

And Zemila woke up to the sound of breaking glass.

It was still dark out. There was a commotion downstairs.

"It should have been me!" Nemo shouted. "We can't just keep trading lives! How could you let this happen?!"

Zemila threw off the covers and raced down the stairs. Nemo had Llowellyn pinned to the wall in the front vestibule. The hall mirror lay broken at their feet. Llowellyn, twice as wide as Nemo and a demigod, would never lose the upper hand.

Not unless he wanted to.

"Nemo?" Zemila said, cautiously.

Llowellyn looked broken, defeated. Jenner and Cam watched, stunned, from the living room doorway. Nemo swung his fist high, bringing it down on Llowellyn's face.

"Nemo!" Zemila cried and rushed forward.

"It should have been me!" Nemo screamed, hitting Llowellyn again and again. "It should have been me!"

"Nemo, stop it!" She tried to pull her brother off. It was no use. Jenner grabbed her arm and dragged her back.

Nemo's blows grew weak. Tears splashed down his face.

"It should have been me," he sobbed, collapsing. Llowellyn caught him before he hit the ground. "I'm sorry," Nemo cried, clutching the demigod. "I'm so sorry."

"As am I," Llowellyn said in his soft deep voice.

"What happened?" Zemila asked.

"They took him," Jenner said.

Zemila gripped his arm as the world spun around her. She must have started to fall because he steadied her before speaking again.

"The Ruiz cartel took Lochlan."

CHAPTER THIRTY-ONE
Lochlan

I looked up through bleary eyes. My hands were chained to the wall above my head.

So medieval, I thought.

I tried to move. Pain shot through my body and everything came rushing back. Heaven. Nemo. The explosion. Zemila.

I was shot, I remembered, looking down at my bloody shirt. Llowellyn tried and failed to heal me. We'd both failed.

I made the mistake of shifting again, and blacked out from the pain.

When I woke up again, I surveyed my body in the darkness. I mentally went over my injuries.

It's still dark, I thought. Or is it dark again?

I had no idea how long I'd been out.

My hands were numb. That wasn't a surprise. They were chained over my head. I scrunched my forehead. A scab cracked and started to bleed.

A scab? I thought. How long have I been here?

That's when I realized how hungry I was.

My left shoulder was dislocated. I thought my right arm might be broken. I called Magic to me, to break my restraints, but I had no strength. I took in a deep breath to try again, but that only revealed more injuries. The bullet wounds in my chest were only partially healed.

I heard the sliding sound of metal on metal. A small rectangular beam of light came into the room.

"I'm impressed," said a vaguely familiar voice.

I needed to focus on calling Magic. I ignored the voice I couldn't place and pulled Magic into my core. Coiled power settled in my gut. I tried to break the chains holding me, but the power dissipated. It moved to my wounds. I tried again. Focusing on the chains this time.

Nothing.

"I didn't think you would be able to hold him," the familiar voice said.

"It's simple," said another voice. This one I didn't recognize at all. "He can't cast if he's half-dead. His Magic is keeping him alive. He can't do anything. We just have to keep him injured. If we do that, he can't spell us or cast his way out. Nothing."

"Well," said the first voice as the door swung open. I squinted against the light flooding in. "Let's see if I can't help keep him here a while longer."

And the Proxy stepped into the room.

φ

Zemila was with me, that's how I knew I was dreaming. She was always with me when I was dreaming. She kept the pain at bay. It hurt less here. It hurt more when I was awake. But for now, with her. I would lie here. I would lie here knowing it was a dream and hoping it lasted forever.

It never did.

Cold water splashed on my face woke me. She was gone, and I was alone in the room again. But I wasn't alone. Someone had thrown the water.

Was it the Proxy? Was he here to question me again?

"Where is the Shannon?" he demanded.

"I don't find her," I said for the thousandth time. "She finds me."

He broke my arm at the wrist.

I screamed.

"Where is the spear?" he asked.

"I don't know," I said. "We were looking for it too."

He stepped on my newly broken arm.

I screamed again.

I didn't used to scream. I knew he liked it. I didn't want to give him the satisfaction. But many weeks had passed since then, and my strength was failing me.

Starved, beaten, bloody. Pain was the only thing that told me I was alive.

Or mayhap this is the afterlife and I am paying for my sins, I thought.

"Where is the sword?" he asked.

On and on it went. Sometimes it was the Proxy. Sometimes it was someone from the cartel.

He was worse.

He knew how to hurt people, and he liked it. He knew what to say to make me question my mind. To make me feel like I was going insane.

He stepped on my arm again. Harder this time.

Blackness took me.

Zemila was there. The pain lessened. I sagged in relief. She was always with me when I was dreaming.

"Oh God, oh God, oh God."

I couldn't see her. I never could. But I felt her. I felt her warm body beside me. I felt her hands in my hair, and her lips on my skin.

These dreams. These dreams are the only reason he hasn't broken me, I thought.

"There is no god but God. There is no god but God. There is no god but God."

No, I thought. No, go away.

"There is no god but God. There is no god but God."

No, I thought as she slipped away from me. No not yet, don't go. Don't leave me.

"There is no god but God. There is no god but God."

What is that chanting? I thought. Why am I hearing that? Why is it taking my pain away?

And it was taking my pain away.

As Zemila slipped from my fingers, I felt my other hand tangle in the chant, in the prayer. It was a lifeline. It was power.

"There is no god but God. There is no god but God—

أشهد أن لا إله إلاّ الله و أشهد أن محمد رسول الله

—oh God, oh God, oh God."

I was back in the room. The room where they hurt me. But I didn't hurt, not as much. And it was this voice that was doing it.

This prayer.

A man was chanting. He was pouring his Spark into the words. Powering the prayer with his lifeforce. With his Spark.

"Though our followers may be gone," I heard Queen Anne's voice echo in my memory, "all those who step into my house, who seek riches here, love here, desire here, all those prayers come to me."

I was stealing this praise from the God it was intended to. I was healing myself with that power. I didn't mean to. I didn't know why it happened. But it felt good.

I could take it, I thought as I held tighter, weaved my mental Magic bonds deeper into the rhythmic chanting.

If I kept pulling, I could heal myself. If I kept pulling, I could free myself.

But, no, my body was too broken for that. I would never be able to heal myself with only the Spark put into prayer.

If you ate his Spark, a voice in the back of my mind said. If you ate it, you would be strong enough to heal yourself. To escape. To get back to Zemila.

Yes, I thought and gripped tighter still to the invisible bonds in the darkness. The bonds that tied the words to the Spark, the Spark to the soul, the soul to the life.

"There is no god but God. There is no god but God—

أشهد أن لا إله إلاّ الله و أشهد أن محمد رسول الله

—Oh God, oh God, oh God."

Eat it, the voice said. And you will be with her.

Yes, I thought, and found the man's spark with my Magic.

Eat it, the voice repeated. She is waiting for you.

Yes, I thought again. And pulled.

φ

CPSIA information can be obtained
at www.ICGtesting.com
Printed in the USA
BVHW032107081020
590653BV00001B/4